THE MERSEY FERRY MURDERS

Mersey Murder Mysteries Book IX

BRIAN L PORTER

Copyright (C) 2021 Brian L Porter

Layout design and Copyright (C) 2021 by Next Chapter

Published 2021 by Next Chapter

Cover art by http://www.thecovercollection.com

Edited by Debbie Poole

This book is a work of fiction. Names, characters, places, and incidents are the product of the author's imagination or are used fictitiously. Any resemblance to actual events, locales, or persons, living or dead, is purely coincidental.

All rights reserved. No part of this book may be reproduced or transmitted in any form or by any means, electronic or mechanical, including photocopying, recording, or by any information storage and retrieval system, without the author's permission.

Dedicated to the memory of Enid Ann Porter and to Sasha, who sat by my side throughout the writing of the first eight books in this series but who sadly never saw book nine come to fruition.

CONTENTS

Introduction	vii
1. June 2007	1
2. Tuesday	7
3. A New Widow	18
4. A New Day Dawns	25
5. The Return of Captain Pugwash	39
6. Another Brick Wall	51
7. Betty	58
8. First Description	69
9. The Trial of Howard Blake	77
10. Ferry Across the Mersey	85
11. Ross Confesses	92
12. Siblings	99
13. Strangeways	116
14. The Bootle Connection	125
15. Love, Life and Everything	136
16. Angela Ryan	142
17. A Bolt Hole	149
18. The Road to Wigan Pier	156
19. Davy Grant	170
20. The Leaving of Liverpool?	191
21. Good News, Bad News	199
22. Polar Star	207
23. Autopsy	221
24. Progress?	230
25. Jean	238
26. Closing In	247
27. Autopsy	256
28. A Council of War	265
29. Arrest	272
30. End Game	279

Dear Reader	289
Acknowledgments	291
About the Author	293
From International Bestselling Author Brian L Porter	295

INTRODUCTION

Welcome to the ninth book in my Mersey Mystery series, featuring the cases of the fictional Merseyside Police's Specialist Murder Investigation Team, led by Detective Inspector Andy Ross. Regular readers of the series will, I'm sure, welcome the return of Detective Sergeant Izzie Drake following her temporary absence on Maternity Leave. The Mersey Ferry Murders also sees a new member joining the team, replacing DC Nick Dodds, tragically killed in the line of duty in the previous book, A Liverpool Lullaby.

For now, though, I hope you enjoy this latest addition to the series, as Ross and the team are faced with yet another seemingly impossible series of murders to solve.

Readers of previous books in the series will be familiar with the central characters, but for newcomers to the series, a little background information to help you settle in with the team.

The Merseyside Police's Specialist Murder Investigation Team is a fictional creation and features a small team of highly skilled detectives, brought together to investigate the more bizarre and often extra-violent crimes that the force is frequently faced with.

INTRODUCTION

Headed by Detective Chief Inspector Oscar Agostini, the squad is run on a day-to-day basis by Detective Inspector Andy Ross and his assistant Detective Sergeant Izzie Drake. At the time of writing this book Drake is absent on maternity leave, having given birth to her first child. The team is a small, select group of some of the finest detectives on the Merseyside Force, hand-picked for their outstanding skills and abilities. Dissent and discord within Ross's team is non-existent as anyone who doesn't fit in to the team and its ideals is rapidly show the door.

As well as Ross and Drake, the team includes Detective Sergeant (DS) Paul Ferris, their resident computer expert who works closely with their civilian Administrative Assistant Kat Bellamy, DS Fenella Church, Acting DS Derek McLennan, and Detective Constables (DCs) Tony Curtis, (real name Leonard but given his nickname due to his striking similarity to the movie star Tony Curtis), Samantha Gable, Gary (Ginger) Devenish, Ishaan Singh, and as you'll soon meet, DC Mitchell, (Mitch) Sinclair.

For readers from the USA and other countries who may be unfamiliar with it, the Liverpudlian accent and dialogue is unique to the Merseyside are of England so readers might find some of the words and grammar used by some of the characters a little different from standard everyday English. This is not a mistake, merely used to create realism.

Finally, I welcome you to the city of Liverpool and to the cases of the Merseyside Police, Specialist Murder Investigation Team.

CHAPTER 1
JUNE 2007

It had been a warm Monday, the skies almost cloudless and the surface of the River Mersey bore barely a ripple as the Mersey Ferry, MV Royal Daffodil tied up at the pier head, quickly disgorging its passengers, mostly daily commuters who worked on the Wirral side of the river. The crossing from the Seacombe Ferry Terminal had taken, as usual, little more than ten minutes and among those disembarking was 55-year-old Wanda Burnside, a solicitor's clerk who worked for the firm of Bertrand and Doyle in Wallasey. Single since her divorce a year ago, Wanda enjoyed life as a single woman, and most people, on seeing her for the first time, could be forgiven for thinking the attractive blonde to be at least ten years younger than her actual age. Her natural blonde hair was wavy and stylishly cut, her face make-up immaculate, and her clothes certainly belied her age. This evening, she was wearing her usual office attire, a royal blue skirt suit, the straight pencil skirt reaching to just above her knees, teamed with a cream blouse and low-heeled black patent leather shoes.

She owned a two-bedroomed house in the Wavertree area of the city, which she shared with her cat, Coco, a tabby she'd adopted from a local rescue shelter soon after her divorce. Occasional evenings out were her main source of social entertainment, but she could hardly be described as a social butterfly, tending to restrict such evening recreation to one evening a week, either on a Friday or Saturday.

Reaching the bus stop on James Street, Wanda took her place in the short queue to wait for her bus. She was one of six people waiting for the bus and once the bus arrived, she settled herself into a seat and casually watched the people on the streets, enjoying people-watching as she was carried home. Alighting at her stop near the Liverpool Bluecoat School, Wanda walked the last few yards to her home, where her Vauxhall Vectra stood on the drive, exactly as she'd left it that morning. She knew she could get to work faster if she took the car and used the tunnel every day, but she enjoyed the relaxed approach that the ferry afforded her, the short crossing, especially in the mornings helped to blow away the cobwebs in her mind and set her up for the working day. Equally, the return crossing was a great way to begin the process of unwinding after a hard day's work.

She reached her front door and extricated her keys from her handbag, blissfully unaware of the soft footsteps that followed her as she placed the key in the lock. The key turned, Wanda pushed the door open, and in less than the time it took her to cross the threshold into her home, a push in the back suddenly sent her sprawling into her hallway, and before she could shout, scream or turn to confront her assailant, a blow to the back of her head ensured Wanda's world turned black as unconsciousness turned her day to instant night.

* * *

Earlier in the day, Detective Inspector Andy Ross arrived especially early for work. After the tragic loss of DC Nick Dodds some months before, killed by the twisted killer known as 'The

Doctor', a replacement member of the squad was due to start work today, and Ross had asked him to arrive early so he could spend some time introducing him the rest of the team.

No matter how early Ross arrived, he always seemed to be beaten into second place by his partner, and squad member, Detective Sergeant Izzie Drake, who'd recently returned to work after a period of maternity leave following the birth of her first child, Alice. Sure enough, he opened the door to his office to find a grinning Detective Sergeant, sitting in one of the two visitors' chairs, with two mugs of steaming hot coffee on his desk, ready for his arrival.

"What time d'you call this then, Detective Inspector?" she laughed, and Ross laughed with her.

"Bloody hell, Izzie, can't I ever beat you in to the office?"

"Not a chance," Izzie replied. "Didn't you know, I've got my secret radar following you so I know when you're leaving home, and I can get here before you, and anyway, if you got here first, who'd make your coffee?"

Ross was so pleased to have Drake back on the team. The pair had worked together for so long that they understood each other perfectly and at times the two of them seemed able to read one another's thoughts, so close was their working relationship. They had an easy but respectful relationship, one that transcended rank, and he wondered how he'd managed during the months she'd been away on leave.

"If I didn't know better," he now responded, "I might even believe you about the bloody radar," and he laughed again.

Drake just tapped her nose with one finger, smiling a knowing smile.

"Who says I'm joking?"

"Izzie Drake, shut up and drink your sodding coffee before it gets cold."

"Yes, sir," she smiled and then the pair spent five minutes

quietly enjoying the hot drinks, before getting down to business.

Ross and Detective Chief Inspector Oscar Agostini had jointly interviewed the candidates for the vacancy in the squad and both agreed without hesitation on the choice of 28-year-old Detective Constable Mitchell (Mitch) Sinclair as the outstanding candidate from some impressive applicants. The squad had been operating under-strength since the death of DC Dodds, as there had been no suitable applicants that met with Agostini and Ross's strict criteria.

No sooner had they finished their coffee than there was a knock on the door, and the team's Admin Assistant, Kat Bellamy opened it and escorted the tall, blonde-haired detective into the office.

"I found this poor soul wandering around the squad room," she said, announcing the arrival of Mitch Sinclair, who walked past her and strode up to the desk and offered his right hand, which Ross, rising from his chair, took and the two men exchanged a firm handshake. Kat quickly withdrew from the room, leaving Sinclair in the hands of the boss and his sergeant.

"Good to see you again, Mitch," Ross said by way of a welcome. "This is my second-in-command, Izzie Drake."

Izzie stood and offered her own hand, and she and the newcomer also shook hands. Sinclair's right eyebrow lifted slightly as he felt the strength in Drake's handshake.

"Pleased to meet you Sarge," he said with a smile, and Drake smiled in return.

"Nice accent," she said, picking up on Sinclair's obvious Australian heritage.

"Yeah, left the old country when I was fourteen when my Mum and Dad decided to settle over here. Dad's a retired captain for the Oceanic Cruise Line, and he was from over here anyway. Mum's Australian, and they met in Sydney years ago, and well, I won't bore you with the sickly-sweet love story."

Drake instantly liked the latest recruit to the team.

"Hope you'll enjoy working with us," Drake said to which Sinclair responded.

"I sure will, no worries."

"You were with the Regional Crime Squad, I hear."

"Correct, Sarge. Spent two years with them before this came up and I put in my application."

"That's enough for now, you two," Ross interrupted. "I think the rest of the team will be in the squad room now, so let's go and introduce you."

"Sure thing, Boss," Sinclair replied, and Ross and Drake led the way from the office into the squad room where, as Ross expected nearly all the team were present already.

The rest of the team knew of the impending arrival of the newest member of the team, and all were present except for DC Ishaan Singh, who was on a week's leave, and not due back for a couple of days. Ross's only slight worry was how DC Tony Curtis would react to Sinclair's arrival. He and Dodds had been close friends and the death of his pal had hit him harder than it had anyone else on the team.

As he and Drake walked Sinclair round the squad room, making the introductions, Ross hesitated for a few seconds after introducing the new man to Curtis. Curtis's real name was Leonard, (Lenny) Curtis but ever since he joined the squad, he'd been known as Tony, due to his uncanny resemblance to the former movie idol of that name. Ross needn't have worried. Curtis was nothing if not a consummate professional.

After shaking hands, he spoke genially to Sinclair.

"Welcome mate, if you need any help settling in, just grab a hold of me, anytime, you hear me?"

"Yeah, thanks Tony," was Sinclair's short reply, before

Drake dragged him across to meet Paul Ferris and Kat Bellamy.

The rest of Mitch Sinclair's first day passed without drama as he learned his way around and made some tentative friendships with the rest of the team. It would soon prove to be nothing more than the calm before the storm.

CHAPTER 2
TUESDAY

Adrian Hill had enjoyed a good day at work. As a repair engineer for Bolton and Son, a local firm in Birkenhead that supplied a full range of household appliances, washing machines, tumble driers, fridge-freezers and so on, he enjoyed getting out and about and dealing with customers needing repairs or service to their appliances. Adrian had held his current job for almost ten years and was popular with his workmates and customers alike. Polite and affable, it could probably be said that Adrian Hill didn't have an enemy in the world.

He enjoyed the daily commute across the Mersey, using the ferry in preference to driving through the rush hour traffic. Adrian and Pam, his wife of fifteen years had saved for years to buy a place of their own and now lived in a two-bedroomed flat in the City Quay Apartments complex on Ellerman Road. Pam had a good job as the manager of a privately owned ladies' clothes shop in the city, so together they had a good income and life was good to them. At fifty-two years of age, Adrian hoped to be able to retire early, perhaps in five years or so, when a couple of his private pension plans could be cashed in, and he and Pam could spend some time enjoying retirement while they were still young enough to do some of the things they'd promised themselves over the years.

Adrian loved walking, jogging, hiking and enjoyed walking to and from the Mersey Ferries Terminal in the morning and evening. As far as he was concerned, he was fit, healthy and happy. He had a wife who looked great for her age, with whom he enjoyed a great sex life and who shared his love for outdoor pursuits. As he alighted from the ferry that evening, he couldn't wait to get home. He'd waited all day to tell her his news. Trevor Bolton the 'son' in the company name, had informed him that he was to be promoted to Service Manager, as Mr Crandell, the current holder of the title had announced his intention to retire, and the job was Adrian's if he wanted it. The job came with a pay rise of course, and the extra money would be sure to help the family finances. He'd picked up a bottle of wine, chardonnay, Pam's favourite, plus a bunch of flowers on his way home and he felt as if nothing could spoil the evening ahead.

Approaching the entrance to the apartment complex, his attention was taken by what appeared to be someone lying on the ground under a car in the car park. He recognised the vehicle as being the Land Rover Discovery owned by his neighbour, Phil Knott. Thinking his friend might need help, and being mechanically minded, Adrian immediately walked across to offer his assistance.

"Hello mate, do you need some help?" he asked. All he could see was the person's legs jutting out from under the car. When he received no reply he asked again, "Phil, is that you? Are you alright under there?"

Adrian grew suddenly suspicious and, bending down and placing the wine and flowers on the ground, he tapped the person's leg, but something felt wrong. He pulled on the leg and the next thing he knew, what appeared to be the bottom half of a mannequin came out as he pulled on it.

"What the hell? Is this some kind of a prank?" he asked nobody in particular.

At that moment, a figure quietly emerged from the other side of the Land Rover, dressed from head to foot in black, topped off by a black hoodie. Quickly making sure there was nobody in the close vicinity, the hooded figure ran round to the other side, where Adrian was still on his knees and before the man on the ground could react, brought a baseball bat down on the back of his head, rendering him instantly unconscious. Another look around, making sure the coast was clear, then the killer quickly pulled the man's trousers and underpants down, and committed a vicious sex act on the victim, using the wooden handle of an old, well-used screwdriver, finally flipping Adrian Hill over onto his back, pulled a seven inch blade from the pouch of the hoodie, and without wasting a second, thrust the blade forcefully into Adrian Hill's chest, directly into the man's heart, before wiping the blade clean on Hill's trouser leg. After checking there was nobody around, the killer rose, stood for a second ensuring the coast was clear, and then quite calmly walked towards the road, not running, as that might draw unwanted attention.

The blood from the stab wound quickly formed a pool on the ground, enveloping the flowers he'd bought for Pam, and staining the label of the bottle of chardonnay a deep shade of red. As the heart ceased its rhythmic beating, the blood flow ceased, as Adrian Hill departed the land of the living. Meanwhile, on the back seat of the Land Rover, the unconscious form of Phil Knott groaned and began to stir.

* * *

The call to the Specialist Murder Investigation Team was received at eight pm that evening. That's to say, the call reached Andy Ross at home, as the squad room wasn't manned twenty-four hours a day. They'd tried that a couple of years previously, and so rare were the referrals to the squad during the night, the idea was abandoned, as they reverted to having an 'on call' officer on duty each night, with the authority to summon more team members if a call of an urgent nature was received.

Ross and his wife, Maria, a local GP, had just sat down to a later than usual evening meal, at their home in Prescot on the outskirts of the city, due to Maria being delayed after evening surgery, when the phone rang. The couple looked at each other, until Ross broke the silence.

"I'll get it. It's probably for me, anyway."

Sure enough, it was the duty officer in the central control room.

"Sorry to disturb you, sir. It's Sergeant Howarth here. Seems CID have been called to a murder scene on Ellerman Road."

"So, why me, Dave?" Ross asked the sergeant, who he'd known for a good few years.

"You're on call for your squad, I believe, sir?"

"That's right. Like I said, Dave, why me?"

"Detective Chief Inspector Lewis from CID asked for your team, I'm afraid. They've had two virtually identical murders in twenty-four hours. No witnesses, no apparent motive, and neither victim has any prior record. Mr Lewis also mentioned that both victims are in their fifties, one male, one female, but signs of sexual assault in both cases."

Ross had heard enough. Sexual assault on both male and female victims was rare and was reason enough for DCI Lewis to have requested the attendance of the Specialist Murder Investigation Team.

"Contact DS Drake and have her meet me there, Dave," Ross instructed, feeling as always a little guilty at pulling Izzie away from home and hearth at night.

"Will do, sir," the Control Room Sergeant acknowledged.

As Ross hung up the phone, Maria was already behind

him, holding his camel overcoat ready, one she'd bought him two Christmases ago. Ross quickly shrugged the coat on, placing his mobile phone in the right-hand pocket, and picking up his car keys from the key tray beside the phone.

"Sorry about this, darling," he apologised but Maria just kissed him and smiled.

"If I'm not used to this sort of thing after all these years, I never will be. Now go, and stay safe."

"I'll call you when I'm on the way home."

"Not if it's after midnight, you won't. Just creep in quietly, and *do not* try to warm your bloody cold feet on my legs, Andrew Ross, or I'll kill you."

Ross laughed. He always made Maria jump when he climbed into bed on a cold night, his icy feet instantly waking her.

"Okay, okay," he promised.

With that, he was out the door and in his car in seconds and on his way to the new murder scene. His next case was about to get under way.

* * *

Upon his arrival at the crime scene, and after parking his Vauxhall Insignia well away from the bustling activity that identified the exact location of the murder, Ross couldn't fail to notice the gleaming new Dacia Duster SUV belonging to Izzie Drake, complete with baby seat on the rear passenger seat. Izzie clearly hadn't wasted any time getting there.

The scene was well lit with lights erected by the crime scene team, headed as usual by Senior Scenes of Crime Officer, Miles Booker, who Ross could see was engaged in conversation with Drake and another officer, who he assumed to be DCI Lewis. Also present was the senior pathologist and Medical Examiner William Nugent and his assistant, Francis Lees, busily flashing away with his camera.

Walking quickly across the car park to join them, Ross nodded to Drake and the others and approached the unknown plain-clothes officer.

"DCI Lewis, I presume?" he said, holding his hand out, which the other man took, and they shook as he confirmed his identity.

"That's right, and you must be DI Ross?"

"Correct, sir. Good to meet you. Sad circumstances of course."

"Indeed it is, Ross. I've met your sergeant here and given her a quick run-down of what we have so far."

Having said that, to his credit, Lewis then gave Ross the details of what he'd found out so far, after which he called his sergeant to him and officially handed the case over to Ross's squad.

"I presume you'd like to keep the uniforms on site until you're done here?" he asked, and Ross acknowledged his help in leaving the six constables who were in attendance, to ensure security of the crime scene and carry out any other tasks Ross deemed necessary.

"I've already had two of them doing a door to door, around the apartments. As always, nobody admits to seeing or hearing anything."

"Typical," Ross replied. "Okay sir, just one thing. I was told this was the second similar killing in the last twenty-four hours, with sexual connotations to both crimes?"

"Yes, and that's the strange thing about these murders," Lewis replied with a look of consternation on his face. "Yesterday evening, fifty-five-year-old Wanda Burnside, an attractive divorcee, was murdered in Wavertree. Seems to be the same MO with what Doctor Nugent has already confirmed to be sexual penetration of both victims. That's why I called your team in. Rape and associated murder aren't uncommon as we know, but such killers usually stick to one gender of victim. This bozo's made a real mess of this poor chap's rear end as

I'm sure Doctor Nugent will point out to you and Sergeant Drake."

"Right," said Ross, grimacing at the mental image Lewis's words conjured up. "And the murder weapon?"

"Seems to be the same in both cases. The victim was apparently rendered unconscious first by some form of blunt force trauma to the head, then they were sexually assaulted, and dispatched with a stab wound to the heart. They both bled to death, quickly."

Ross pulled a face at the thought of two such brutal murders. Despite his job, he always felt a sense of revulsion at the innate cruelty of some killers, who could display such depravity in their methods of disposing of their victims.

"I'll have a copy of the report on Mrs Burnside's murder on your desk by the morning, plus what we've already discovered here, which isn't much as I called you in as soon as I recognised the similarity in the cases."

Ross pointed out a male figure sitting on the steps of the waiting ambulance, being attended to by a paramedic.

"Who's the patient?"

"The owner of the Range Rover, name's Phillip Knott. He's a bit groggy but far as I can make out, he was decoyed out to his car by a phone call to tell him there were a couple of scallys trying to break into his car. He never thought to ask who was calling, just ran down to the car park and as soon as he reached his car, someone whacked him over the head, bundled him into the car, and he was just coming round on the back seat when we arrived."

"That's interesting," Ross mused, "It shows our killer had this all planned and well thought through. How, for example, did he know who the neighbour was? How did he get his phone number? How did he know the man was known to the victim and that Mr Hill would immediately play the Good Samaritan? That business with the mannequin was damned clever," as Lewis explained the significance of the half mannequin which still lay where Hill had begun to pull it out from beneath the vehicle. "I think we're up against a very clever killer."

"Let's just say I'm glad it's your problem now, not mine," said Lewis, his voice tinged with relief.

* * *

Lewis and his DS, Sergeant Wallace, took their leave of the scene and Ross and Drake made their way to the crime scene. As they approached the activity taking place, they spoke briefly.

"Sorry to call you out at night," Ross apologised.

"Don't be daft," Izzie replied. "It's the job, isn't it?"

"You and Peter weren't doing anything special, then?"

"Sort of, yeah, but I didn't mind having an excuse to leave him bathing Alice and putting her to bed," she said with a wide grin.

"Right, ok, I think I get it," Ross smiled in return. "Had enough of the joys of motherhood already, have you?"

"Not at all, but babies can sometimes be more demanding than Detective Inspectors, especially at bath time, and it's good to have an excuse to leave Pete to see to her while I get my teeth into a nice, juicy new case. Anyway, he loves it."

"Hello there, Inspector, Sergeant," the dulcet Scottish tones of Doctor William Nugent interrupted their brief conversation as they neared the death scene.

"Evening, Doc," Ross called to him, as Drake nodded her greeting to him.

Ross and Drake approached the body and Francis Lees stopped exercising his shutter finger and stepped back a couple of paces to allow them a better view of the dead man.

"Aye, well, there's nae a lot good about it for this poor soul," Nugent's native Glasgow accent always came to the fore when the doctor felt angry or stressed. He may have lived and worked in Liverpool for over twenty years, but that Glaswegian lilt was never far from the surface.

"Tell me," Ross said.

"Same as the poor lassie I autopsied earlier today. As I hear it's your case now, I'll send you the report first thing tomorrow."

"Thanks, Doc, but what can you tell me so far. Start with this victim, okay?"

"Okay. Name's Adrian Hill, aged fifty-two, and before ye ask, the poor widow's sat upstairs in their apartment, breaking her heart as we speak. One of the chief inspector's lads, doing the house-to-house broke the news to her. His ID was in his wallet in his jacket pocket. He's still with her as far as I know, waiting until you got here, I've nae doubt."

"What exactly happened, Doctor, do we know?" Drake asked.

"See that?" the doctor pointed to the half mannequin still positioned half under the Range Rover where Hill had left it. "It's ma guess yer killer used it as a kind of decoy to get the man's attention and when he bent down to look he hit him over the head with a blunt object, knocked him out, carried out a particularly nasty sexual assault on him as he lay unconscious and then stabbed him in the heart, one very precise stab wound, as if he knew his way around the human body,."

"How nasty was the sexual assault?" Ross asked.

Pulling aside a sheet that had been used to cover the body, Nugent pointed and simply said, "See for yourself."

Despite his years of experience, Ross was shocked when he looked at the body of Adrian Hill. Drake put her hand over her mouth to counter a gag reflex.

"Fuckin' hell," Ross exclaimed. Drake was silent.

"What the hell did he do?"

"It's ma guess he inserted a large object into the anus, causing massive tearing and haemorrhaging.

Both detectives stared in horror at the terrible wound that gaped from the man's rear.

"Only terrible rage could have caused someone to carry out such a brutal attack," Drake commented.

"This was definitely a very personal attack," Ross said immediately. "Any similarities with the woman?"

"Unfortunately, yes," Nugent nodded gravely. "Her vagina and anus were both torn in similar fashion, and before ye ask, both attacks were carried out premortem, probably while the victims were unconscious. If they'd been conscious, the pain of such brutality would have had them screaming the neighbourhood down. Someone would have been bound to hear them and either gone to investigate the screams or called the police."

"Was the woman killed in the same way?" Drake asked the doctor.

"Aye she was. Looks like yer man followed her home, then hit her over the head as she opened her door, pushed her into the house and attacked her in the hallway. The crime scene photos do not make pleasant viewing."

Miles Booker the head of the Scenes of Crime Team spoke up from behind Ross. His team were standing by, waiting for the doctor to finish his on-scene examination of the body before getting to work on the scene.

"She was posed in death, Andy. Skirt lifted up above her waist, underwear around one ankle and legs spread in a blatant sexual invitation, a classic rape scene."

"This is some sick bastard," Ross said. He was angry, as he always was when lives were taken in such brutal and vicious ways. "Anybody questioned the owner of the Range Rover yet?"

"He wasn't up to it, according to DCI Lewis," Booker provided the answer to Ross's question.

"Well, let's us go and have a word with him, Izzie, while your people see what they can find, Miles."

"Unless he's been careless, and there was no sign of carelessness at last night's scene, I doubt we'll find much to help you, Andy," Booker replied with a look of resignation on his face. Ross and Drake walked across to the ambulance as Doctor Nugent gave the okay for the body to be removed and transported to the morgue.

"What about the wife?" Drake asked.

"Just a word with this guy and then we'll go up and see her. Hopefully, by then, the officer who's with her will have managed to calm her down a bit."

"Don't bet on it," Drake was doubtful, but dutifully followed Ross to the ambulance, where a two-minute conversation with Phil Knott proved fruitless.

He understandably hadn't thought to ask who was calling when a voice told him a pair of young men were attempting to break into his car. He hadn't recognised the voice, which he said sounded strange, he couldn't say whether it was male or female, and on emerging from the apartment block, he hadn't noticed anyone looking suspicious in the vicinity. He remembered opening the driver's door of his car, after which everything went black and all he knew was waking up, and a policeman was shaking him, with a lump the size of an egg on the back of his head.

"Strange he couldn't tell if the phone caller was a man or a woman," Drake made a point of mentioning as they entered the apartment block.

"I agree," Ross replied. "He might be just confused, concussed perhaps, or our killer might have been deliberately disguising their voice."

Arriving outside the victim's apartment, both Ross and Drake sighed, and each took a deep breath.

Next on the agenda was what was going to be a painful conversation with the newly widowed Pamela Hill.

CHAPTER 3
A NEW WIDOW

A knock on the door of the Hill's apartment was answered by a petite woman police officer. Ross was pleased that DCI Lewis had possessed the sensitivity to send a woman to break the news to Adrian Hill's wife.

He identified himself and Izzie Drake to the young officer, thinking to himself how young she looked, (or was he getting older?).

"Constable Brenda Fry, sir," she said, her voice firm and professional sounding. "She's through here," as she led Ross and Drake into the well-appointed lounge/dining area of the apartment. There, sitting on a new-looking black leather sofa, her head down, her body clearly wracked with tears, was the grief-stricken figure of Pamela Hill.

"She's hardly said a word sir," Fry whispered, and then, in a louder voice, "Pam, this is Detective Inspector Ross and Detective Sergeant Drake. They're going to need to speak to you."

"Thank you, Constable," Ross moved towards the woman on the sofa, as Fry hesitated before asking Drake, "Do you need me to stay?"

Drake looked at Ross who gave a brief shake of his head,

allowing her to reply, "No thank you, Constable. You can go now. Thanks for doing a difficult job and holding the fort till we got here. The other officers are helping with a house to house, and you can see how they're getting on, and join them."

Ross interrupted. "Hang on, Constable Fry, you can do something for me,"

"Sir?"

"Go and see the man sitting on the step of the ambulance outside. His name's Knott. Ask him if he's seen any strangers hanging around the complex in the last couple of weeks or received any strange phone calls. He was pretty much out of it when we spoke to him. Hopefully, he'll have his wits about him by now. Do that and wait for us with the Crime Scene people, please."

Delighted to have been asked to do something she considered important to the investigation, Fry almost stood to attention as she replied, "Yes sir, I can do that," and she turned on her heel and almost skipped her way out of the apartment.

Ross now turned to the matter in hand.

"Mrs Hill, I'm so sorry for your loss. I know you must be absolutely devastated, but we have to ask you some questions."

It seemed to take a great effort for the sobbing woman to raise her head to look at Ross. When she did, Ross saw a good-looking woman, probably in her late forties, whose face was a mask of tears. Her make-up had run and smudged, and he noticed a half-empty box of tissues that he guessed PC Fry strategically placed beside her on the arm of the sofa, which she reached for, taking another tissue from the box, and blowing her nose. A second tissue followed which she used to wipe her already tear-reddened eyes.

"Why?" she sobbed, and then, "Why Adrian? He never harmed a soul."

Ross took her words to lead into his first question.

"I know this is terribly difficult for you, but can you think of anyone who might have wanted to harm your husband?"

"Nobody," she exclaimed, her voice weak and trembling. "The policewoman said he'd been stabbed. Is that what happened? Did someone try to mug him or something like that?"

Ross was glad that PC Fry hadn't gone into any details of the murder with the unfortunate woman.

"We're not sure exactly what took place yet, Mrs Hill. We're still trying to piece things together."

Izzie Drake pitched in with a question.

"How well did Adrian know Phillip Knott? Was he a close friend?"

"Phil, what's he got to do with it? You don't think he had anything to do with Adrian being attacked, surely."

"No, not at all," Drake reassured her. "It's just that Adrian's attacker used Mr Knott's car as a decoy, a blind to draw your husband in. Mr Knott was also attacked and knocked unconscious."

"Oh God, is he okay?"

"He's not badly hurt, but please, can you answer my question?" Drake pressed for a reply.

"Oh yes, sorry. They weren't what you'd call good friends. We knew Phil and Rosie, her real name's Rosemary, as good neighbours. Adrian and Phil occasionally went for a drink together, but that's as far as it went."

"What did your husband do for a living?" Ross asked, and over the next fifteen minutes, he and Drake managed to draw out as much relevant information as they could about the dead man, from his widow, who was finding it increasingly difficult to maintain her equilibrium in the face of her terrible loss.

"We're going to leave you for now, Mrs Hill," he eventually said as he and Drake prepared to depart, "but we will need you to perform the official identification of your husband's body. That can wait till tomorrow. Have you anyone, a relative or friend who can come and be with you for now?"

Pam had appeared to drift off into her own world of all-encompassing grief and Ross had to repeat his question, eventually receiving a reply.

"Yes, my sister, Ann, lives in Formby. The young policewoman called her before you got here. As soon as her husband, Sam gets home from work, to take care of the kids, she'll be coming over. She should be here any time now."

Right on cue, the doorbell rang, and Izzie Drake made Pam Hill stay seated while she answered the door, returning to the room a minute later with Ann Terry in tow. The two sisters immediately collapsed into each other's arms and Ross and Drake took this as sign that it was a good time to leave.

Ross left one of his cards on the coffee table in the centre of the lounge, and said, "My card's on the table, Mrs Hill. Please call me if you think of anything that might help, or if you remember anything you may have forgotten."

It was the sister who replied, having quickly assumed the role of big sister and taken charge of the situation.

"She will, Inspector, but I think my sister needs some time to come to terms with all this, don't you?"

"Yes, of course," Ross replied, happy at least that the newly widowed Pam Hill wouldn't be on her own after he and Drake took their leave of her.

As he and Drake reached the fresh air, he could see that Miles Booker and his crime scenes technicians were still hard at work, going over Phil Knott's Range Rover and the rest of the car park and entrance to the apartment block. Young Brenda Fry was sitting in the back of Booker's car with Knott, the ambulance having left with the body, followed by Nugent and Lees some minutes earlier.

Fry caught sight of him and Drake and appeared to take a few seconds to wrap up her conversation with Knott, before releasing him, and allowing the shaken man, his head heavily bandaged, to return to his apartment with his wife Rosie, who'd come out into the car park to look for her husband and much to her shock and horror, become wrapped up in the organised chaos that always accompanied such a terrible event. Fry then walked across to Ross and Drake, smiling and looking pleased with herself.

"You look as if you might have something for us, Constable," Drake said, before Ross could speak,

"Kind of," Fry replied. "Over the last three weeks, Mr Knott remembers at least three 'silent' calls, you know, when the caller doesn't say a word and leaves you…"

"Yes, I think we know what a silent call is, please go on," Ross encouraged her to continue.

"Sorry sir, of course you do. Anyway, Mr Knott did a 1471 to try and find out who was calling, but the caller had blocked their number. Then, he was in the pub, the Flying Horse, two weeks ago when he had his smartphone stolen. It had been in his jacket pocket, which he'd placed over the back of his chair while he talked to his friends, including poor Mr Hill. It wasn't till they left the pub, and he tried to call his wife to let her know he was on his way home that he realised the phone had gone. Mr Hill and another mate went back to the pub, checking the paths along the way, but the landlord told him that nobody had handed a phone in. So, it seems someone nicked it, and possibly accessed all his information."

"Didn't he have a password on it?" Ross asked.

"No, the daft bugger," Fry said. "He said he can never remember passwords and never bothered to set one on his phone."

"Looks like our killer might have taken it and found out quite a bit about Knott, enough to maybe work out his routine and know when he'd be at home or at work," Drake nodded. "He planned this murder in detail right down to using the man's friend as a decoy."

"In which case, we can assume he's been watching Hill for quite some time. He probably saw him and Knott talking or going to the pub together and decided on his strategy based on the two men knowing each other," Ross said, thinking on his feet.

"How about any strangers suddenly showing an interest in him, or his little gang of mates in the pub?" Drake asked.

"I asked him that, Sergeant, and all he recalls is a bloke who sat with them a fortnight ago and joined in a conversation they were having about the upcoming football season and a young woman who'd had a few drinks who ended up draped around the neck of one of his mates, a Gerald Hunt. I have his addresses, both home and work. That's about it really."

"Good work, Constable," Ross smiled at the young officer. "You've done well. Give those addresses and the name of the man in the pub to Sergeant Drake, then you can get away for the night. Call up your mates on your radio, tell them all to report back here, and if no one has anything useful for us, they can all call it a night as well,"

"Yes, sir, and thank you."

"Don't thank me, Fry. You did the work and got the information. Good job."

Fry wandered off, speaking into her radio to her colleagues from the station.

"You just made her day," Drake told Ross.

"A bit of encouragement never hurts when they're young and keen, you know that Izzie."

"I sure do. God, was I ever that young and keen as mustard?"

Miles Booker was their next port of call, but sadly, the Crime Scenes officer had no good news for them.

"All we've come up with are a few alien fibres, Andy, on Knott's shirt. My guess is your man wore a black hoodie or something similar. They're the right type of fibres. We'll know more tomorrow. A look at his head showed a couple of traces of material in his hair, as well as a hair that might be from the killer or maybe from his wife. We've got a tech up there now getting a sample from his wife for comparison purposes."

"We always seem to give you the next to impossible jobs, Miles. Sorry mate," Ross apologised, knowing how frustrating some of their cases could be for the forensics people, as well as for his own team.

"You know what I always say, Andy," Booker grinned. "The impossible just takes us a bit longer than normal, but we usually get there in the end."

"I know you'll do your best, Miles."

"Yeah, we will, and if there's anything else to find, we're damn well going to find it. Got two lads giving the Range Rover a second going over."

"You'll let me know if you come up with anything, right?"

"Sure will," Booker replied. "You and Izzie heading home for now, I take it?"

"Dead right we are. Not much more we can do here tonight. The uniform lads haven't come up with anything from the residents, so we'll start looking into the victims' lives first thing in the morning."

"Let's just hope your killer doesn't have any more victims lined up," Booker said, voicing a thought that both Ross and Drake had been harbouring themselves.

"Too right, Miles. This could get sticky if he has,"

Ross and Drake were soon back in their respective cars, heading home for what was left of the night. Tomorrow promised to be a busy day.

CHAPTER 4
A NEW DAY DAWNS

Having first reported the latest case to DCI Oscar Agostini, who accompanied him as Ross now faced the rest of the team waiting in the squad room, where Izzie Drake had brought everyone up to date with the events of the previous night, and the link to the first murder, Ross seated himself on the edge of Singh's vacant desk as he addressed his team.

"Okay everyone, Izzie's told you what we're facing, yes?"

Everyone agreed that she had, and Ross went on.

"DCI Agostini is here to make sure he's up to speed with the new investigation. There's a niggling worry in the back of my mind that we might not have heard the last of this killer. Two murders in two days, with no real clues, one female and one male, both sexually assaulted and the real possibility that he might strike again."

Agostini broke into Ross's narrative to offer his thoughts.

"From what DI Ross has told me this perpetrator is a clever bastard who appears to have planned his killings down to the last detail. Doctor Nugent is carrying out the autopsy as we speak and I'm hoping he can provide us with something we can use to help identify the killer."

Ross spoke again, addressing his comments to Sergeant Paul Ferris, the team's resident computer expert.

"Paul, you should have received the reports on last night's murder and the previous killing of the woman in Wavertree. I want you all to go through those reports and try to find anything that you think the two victims have in common. What Izzie and I found when we attended last night's murder scene was pretty gruesome, and I'd hate to think this bastard is going to kill again."

"Do we have any reason to think he won't… kill again, that is?" DC Tony Curtis asked.

"No reason at all, Tony," Drake gave him the reply that nobody really wanted to hear.

Paul Ferris interrupted, with the news that he'd now received both reports.

After perusing the scant information available so far, Ross decided on a course of action.

"We're not going to get very far until we know more about the victims. Something somewhere has to link the victims to the killer. They must have something in common, and it's our first priority to find out what that is. Tony, I want you and Mitch to work together on investigating the background of the woman, Wanda Burnside. Go and talk to her employer, Bertrand and Doyle in Wallasey. Talk to her co-workers, find out if she'd mentioned anything unusual taking place in her life in recent weeks. Find out who her next of kin is. Go and see them, get a statement. We need to find out everything we can about this lady, and fast.

Next, Ross addressed Sergeant Fenella Church.

"Fee," he used her nickname, "I want you to go see Adrian Hill's widow. She should be thinking a little more clearly this morning. See if her husband mentioned anything strange going on in his life, then go talk to his employer and friends at work. Same scenario as Tony and Mitch, you know what to ask."

"What about the guy who was knocked on the head?" Church asked. "Should I talk to him again? I see here a young PC spoke to him last night and got some info from him."

"Yes, PC Fry, seemed like a bright girl. By all means, go see him, though he might have gone into work today."

"I doubt that," Drake interrupted. "Did you see the size of that lump on his head? He must have a Titanic-sized headache this morning."

"Alright, clever clogs," Ross replied. "Check him out anyway, Fee."

Sam Gable and Gary, (Ginger) Devenish were given the unenviable task of visiting the mortuary, where Doctor Nugent would be busily examining the two murder victims' remains. Ross wanted to be certain that anything he discovered was communicated to him as soon as it became available.

"Oh wow, thanks a lot, Boss. Just what I needed this morning. Formaldehyde and disinfectant," Gable groaned, and Ginger Devenish placed a sympathetic arm on her shoulder.

"Don't worry, Sam," he said, reassuringly, "I've got a nice jar of Vicks in my pocket."

He was referring to the fact that the detectives usually smeared the strong-smelling inhalant under their noses to help counter the less than savoury odours that seemed to permeate every wall, floor and other surfaces in the city mortuary.

"Oh wow, you sure know how to treat a girl, don't you, Ginge?" Gable laughed.

"You know me, Sam, I always aim to please," Devenish smiled as he replied.

"Oh well, let's not delay the inevitable," Gable said, resigned to her fate. "Let's go," and she and Devenish made for the squad room door and were gone in seconds.

"What about me, sir?" Derek McLennan asked.

"Derek, I want you to have a day on the water. Go and talk to the ferry crews. Show them photos of both victims. If they used the ferries regularly, some of the crew may have talked to them, chatted with them. We can't know if they caught any particular ferry, so you'll need to speak to them all. See if they recall anyone else interacting with the victims, or maybe saw them getting upset by anyone. It's a long shot, but if anyone can prise anything out of them, maybe something they haven't realised they've seen, you can do it."

"Why do I think that last sentence was a load of old flannel, Boss?"

"I mean it, Derek. You have a way with people, and anyway, it's a nice day, the sun's shining and you should have a pleasant time cruising the river all day."

At that, Tony Curtis began whistling the tune to the old Gerry and the Pacemakers sixties hit song, *Ferry Cross the Mersey*. He was immediately joined by Sam Gable who began singing the words to accompany him. Ross smiled and stopped the reverie with a firm,

"Now then kiddies. That's enough of the frivolity. Get to work, both of you."

"Sure Boss, Sorry Boss," Gable and Curtis replied in turn, both grinning like Cheshire cats.

With that, the team headed out, leaving Ross and Drake in the squad room with Ferris, Admin Assistant Kat Bellamy, and DCI Agostini.

"So, what are we doing?" Drake asked Ross who shrugged his shoulders, as if to say, I don't know, leaving Agostini to reply.

"Sorry, Izzie, I need a private word with both of you, in your office Andy, if you don't mind." Agostini interrupted from his position near the squad room door.

Ross and Drake preceded the DCI into Ross's office. Agostini followed them and then closed the door behind, giving him the privacy, he required for what he had to say. In the squad room, Kat asked Ferris if he knew what was going on. He just shook his head.

"What's happening, Oscar?" Ross asked his old friend.

"Andy, you might know the squad has been under review for a while, and the DCS has asked me to relay the results of that review to you both."

Detective Chief Superintendent Sarah Hollingsworth was in overall control of the plain clothes detective division of the force, and her word was law as far as the team was concerned. Agostini continued.

"It's been decided to upgrade the team. Over the next six months, we'll be recruiting four more detectives, the idea being that we can provide a sort of rapid response unit, to assist other forces in the vicinity with the kind of cases you're handling at present. In order to properly fulfil our new, expanded role, there are going to be some organisational changes. First of all, I will remain in overall charge of the new unit, but will be promoted to superintendent, while you, Andy, will be promoted to Detective Chief Inspector, and before you say anything, you will remain in operational command, much as you are at present. You've turned down promotion in the past because you want to lead from the front. Well, now, you can do that as well as accepting the higher rank, which, by the way, you fully deserve."

Ross looked stunned and for a moment he remained silent as Agostini went on,

"You, Sergeant Drake, are to be promoted to Detective Inspector and will continue to work as second-in-command of the team, with a rank commensurate with the responsibility."

"Bloody hell, oops, sorry sir," Drake couldn't help herself.

"Don't apologise, Izzie, it's well-earned and I know it's a bit of a shock. As for the rest of the team, Derek McLennan's acting sergeant position will be made up to substantive rank, so he'll be a full sergeant as of now. He and Sergeant Church will, when necessary, lead your small rapid response teams in assisting other forces in the region when called upon. From an administrative viewpoint, you're going to need another pair of hands, so you'll be getting another admin assistant. I'm sure

Kat Bellamy and Sergeant Ferris will soon bring the new assistant up to speed. Don't worry, I've made sure that computer skills are at the top of the list when it comes to the requirements of the job. I think that's about all for now. So, do you have anything to say, any questions, anything at all?"

Ross and Drake looked at each other, looked at Agostini, and finally, Ross broke the silence.

"I'm surprised, shocked, and stunned, to tell the truth."

"Me too," Drake managed to blurt out, almost breathlessly.

"I suppose you arranged it so I retain day to day operational control?"

"I did. I knew you'd never accept the promotion if they stuck you in an office behind a desk. So did DCS Hollingsworth. Nobody wants to lose your operational detecting skills Andy. You're too good in the field."

"Thanks, Oscar. I'm totally gobsmacked, if I'm being truthful."

"What about you, Izzie?" Agostini smiled as he waited for Drake to put a coherent sentence together.

"I don't know what to say, sir. I'm delighted, of course, but like DI Ross, this has come as something of a shock."

"At least now you know why I asked the two of you to remain here while your team went to work. Now, I suggest you get back to work. I'm sure you have a DS and a young Admin assistant out there wondering what the hell is going on in here."

"Is it okay to tell our people?" Ross asked.

"Yes, of course it is. Oh, and you and Izzie will be closely involved in the interviews for your new team members once we begin recruiting."

"When is all this going to take place?" Drake asked, just as Ross was about to ask the same question.

"There's quite a bit of organising involved before we begin recruiting your new team members, so I'm thinking it'll be about three months before anything happens. For now, we carry on as normal, okay?"

"Okay, sir. Well, this is a real turn up for the books."

"It's just a shame Nick isn't with us to see all this happening," Drake commented, referring to DC Nick Dodds, a long-standing member of the team who was killed by the serial killer known as 'The Doctor' a few months previously.

"He'd have been dead chuffed, Izzie, that's for sure," Ross said sadly.

"I'm sure he would've been," Agostini agreed, then handed a file to Ross before leaving the office. "All the details of the proposed changes are in here. Study everything thoroughly and if you've any questions, my office door is always open."

With that, the DCI left them in peace to peruse the details of the proposals. Ross and Drake spent the next few minutes assimilating everything that Agostini had just told them.

"Well, that was a turn up for the books," Drake said, at a loss for anything else to say, such was the shock she felt at the news.

"Couldn't have put it better," Ross replied. "The rest of the team are in for a big surprise, that's for sure."

"Derek's going to be dead chuffed to be made up to full DS, isn't he?"

"No more than he deserves," Ross replied.

"But, what about this expansion to the team? Are you happy to become a DCI, after years of turning promotion down?"

"You know I only turned it down because I didn't want to lose overall daily control of the team. This way, thanks to Oscar and the Chief Super, I get to stay in charge as I am now."

"You're a bloody lucky bugger," Drake laughed. "You must have a charmed life. You could fall into a vat of shite and come up smelling of roses."

Ross roared with laughter. With their close and easy relationship, nobody other than Izzie Drake could get away with using such language to the boss.

"You're probably right, Izzie. But I'm not going to rock the boat. If the brass wants to give me exactly what I want, then who am I to refuse it?"

"But me, a DI? I can hardly believe it. I'm a wife and mum for God's sake."

"And a damn good, no, make that brilliant detective."

"Thanks for that. So, what do we do now?"

"We do what we always do, Izzie. We solve the cases that get thrown at us. According to that document, they are expanding the unit because we can handle maybe two cases at a time at present but if a third case suddenly dropped in our laps we'd be hard pushed to cope. As far as I'm concerned, nothing's changed. At least until we know more about any organisational changes that might come about once we have the extra manpower, and we know exactly how they want us to operate."

"Speaking of cases, what can we do with this one for now?"

"For the moment, my dear Sergeant, soon to be DI Drake, we go out there and break the news to Paul and Kat, who are probably wearing out the realms of possibilities after Oscar's visit, and then we wait for the reports to start coming in from the others."

Sure enough Paul Ferris and Kat Bellamy had been speculating on all kinds of reasons for the DCI's meeting with Ross and Drake and when Ross broke the news to them, they were both delighted with the new developments.

"So, we're really getting noticed eh, Boss?"

"It would seem that way, Paul".

"And it's so well deserved," Kat Bellamy added.

"Maybe we'll have to make you senior admin when we get

the new administrator, Kat," Drake suggested, planting the seed of an idea in Ross's mind.

Ross, Drake, Ferris and Bellamy spent the next hour discussing the possibilities that would be open to the expanded team once it became a reality. The first of the teams sent out that morning to return were DCs Gable and Devenish, fresh from their visit to the morgue, and Dr. Nugent's autopsy suite.

"God, that's one of my worst favourite places in the entire world," Gable gasped, as Devenish, taking pity on her, quickly placed a mug of coffee in front of her as she flopped into her chair at her desk.

"Well, Sam, Ginge, sounds as if you had an interesting morning," Ross said, with a lopsided grin.

"You, my dear, esteemed gaffer, are a bloody closet sadist, d'you know that?" Gable groaned. "The sight of Fat Willy slicing and dicing a human being to pieces just doesn't float my boat, if you know what I mean, and as for the smell…"

Ross stifled a laugh at Gable's reference to the pathologist's in-house nickname for the overtly obese William Nugent.

"Now, now, Samantha," he tried to sound sympathetic, "You've attended enough autopsies over the years. Surely you're at least partially immune from the odours if the autopsy suite."

"And you used plenty of my Vicks," Devenish added.

"You can shut it and all, Ginge. You weren't much better, and you know it."

"I admit I'd rather fall into the hold of a fully laden trawler than be in that place," Devenish pulled a wry face, "but it's an occupational hazard, isn't it?"

"That's the spirit, Ginge," Drake smiled as she spoke. "Now, what did the doctor have for us?"

Devenish made an expansive hand gesture, indicating to Gable that she should deliver the information.

"Well," she began, "He's fairly sure that both victims were

rendered unconscious with the same, or incredibly similar weapon. The shape of the head wounds contained minute traces of wood and a nylon polymer, which Dr Nugent felt certain had come from something like a baseball bat, or something of the same shape. The interesting thing about the sexual attacks on both victims showed no ejaculate in either victim. Bear in mind that Wanda Burnside was assaulted both vaginally and anally and that Adrian Hill was anally raped, and yet there was no trace of semen or condom lubricant present in either victim."

"So, what did he conclude about the attacks?" Ross asked.

Gable pulled a face as she prepared to reply.

"The doctor is of the opinion that either the killer is a non-secretor, but he doubted that, or that no penile penetration took place."

"Why did he think that?" Drake asked, and Ginger Devenish provided the answer.

"Because there was a complete lack of seminal fluid present in either victim. A non-secretor would still produce fluid which would be deposited in the vagina or anus, it would just be lacking in any personal DNA and …"

"Yeah, we get the picture, thanks, Ginge," Ross said, his brow creased as an idea began to form in his mind. "But there's another possible conclusion we can some to from that information."

"I thought that as well, sir," Gable returned to the conversation.

"Go on, Sam," Ross urged her to propound her theory.

"As we know, non-secretors leave virtually no trace of DNA behind in the fluids, or indeed in their prints, but the lack of either can also mean that we're not looking for a man at all. Our killer could be a woman."

"Very good, Sam. That's exactly what I think Doc Nugent was suggesting to you and Ginger."

"That's what he intimated to us, yes sir," Devenish confirmed. "The doctor pointed out that he had found splinters in and around the entry and internally in the penetrated orifices. The killer could have used the handle of some kind of wooden tool."

"Would probably be an old one then, most modern tools I've seen tend to have plastic or resin handles." Drake commented. "But the head wounds, he said may have been caused by a baseball bat. I didn't think it was a popular sport over here, more an American thing."

"It isn't really," Gable replied. "But kids often play it, and softball too, especially in schools, so there's a call for them in sports shops and so on."

"So, our killer could be a man or a woman," Ross concluded. "Let's not rule anything out yet. That's a good point about the tools Izzie. I didn't know you were an expert with DIY tools. It could be a man who can't get an erection, or who is deliberately making us think he's a female, for any number of reasons."

"I'm no expert," Drake replied, "but when you've been dragged round every bloody DIY store in Liverpool, as I have, you get to know these things. Peter's become obsessed with sodding DIY."

Ross laughed at the thought of Peter dragging Izzie and the baby round the large DIY superstores on a Sunday afternoon.

"Doctor Nugent also said there were traces of a lubricant having been applied to the weapon used to inflict the penetrative damage to both victims," Devenish added.

"So, no spermicide as in a condom, but some form of lubricant to ensure he or she could inflict maximum pain and tearing of the points of entry on both victims, and internally too, I expect," Ross found the prospect terrifying, and he'd seen some horrors during his years on the force.

"Doctor Nugent said the internal damage to both victims was appalling, as if they'd been subjected to impalement," Gable shuddered at the thought of what the man and woman had been subjected to by an obviously deranged and sadistic killer. "As for the murder weapon, he estimates that they were both killed by a single stab wound to the heart, from a long, slim blade, probably seven to eight inches long, and that the killer knew precisely where the heart is, as there were no hesitation cuts on either victim."

"So, we could be looking for someone with medical knowledge," Ross was thinking aloud.

"I hate to ask this," Drake interrupted. "But why didn't he use the baseball bat, if that's what was used, to carry out the rapes, for want of a better word?"

"I asked that question," Devenish responded. "The doctor said that if it had been a baseball bat, even the narrow end would have been too big to insert in a human anal passage, even with lubrication, without causing devastating injuries, greater than were present on the victims."

"Okay, I think we've heard enough of this horror story for the moment. One last question though. Did Nugent give any indication that anything connected the victims, apart from the method of their deaths?"

"He found nothing among their clothing or possessions to link them together," Gable replied.

"Apart from the tickets, remember, Sam," Devenish corrected her.

"Tickets? What tickets?" Ross asked.

"Adrian Hill's shirt pocket contained a ticket stub from the Royal Daffodil, and a similar stub was found in Mrs Burnside's purse."

"Which simply proves that both victims caught the Mersey Ferry on their way to or from work," Drake observed. "As they both worked across the river, that's not really a damning piece of evidence."

"I know, Sarge, but you did ask the question."

"I know Ginge, I'm not having a dig at you. It's just bloody weird. Two people, with seemingly nothing in common and nothing to connect their lives together, both savagely murdered by some perverted bastard, for no apparent reason."

"That's exactly why it's fallen to us to solve the bloody thing," Ross growled, sharing Drake's frustration. "Anyway, before we go on, I've some news for you both." Despite originally intending to address the whole team when they were back in the office, he'd decided to tell each pair of his detectives as they returned from their current tasks.

Gable and Devenish were predictably surprised and delighted to hear the news of the impending changes to the squad and both immediately congratulated Ross and Drake on their respective promotions.

"Bloody hell, Boss. You, a DCI? Will we have to bow when we want to speak with you?" Gable asked with a cheeky grin spreading from ear to ear.

"Samantha Gable, you're a bloody cheeky bugger. Behave yourself or I just might insist on you doing just that," Ross sniggered.

"And you, Sarge," Devenish held a congratulatory hand out to Both Ross and Drake in turn, shaking both of their hands firmly. "Fancy you being a DI. Couldn't have happened to nicer lady. Congratulations to you both. When does all this happen?"

"Not for a while yet, Ginge," Ross replied. "There's a lot of work to be done setting it all up first."

"I'm right chuffed for Derek too," Gable added. "He's done well as an acting DS, in my own opinion anyway."

"Indeed he has, Sam. Now remember, not a word to the others as they return. I'd like to tell them myself if you don't mind," Ross warned them.

"Our lips are sealed, Boss," Gable promised for both of them, using her hand to make a zipping movement across her face. "I presume Paul and Kat know already?"

"Yes, we do," Ferris said loudly, from his seat at his computer.

"Remember, not a word to the others," Ross reminded them, just in time as a minute later, the squad room doors open to admit DS Fenella Church.

Ross hoped she'd have something positive to report.

CHAPTER 5
THE RETURN OF CAPTAIN PUGWASH

"Okay, what's happened?" Fenella Church immediately detected the frisson of an atmosphere in the squad room as soon as walked across the floor towards her desk. Nothing appeared to get past her empathic nature, and Ross knew he had to tell her the news before getting her report.

"That's fantastic, sir. Congratulations, to you both."

Ross and Drake both voiced their thanks but then rather than ask any questions, of which she had many, Church's business-like brain took over and she commenced with her report. She began with her visit to the home of Adrian and Pamela Hill.

"The widow wasn't exactly helpful to be honest. She couldn't tell me much more than she imparted to you and Izzie last night, sir. Her sister was very protective of her and if she hadn't been there, I'd have been worried about the possibility of Pamela harming herself.

The neighbour, Mrs Knott wasn't much help either. She did say that Phil had gone out and bought a new phone the day after his old one was nicked in the pub. I asked if he'd informed his service provider so they could put a block on it, but she didn't know. I'm hoping Paul can find that out for us. I tried phoning Vodafone, but they wouldn't give me the information I required, without some proof of who I was."

"Give me the number Fee, and I'll get on it now," Ferris immediately said.

Church gave him a piece of paper containing the number and then continued her report.

"Pamela Hill is definitely in the clear as far as I'm concerned. I did think maybe she was behind her husband's murder, you know, maybe for insurance money or something, but no way could grief like that have been faked. She also had no idea why her husband had come home bearing wine and flowers, but I'll get to that in a minute. Plus, I don't see how she could have been connected to the first murder, unless it was a random killing as a trial run for the real thing."

"Highly unlikely," Ross ventured to interrupt.

"My thoughts exactly, just mentioned it to dismiss it really. Anyway, next I took the ferry to Wallasey. I know, I could have used the tunnel, but I wanted to get a feel of how Hill would have felt crossing the river twice a day. His boss, Trevor Bolton, at Bolton and Son, a company specialising in the supply and maintenance of household appliances couldn't praise Adrian Hill enough. He'd been with the company for years, and was so highly thought of, that on the day of his murder, he'd been promoted to the post of Service Manager, on the retirement of the previous incumbent. That explained the wine and flowers. He obviously intended to celebrate his promotion with his wife."

"Poor bastard," DS Ferris commented from his desk.

"Mmm, that's what I thought, Paul," Church agreed, before continuing. "It was probably one of the happiest days of his life, right up until someone decided to end it before his wife could share it with him. So, his boss thought the world of this guy and couldn't think of any reason why anyone would want to hurt him. It was pretty much the same when I spoke to his fellow workers. Between them they told me that he was well respected, friendly and courteous to them and the customers he came into contact with. In fact, some customers phoning up for a service call would often ask for him by name when they needed an engineer call out."

"Sounds too good to be true," Drake commented. "Didn't anyone have a bad word for him?"

"Not as such," Church replied, "But one of his colleagues said that Hill was very outspoken on any issues relating to crime and punishment. He thought the law was too soft and that criminals got off too easy. He was quite passionate about it, apparently."

"Sounds like he'd have made a good copper," Ferris responded.

"I was thinking that, too," Ross added. "I don't think that would have given anyone a reason to kill the guy."

"I know," Church went on. "In short, nobody could think of a reason for his murder. I asked everyone if they'd heard of Wanda Burnside, but the name didn't mean a thing to anyone."

"You don't think maybe he was having an affair with the dead woman?" Drake had a sudden thought.

"I doubt it," Church replied. "From what I've learned today, he was very much a home bird, spent most of his time with his wife, apart from going to the pub for an occasional drink with friends. One thing's really bugging me though," she went on to say.

"What's that, Fee?" Ross asked.

"This business of the phone calls. Phil Knott told his wife, and PC Fry, he couldn't tell if his anonymous caller was male or female, and before I came back here, I've had the emergency operator play me the calls they received notifying them of both murders. If I had to guess, I'd say the caller was using one of those gadgets that masks or changes your voice."

After a few seconds thought, Ross concluded, "Which raises the possibility that both victims and possibly Phil Knott knew the killer or it's a deliberate ploy to confuse us. If we don't know what gender our killer is, it makes it double difficult for us to identify them."

"More likely the second one, sir, I think," said Drake. "The killer didn't speak to either victim, as far as we know, so why disguise their voice."

"Point taken, Izzie" Ross agreed.

Before they could say more, the squad room door opened, and Derek McLennan strode into the room.

"I need coffee, I'm parched," he gasped, and Drake joked,

"Well, if it isn't Captain Pugwash," recalling the children's cartoon TV series of her youth.

"Don't you start, Izzie Drake," McLennan retorted. "Tony friggin' Curtis is bad enough without Sam Gable and now you backing him up, with his wisecracks".

"Oh, come on, Derek, we need to hear what you've discovered, and anyway, DI Ross has something to tell you first. Tell you what, sit down and the DI can fill you in before you give us your report."

"Alright, something's going on here that I'm in the dark about. Sir, are you going to tell me what it is?" McLennan asked, just as Drake plonked a mug of coffee on his desk.

"Have you enjoyed your stint as an acting sergeant, Derek?" Ross began.

McLennan instantly thought that Ross was about to inform him that he was being returned to the rank of detective constable, now that Izzie Drake was back in her position in the squad.

"Of course I have, sir. You know that, I hope."

"I do, Derek, and I'm afraid it's time for you to relinquish your acting rank."

I knew it, McLennan thought, resigning himself to being a DC once again.

"I see sir," he spoke quietly.

"No, I don't think you do, Derek," Ross said, ready to reveal the surprise.

McLennan waited with a quizzical look on his face. He raised his coffee mug and was about to take a sip of the hot liquid when Ross said,

"How'd you like to be full sergeant instead of an acting one?"

McLennan almost dropped the mug in his hand.

"What? Really? Do you mean it?"

"Of course I do, I wouldn't say so otherwise."

As McLennan sat looking shell-shocked, his coffee mug seemingly suspended in mid-air, Ross outlined all that DCI Agostini had informed him and Drake earlier in the day. As he finished, he waited for McLennan's response.

"I don't really know what to say, except thank you, sir. I'm delighted, obviously but I do have one question."

"Only one, Derek? Go ahead, ask away."

"Well sir, you say me and Fenella are going to be team leaders within the expanded squad, right?"

"That's right Derek."

McLennan's next response had everyone in the room in paroxysms of laughter.

"If it's possible, can I *please, not* have Tony on my team? He's a great detective but his jokes would probably have me admitted to a psychiatric ward by the end of the first week."

Ross held a hand up to bring the laughter to a halt.

"You mean you could last a whole week, Derek? You surprise me. What do you think Fee? Could you cope with Tony's sense of humour in your team?"

Church managed to appear serious as she replied to Ross's question.

"Don't worry about that, sir. I think I can handle Tony, and his crazy jokes. We seem to have an understanding."

"That's settled then," Ross said. "We've just made our first appointments towards the new set-up. Now then Derek, if you can contain your excitement for a few minutes, how did you get on with your ferry inquiries?"

"Better than I expected, sir. To tell the truth I wasn't expecting much, but the ferry crews proved to be most informative. They take a great interest in their regulars and some of the crew get to know their passengers quite well. A couple of lads on the *Royal Daffodil* remember Wanda Burnside quite well and another used to speak to Adrian Hill quite often, Same type of thing on the *Snowdrop*".

Referring to his notebook, he began,

"Eric Myers, crewman aboard the *Royal Daffodil*, remembers Wanda very well. She would always talk to him, and according to Myers, he knew she was quite a lot older than him, but he still considered her to be drop-dead gorgeous, with a fantastic figure, always sexily dressed in what he called 'those power suits' with skirts that showed what great legs she had, and high heels. He told me he'd advised her to wear lower heels while on board as she was prone to trip and almost fall at times with the movement of the ship, but she said it would spoil her look if she did that. She'd told him she was single and worked for a law firm and he couldn't imagine anyone wanting to hurt her. A couple of the other lads said similar things, she was always friendly, had a smile and a good word for everyone, and more than one of them felt like Myers about her. As for Adrian Hill, the ship's first officer apparently often spoke with the man who seemed knowledgeable about nautical matters, and they often had short conversations about the war at sea during World War Two, He knew what Hill did for a living and told me he even bought his wife a new washing machine from Hill's employers. I was told similar things by the crew of the *Snowdrop*. The conclusion I came to was that these were two pretty ordinary but popular people who had no air and graces and enjoyed riding the ferries and conversing with the crews when the opportunity presented itself. There was one thing though, Mike Thomas, a crewman on the *Snowdrop* said Mrs Burnside told him a couple of weeks ago that she felt as if she was being followed. She couldn't identify anyone, it was just a feeling, but Thomas kept an eye on her whenever he could after that. Most men would turn and look at her, she was a good-looking woman after all, but he couldn't say that any one man was paying special interest in her. There was a woman who struck up a conversation with her one day and she was there again a few days later, but he never saw her again."

"Did you get a description of this woman?" Ross asked, and McLennan nodded.

"I did, sir, though it's not very detailed."

"Whatever it is, it may be helpful, so let's hear it."

McLennan quickly checked in his notebook and went on,

"She was about five feet two or three, wore jeans, black trainers, possibly Reeboks, and a black hoodie with a baseball hat. From what Paul Jennings, the witness could see of her hair, it appeared to be blonde, but he'd no idea of how long or what style. The hat and hoodie prevented him getting a good look at her hair and as he told me, he wasn't taking that much notice. He just saw them talking a couple of times, and that was all."

This mystery woman instantly jumped to the top of Ross's suspect list. In truth, she was the only suspect and a tentative one at that,

"So, we might be looking for a five-foot two-inch blonde woman whose face is unknown, who probably doesn't wear the same clothes every day and maybe hasn't caught a ferry since her interactions with the first victim."

"I wouldn't put too much credence on the blonde hair either, sir," Fenella Church said in response to Ross's words. "Don't forget, I can change my hair colour and style in a couple of minutes, and most women could probably do the same thing, so this woman could be a redhead, a brunette, anything."

"Damn, you're right of course, Fee," Ross agreed.

Church had lost her own hair when she suffered severe burns when she ran into a burning house in order to save a child almost four years ago. In addition to losing her hair she'd also suffered extensive burns to her upper body, leaving her with a deep scar, visible on the right side of her face, which recreative surgery had mostly managed to repair, but though smaller than it had been originally, it was still clearly visible. She wore wigs to conceal her lack of hair and had grown to enjoy the freedom to change hair styles, colours and length at any time, without spending a fortune at the hairdressers. She was in fact, a beautiful woman, who, after a long stay in the burns unit at Whiston Hospital in Prescot, which included three skin graft operations, had fought her way back to fitness and a return to duty. She'd been assigned to the Force's Cold Case Unit, where she spent two years, before coming to the attention of Andy Ross at just the right time, when he was looking for a replacement for Sofie Meyer, the German detective who'd returned to the Bundeskrimilamt at the end of her attachment to the Merseyside Police Force. She'd since proved herself to be a highly intelligent and superbly motivated member of Ross's team.

"So, we don't really know who she is, what she looks like, and even whether she has anything to do with the deaths of Wanda and Adrian," Ross looked deflated.

"Sorry, Boss," McLennan apologised. "Not much help, is it?"

"Never mind, Derek. At least we know both victims were regular users of the ferry service, and maybe that's the thing that links them together as far as the case is concerned."

"Have we missed anything?" the voice of Tony Curtis announced his return, together with Mitch Sinclair, as the pair breezed through the squad room door.

"You've survived your first job with Tony, then Mitch?" Sam Gable joked and Sinclair laughed.

"Oh, he wasn't so bad, once I gave him a kick or two," Sinclair responded, only for Curtis to turn to him and give him a friendly slap on the back of his head.

"Watch it, you big lumbering Aussie twerp," he said and then jumped back before Sinclair could respond in kind.

"I see you have a new sparring partner, DC Curtis," Ross spoke sternly, though he had a smirk on his face. He'd deliberately paired the two together, wanting Curtis to help Sinclair settle in with the team. He'd been badly affected by the loss of Nick Dodds, his best friend, and Ross knew that Curtis had been treated for depression since Dodds' demise. He hoped pairing him with the tall half-Australian detective would prove to be good therapy for one of his most experienced and valued team members. From first impressions, it appeared to be working, so far at least.

"Don't take him too seriously, Mitch," Drake added, "except when he's working. He does know what he's doing when he stops his jokes."

"Aye, I've already gathered that, Sarge," Sinclair replied.

"Before we hear from you two, we need to fill you in on some rather massive developments for the team," Ross said, above the general atmosphere of frivolity that Curtis and Sinclair's return had generated.

It took Ross around five minutes to impart the relevant details to the two detectives. Sinclair, being new to the team, aside from giving his congratulations by way of a very Australian, "That's bonzer, Skip," and expressing his excitement at being involved in the team's expansion, had little to say, not so DC Tony Curtis.

"Bloody fantastic, Boss. That's all I can say, apart from the fact that you and Izzie totally deserve your promotions and you can count on me to help the new guys settle in and anything else you need me to do."

"Yes, right, Tony, thanks for that. I know I can count on you, always have and always will," Ross beamed. "Now, can you and Mitch please tell what, if anything you found out from Wanda's employers?"

"Yeah, of course, sorry Boss. Bertrand and Doyle have been in business in Wallasey for years, with Wanda Burnside working for them for nearly eight years. We spoke first to the firm's chief legal clerk, Giles Ackland, and before you say anything we thought the same. With a name like that he could only be in the legal business. Ackland's been employed by the firm for over twenty years and nothing gets by him, and I mean nothing. He knows everyone who works for them and what he doesn't know about each employee isn't worth knowing. You want to tell them about Wanda, Mitch?" Curtis allowed the new man to continue.

"Sure, cheers Mate," Sinclair took up the narrative. "Wanda Burnside, as Tony said, had worked for the firm for nearly eight years, until some bastard cut her life short. She was happily married up until five years ago when she discovered her husband, Roger Steven Burnside, was having an affair with a woman she'd thought of as a friend, Linda Gray. Bertrand and Doyle handled her divorce and she and Roger came to an amicable settlement. She got the house, he moved in with Ms Gray, who was already divorced, and they apparently maintained a civilised relationship if they ever came into contact with each other since the split. I suggest we speak to Mr Burnside if only to eliminate him from our inquiries."

"One of Wanda's workmates told us that Roger works as a self-employed plumber," Curtis interjected. "They have his address on file at Bertrand and Doyle, and we tried calling him, but his phone was turned off, probably busy on a job, stuck under a broken sink or up a ladder maybe. We're going to try again after normal working hours."

Okay, well done you two. We still don't have much to go on, but every little scrap of information helps us to build a better picture of our victims," Ross said, scratching his hair. So far, they hadn't got much. Both victims stood out only for their ordinariness. He couldn't for the life of him think what had made them into targets for murder.

"Where does the ex-husband live? Did anyone know."

"Sure thing, Skip," Sinclair replied. "We even got an up-to-date address on the joker."

"Then, as there's plenty of day left, I suggest you two get out there and have a word with him. Forget phone calls, see the man in person. Where is it, by the way?"

"Formby," both Sinclair and Curtis voiced in tandem.

"Well, what are you both still doing here? Go, now," Ross waved them towards the door and the two detectives swiftly departed."

"What do you think of Sinclair?" he asked Drake a few minutes later, in the privacy of his office.

"I like him. Looks like he's going to fit in nicely. Why do you ask?" Drake had a feeling she already knew the answer to her question.

"I'm not sure I can get used to being called Skip, that's all. Sounds very Australian to me."

"Well, he is Australian, after all," Drake couldn't help stating the obvious.

"Oh well," Ross mused. "I don't want to stifle his natural personality. I suppose I'll get used to it, in time. The important thing is how well he does the job, right?"

"Too right...Skip," Drake laughed and then ducked as Ross launched a pad of yellow post-its in her direction.

The pair of them laughed in unison. She may have been absent for months on maternity leave, but Ross was pleased to see that Izzie hadn't changed one iota in her absence.

"Let's wait and see what he and Curtis find out from the husband. Hopefully we'll at least have more information about the dead woman to work with."

"Or maybe not," said Drake. "If they're divorced, they might not have remained in touch, especially as there were no kids from the marriage."

"Well, let's you and I go and find Miles Booker and see if his Crime Scene techs have found anything helpful. I know he said he'd ring me, but…"

With that, Ross and Drake marched quickly out of the office, next stop, the forensic lab and workplace home of Miles Booker.

CHAPTER 6
ANOTHER BRICK WALL

At first sight the address the police possessed for Roger Burnside appeared to be a typical mid-twentieth century detached house on Andrews Lane but had in fact been modernised and converted into well-appointed flats, one of which was the rented home of the man they sought. Curtis had tried ringing Wanda's ex-husband while Sinclair drove the few miles from headquarters to Formby. This time, Burnside answered his mobile, and apologised for not replying earlier, explaining he'd been working in a client's cellar where there was no signal. Burnside was intrigued at receiving a call from the police but when Curtis refused to tell him the reason for their visit over the phone, he rightly assumed it must be a serious matter they wished to discuss with him.

Opening the door to his flat after one ring on the doorbell, Roger Burnside checked the two detectives' identities before fully admitting them to his home.

"Can't be too careful, you know," he explained, apologetically.

After Sinclair agreed with him, DC Curtis informed him of the reason for their visit.

"You what?" Burnside exclaimed on being informed of his

ex-wife's murder. "Wanda? Murdered and raped? Listen to me DC Curtis, Wanda and me might have been divorced, and that was down to me being stupid and playing away from home, if you know what I mean, but I still thought the world of that woman. So, if you're thinking I might have something to do with this, you can forget it. When did it happen?"

"Two evenings ago, just as she arrived home from work."

"Still catching the ferry every day, was she?"

"Yes, she was," Curtis confirmed.

"So, you reckon some pervert followed her home and did this to her?"

"Possibly, Mr Burnside," this was Sinclair, "but the next evening, there was a second victim, a man, attacked in the same way."

"A man?" Burnside looked confused. "I don't understand. How could a man…?" He left the question hanging, and Curtis responded.

"The killer used some kind of implement, Mr Burnside, maybe the end of a wrench, or a screwdriver."

"Don't you dare accuse me of this, just because I'm a plumber and use such tools for my job. I'm telling you, me and Wanda got on alright on the rare occasions we met each other."

"I'm not suggesting that at all, Mr Burnside," Curtis assured him. "But do you know a man called Adrian Hill?"

"Was that the second victim?" Burnside asked and Curtis nodded in confirmation.

"No, I've never heard the name before. That's not to say Wanda didn't know him. I've no idea what she did in her private life since we split up."

"What about the lady involved in your divorce? Linda Gray, was it?" Sinclair asked.

"Bloody Hell, do you guys know everything about me? Listen, I made a big mistake getting involved with Linda. She was Wanda's best friend, but she was jealous of Wanda. She only wanted me because I was Wanda's husband. I was an idiot, falling for a pair of great legs, short skirts and great tits. She never really cared for me. I was too blinded by lust to see it. She stuck it with me for about a year, then buggered off with some guy in a flash Porsche, who had a bigger house than me and a bigger fucking bank balance."

"So, you don't think she could have had any kind of grudge against Wanda?" Curtis asked.

"No way," Burnside replied instantly. "She got what she wanted from Wanda…Me. Why should she bear a grudge against her? No, detectives, you're going to have to look further afield for Wanda's killer, I'm afraid."

"So, you've no idea who might have wanted her dead?" Sinclair asked, and Burnside slowly shook his head.

"Sorry, no idea at all. We weren't close at all since the divorce. She led her own life, and I led mine."

The detectives both realised they were unlikely to learn anything useful from Roger Burnside, and Curtis brought the interview to an end, and it wasn't long before he and Sinclair were motoring back in the direction of headquarters. As they exited the door to Burnside's flat, Sinclair however, had asked on last question.

"Can you give us Linda Gray's address? You never know, she might be able to tell us something you might not know about your ex?"

Burnside laughed.

"Sorry mate, I've no idea where she's living now. Last I heard, the bloke she'd shacked up with threw her out. Guess what? She'd been sleeping around again, the bloody tart."

"What d'you think of him, Tony?" Sinclair asked as they approached their destination.

"I'd say Burnside's clean," Curtis replied. "If we believe what he told us, he and Wanda didn't stay in touch after the divorce and if anyone had a motive for murder, it would have been her. He was the one who did the dirty on her after all."

"Yeah, you're right. What about the tart he had the affair with?"

"Forget her, Mitch. I doubt she's given Wanda a second thought since she nicked her husband."

"I suppose you're right. Not really learned much have we?"

"That's the way it goes sometimes, one brick wall after another," Curtis responded. "But often, once we eliminate all the negatives, we're left with a clearer picture of who it might have been, and we can save ourselves a lot of wasted time following dead-end leads."

"I suppose you're right. It's a bit different from the usual cases I've worked in the past."

Curtis laughed, "Hey, that's why this squad was put together. We get the cases everyone else would turn their noses up at. We're supposed to work fucking miracles, Mitch. Didn't you know that?"

"I don't suppose I did, but I'm learning fast," Sinclair grinned as he brought the car to a halt in the headquarters car park.

Soon after Curtis and Sinclair arrived back at headquarters and given their less than informative report to Ross, the Mersey Ferry, Ross called the team together for a rather subdued briefing.

"I've talked to Miles Booker, and he's assured me that his people have gone over both crime scenes meticulously, as they always do of course, without finding anything that might assist us in finding this bastard, whether it be a man or a woman," he told the gathered detectives. All of our initial inquiries have produced similar, negative results. I've said before, unless we're dealing with some random psycho, there has to be something that links both victims together and by that connection, to their killer. It's our job to find that connection. So far, we've concentrated on the present and the relatively recent past, but what if the connection lies even further back in time?"

"How far back, Boss?" DC Devenish asked.

"Ah, that's the sixty-thousand-dollar question, Ginger," Ross grimaced as he spoke. "I don't know."

"So, where do we start?" DC Gable asked.

Before Ross could reply, Fenella Church interrupted with one word, "Birth."

"Explain that, please, Fee," Ross said, giving the sergeant the opportunity to expand on the word.

"When I was with the Cold Case Squad, some of our cases could look totally impossible to solve, especially if they'd taken place years ago. Quite often, we could only make progress by going back to the beginning, that is, the birth dates of those involved. It would be like a jigsaw puzzle, collating scraps of information, and hoping that we ended up with enough scraps that eventually two or more of them would suddenly fit together and give us a clue that would help bring the case together. It didn't always work but as a last resort it often produced a result."

Ross clapped his hands together.

"DS Church, I knew there was a reason why I stole you from the Cold Case Squad. You might have given us a way to unlock the case. I'd like you and Derek, assisted by Ginger and Sam, to delve into the histories of both victims, and try and find something in their timelines that puts them in the same place at the same time. Derek, Sam, Ginger, as Fee knows how to go about this, let her give you a run through on the procedures she's used on Cold Cases and then split into two teams and get started. Does that sound workable?" he aimed his last remark to Church.

"Yes, but we need to work closely together. It won't work if we work as two separate entities and then hope to find something at the end. We've got to keep in close contact as we highlight their life events and so on. It could take a while though."

"Well, what are you waiting for? Get to it, people and use

Paul and his computer as much as you need. Got that, Paul?" he asked Ferris.

"Whatever they need, Boss," Ferris replied.

Church quickly gathered her team together and began laying out the procedure she wanted them all to follow. It may not produce the result Ross wanted but at least they felt they were doing something positive in the search for the killer.

"Something else we need to consider," Ross said.

"What's that, Skip?" Sinclair asked.

"South of the river," was Ross's reply.

"Eh?" Sinclair responded, looking rather mystified.

"I've just been doing a spot of lateral thinking," Ross now had everyone's attention. "By default, we've all been thinking our killer is based, or lives in Liverpool. What if he or she is located south of the Mersey, but they could just as easily live and work in Wallasey, Birkenhead, Bebington or Ellesmere Port for example. All I'm saying is we need to look at every possible option."

"Bloody Hell, sir. That's a fucking big area," Curtis intoned.

"I know, Tony, which is precisely why the brass is expanding the size of our unit. Unfortunately, until I get the extra personnel, I'm stuck with you lot," Ross replied, a sardonic grin on his face.

"You trying to tell us something, Boss?" Ginger Devenish added.

"Who? Me? Of course I bloody am, Ginger. What I'm saying is that we're going to have to use every bit of detecting skill at our disposal, and cover as much ground as we can. Ishaan is due back tomorrow, which will help, but in the meantime, I'm going to have a word with the DCI and see if we can get a couple of extra bodies to assist us with the investigation. Who knows, we can maybe use their time with us as an extended trial, a sort of 'on the job' interview for the new bodies we'll be recruiting."

After a brief discussion with the whole squad, Ross made his way upstairs, accompanied by Izzie Drake, where they put their case for the extra help to Oscar Agostini who received the request for additional help with the case enthusiastically.

"I don't have a problem with the idea," Agostini responded. "I'll clear it with DCS Hollingsworth and then put a request out to a couple of friends of mine who might have suitable candidates for the job, if I can persuade them to release some of their best people."

Satisfied that they would at least, in all probability receive reinforcements to assist in the investigation, particularly south of the Mersey, Ross and Drake returned to the squad room. There wasn't much more they could hope to achieve that day, and Ross intended to send the team to their homes to get some rest, ready for a busy day tomorrow.

As he relayed the results of his meeting with Agostini to the team, events elsewhere were conspiring to thwart his plans for a restful evening and an early night.

CHAPTER 7
BETTY

Elizabeth, (Betty) Morton had enjoyed her day, visiting her daughter in Birkenhead. Paula, her daughter, was thirty-five and the mother of two young children, who idolised their grandma, Betty likewise loved the children and always looked forward to her weekly trip to see Paula, and the two girls, Gemma and Sally. Paula's husband, Bobby, was the area manager for a small retail furniture chain and spent two days a week working out of the company head office in Warrington, which left Paula free to spend some quality time with her Mum.

As usual, after a day of fun and games, Paula and the girls went with Betty to see her off on the short ferry ride back to Liverpool. Promising to bring the girls over to Knotty Ash to see their grandad at the weekend, they happily waved to Betty as the ferry departed from the Woodside ferry terminal, Betty smiling as she waved back, knowing she'd be home in time to make the evening meal in time for her husband, Charlie, the girls' grandad, arriving home from work.

Betty never sensed the malevolent form of the figure that followed her all the way from the ferry to her house, where she soon had her coat off, and the kettle on. A cup of tea would be nice, she thought, before chopping the veg for Charlie's dinner. The pork chops wouldn't need to come out of the fridge until the veg was boiling on the hob. Just as the kettle boiled and switched itself off, the doorbell rang and Betty cheerfully walked from the kitchen, through the hall to the front door. She opened it and was surprised to be confronted by a black-hooded figure, who wasted no time in pushing Betty backwards, spinning her round, pushing her to her knees, and bringing a heavy object down with considerable force on the back of her head. At that point, Betty Morton's world turned black, and it was her husband, Charlie, sixty-four, and a year away from retirement, who would find her, much to his shock and horror lying half-naked and apparently horribly mutilated, on his return from work an hour later. Charlie managed to keep his wits about him long enough to dial 999, summoning the police and ambulance service, before breaking down in tears, falling to his knees, taking hold of Betty's lifeless hand, and sobbing like a child, which was precisely where Detective Inspector Andy Ross and Detective Sergeant Izzie Drake found him as they arrived on the scene just twenty minutes after being summoned by a knowledgeable emergency operator supervisor, who, knowing of the two previous murders, directed the emergency request straight to the Specialist Murder Investigation Team.

* * *

Ross and Drake were first on the scene, for once even beating Doctor Nugent the Medical Examiner to the murder site. They were followed by DS McLennan, DS Church and DCs Curtis and Sinclair. Ross didn't want to flood the scene with too many officers at this point in time, so much to their disgust, the rest of the team were instructed to stick to the original plan, go home, get some rest, but be ready in case Ross needed them to join him at the murder scene.

He's ensured that there was a uniform presence at the house in Knotty Ash and a fresh-faced constable, having checked the identities of the detectives, lifted the police tape he and his partner had erected across the garden gate to allow them entry. The second uniformed constable was just inside the hall as Ross pushed the front door open, Charlie Morton easily identifiable as the deceased's husband, on his knees, pitifully sobbing.

"PC Shorrocks, sir," the constable introduced himself. "I didn't have the heart to pull him away, sir, but I've made sure he hasn't touched anything since me and Constable Billings arrived. He hasn't said a word, apart from telling me his name. It's Charlie, Charlie Morton, by the way. He's the husband."

"OK, Shorrocks, you've not done anything wrong if that's what you were thinking, by allowing him to stay with his wife. None of us are that heartless."

"Thank you, sir," Shorrocks replied, "greatly relieved at Ross's reassurance. In truth, he had thought he might get a rollocking for not removing the grieving husband from the immediate vicinity of what was clearly a 'live' murder scene.

"Now, be a good lad and position yourself outside the door and make sure the only people you allow into this house are the ME and his assistant, and the SOC team," Ross instructed, hoping the lad understood that SOC meant the Scenes of Crime team. He was relieved when Shorrocks replied,

"No problem, sir. I take it Scenes of Crime are already on their way?"

"They are, so you won't have long to wait."

That sorted, Ross and Drake quietly approached Charlie Morton, where he knelt, lovingly stroking the hand of his dead wife, his face they could see was a mask of tears. Ross nodded to Drake, who made the first move to speak to the grieving husband. Ross knew that a female voice could often be most effective at times like this.

Slowly, Izzie Drake dropped to one knee beside the man, and very gently laid a hand on his shoulder as she spoke.

"Mr Morton," she spoke softly, not wanting to surprise him. "It's Charlie, isn't it? My name is Detective Sergeant Drake. I know you're upset, but I really need you to step away from your wife now and answer a couple of questions for me. Can you do that, please?"

Almost trance-like, Charlie Morton lifted his head, looked tearfully at Drake and with what Drake took to be a Herculean effort, he began to rise to his feet. She placed a hand under his arm to assist him as he slowly stood, and at last, he spoke.

"She's dead, lass. My Betty, she's dead. Some bastard did this to her."

With Charlie Morton at last on his feet, Ross and Drake could see for the first time the full horror that had been perpetrated on Betty Morton. With Church and the other detectives standing near the front door, keeping a respectful distance for the time being, it was immediately evident to Ross and Drake that Betty had fallen victim to the killer of Wanda Burnside and Adrian Hill.

She lay face down, her summer dress pulled up beyond her waist. There was blood visible where she'd been struck by a heavy, blunt object, her underwear had been removed and the blood visible between her legs, indicated to the detectives that she'd been assaulted in the same way as the first two victims. Ross didn't want to turn her over until Nugent arrived, but for now they worked on the reasonably safe assumption that she'd died from a stab wound to the heart, there being no other signs of violence immediately visible.

Ross nodded to Church and McLennan, and they began a preliminary examination of the scene. Church whispered something to Curtis, and he and Sinclair exited the front door, their task being to talk to the Morton's immediate neighbours, to find out if they'd seen or heard anything suspicious.

Between them, Ross and Drake gently led a shaking Charlie Morton through the first door that led off the hallway and entered the neat little home's sitting room.

Ross quietly began the painful questioning of the heart-broken man. He asked if there was anyone who could come and sit with and help Charlie, to which the man replied, haltingly,

"Paula, daughter, Birkenhead. Betty's been to see her, today. Phone number's in the book," and he pointed to a small table in the corner of the room which held a telephone and an old-fashioned address and telephone book.

Drake crossed the room, picked up the book and after finding the number she called Paula's number. It was an awful task, informing Paula Simmons of her mother's brutal murder. Once she'd recovered from the initial shock, Paula informed Drake that she'd be there as soon as she could.

"Paula's on her way, Mr Morton," she told Charlie Morton who nodded and mouthed "Thanks" to her. Ross made a hand signal to Drake who quickly made her way to the kitchen to make the man a drink.

The next ten minutes were excruciating for the detectives and the bereaved man as Ross and Drake, who'd made hot, sweet tea and placed it down on a side table next to Charlie's chair, tried to question him on his wife's movements and habits. Gradually, Charlie Morton regained a modicum of composure and was able to provide the detectives with the answers to some of their questions, none of which threw any light on who might have held a grudge against his wife, much less anyone who might have wished her harm. Ross couldn't help feeling that they may be up against a killer who was selecting their victims at random, though that went against everything he'd learned in over twenty years as a detective. Still, it would have to be considered.

Izzie Drake then asked a question which might, just might have produced an answer that would later prove helpful to the investigation.

"Charlie," she began, as the man had sked them to use his first name, "Apart from home and family, did Betty have any other interests, things that she engaged in and didn't include your participation?"

Charlie looked a little mystified at first but then, realising what she meant, he produced a response.

"She were interested in what she called Current Affairs. It were all a bit above my head, but she loved watching TV shows about true crime, and followed all the big cases in the news. I thought it were a waste of time meself. I mean, what use were it for her to spend time reading newspaper articles about crimes from years ago? You name it, fraud cases, embezzlement, murder, rape, she'd read and watch anything about stuff like that. Stuff and nonsense, I called it, but Betty just called me a phil…phil…"

"Philistine?" Drake offered.

"Aye, lass, that's the word she used. She called me one of them and said I should be better informed about what were going on in the world. Lord's sakes, she even kept a scrapbook wi' press cuttings and the like in it, silly woman. What good's any of that ever going to do anyone? I asked her."

It wasn't until later that Charlie's words would prove to be of great significance, but for now, it was taken to be simply an old lady's hobby, nothing more.

* * *

Doctor William Nugent and his assistant, Francis Lees were already working on the body of Betty Morton, when Ross and Drake emerged from the sitting room, leaving her grieving husband alone for a few minutes. Ross asked DS McLennan to sit with Charlie for a while, knowing the daughter would be arriving soon. McLennan would be just the man to exhibit sympathy while maybe asking a couple of pertinent questions that might help the investigation.

"Anything so far, Doc?" Ross addressed the ME, who was on his knees beside the body, while Lees, as usual, was busy photographing the scene from every possible angle.

"Well, hello to you too, Inspector," Nugent replied sarcastically. "Do ye mind if I actually have a few minutes to examine the poor woman, before delivering any opinions?"

"Sorry, Doc. Have you been here long? As you could see, Izzie and I have been busy with the husband."

"Aye, I kinda guessed that. Francis and I have been here about ten minutes, if you must know. Your two sergeants were busy trampling all over my crime scene when I arrived."

"We were not, Doctor, and you know it. Derek and I were merely examining the area around the body and the doorway for anything pertinent to the investigation," Church quickly snapped back. She wasn't the type of person to allow anyone, even the city's Chief Pathologist make spurious allegations about her professionalism.

"I'm sure Doctor Nugent meant nothing by that remark, Fee," Ross tried to placate the sergeant.

"Aye, just me and ma big mouth, as usual," Nugent growled from his place on the floor. "Dinna take a bit o'notice of me lassie."

About to remind him her title was Detective Sergeant, Church fell silent as Ross indicated with a finger over his lips. Instead, he pulled her to one side and quietly asked her if she and McLennan had found anything prior to the Medical Examiner's arrival.

Church quietly pointed to an area of blood spatter on one wall.

"Derek and I think the killer got angry and extra-violent when they were penetrating the poor woman with whatever they used. We didn't see anything quite like this in the first two cases."

Ross was forced to agree, and Drake quickly concurred with Church's opinion. Before they could discuss anything further, Doctor Nugent announced that he was about to turn the body over, and the detectives waited as Nugent and Lees carefully rolled Betty Morton face-up to reveal the expected stab wound in the chest.

"Looks like the same killer," Nugent said, "As if you needed me to tell you that."

Ross pointed to the blood spatter on the wall.

"Fee and Derek think the killer got angry. Can you tell if there's any sign of such anger around the areas of penetration?"

"Let's wait till I get the poor woman back to the morgue and I can do a full examination."

As he spoke there came the sound of voices outside the front door. Ross correctly guessed this heralded the arrival of Paula, the daughter. PC Shorrocks appeared in the doorway, and announced, "There's a Mrs Simmons here, sir. She says she's Mr Morton's daughter."

William Nugent quickly covered the body with a plastic sheet on hearing Shorrocks' words. Ross then turned to the constable.

"That's okay, Shorrocks, please show Mrs Simmons in."

Paula Simmons tearful face looked even more horrified as she took in the sight of the covered body in the hall, and the numerous people filling the cramped space.

"Oh, my God. Is that my Mum?" she was clearly distraught. "Where's my dad?"

Drake tried to usher her towards the living room door.

"He's in the living room, Mrs Simmons, if you'd like to come with me?"

"I want to see my Mum," Paula cried loudly. "Please, let me see my Mum".

Ross nodded to Nugent who pulled the sheet back just enough for the woman to look upon the face of her dead mother. Sensing she was about to faint Fenella Church quickly moved to support her, and virtually pushed her into the waiting arms of Izzie Drake, and the pair of them carefully escorted the crying woman into the room where her father sat, head in hands, still sobbing quietly to himself.

Before they left father and daughter together, Paula Simmons asked the detectives, "What happened? Who did this? Do you know who killed my Mum? For God's sake I only waved her off on the ferry a couple of hours ago."

There it was again, Drake and Church realised, the ferry! Somehow the Mersey Ferry had to be the link between all three victims.

Drake replied to Paula's questions.

"We don't know anything at present Mrs Simmons. It's early days in the investigation, but I'd like to ask you a few questions, when you're up to it."

"Sure," Paula sniffed. "Just let me see to Dad and I'll answer any questions you have."

Sometime later, Drake sat with Paula in her parents' kitchen. Paula, trying to cope the best way she could, had made tea for herself and coffee for Drake, who proceeded to ask the tearful daughter a few questions. Paula explained that her mother had spent most of the day with her and her children in Birkenhead, which, she confirmed was a regular weekly occurrence. It would therefore have been easy for anyone to work out her mother's routine and be lying in wait for her as she arrived home. On the other hand, when Paula made the point that Betty didn't always catch the ferry back to Liverpool at the same time, making Drake conclude that Betty's killer was probably stalking her and would have been aboard the ferry, and would have followed her home, striking as soon as the poor woman arrived home. Almost as if she'd read Drake's thoughts, Paula said, "I was always offering to bring her home in the car. I've got a lovely new Focus out there, but she insisted she enjoyed riding the ferry, and wouldn't dream of putting me out by having to drive in all that traffic just to run her home. Perhaps if I had…"

"I don't think it would have made any difference, Paula," Drake attempted to placate the woman. "You probably don't know this yet, but there've been two similar murders to your Mum's in the past two days."

Paula's hand shot up to cover her mouth, before she exclaimed,

"Oh no. Those news soundbites about the police seeking the killer of a woman the other day….?"

"Yes, and yesterday a man was murdered in the same way."

A sudden realisation gripped Paula Simmons.

"Was my mum…you know…sexually assaulted?"

Drake couldn't lie to the woman but kept her reply as non-committal as possible.

"Nothing's been confirmed as yet, Paula. The Medical Examiner was still with your Mum as you arrived. There'll be a post-mortem of course. We'll know more then."

Paula nodded her understanding, then broke down once again, the tears flowing freely before she managed to pull herself together a minute later. When she'd dried her eyes, Drake asked her if she'd be staying with her father when the police left. Paula assured her that she would be. Her husband had arranged to stay at home to look after the children for a couple of days.

"You can go back and sit with your dad now, Paula," Drake let her go, as she went to join Ross and the others, after assuring the woman that she'd also arrange for a police Family Liaison Officer to come and stay with her father for the next couple of days, at least. "If you think of anything else that might be of help to us in finding out who did this to your Mum, please call us," and she handed Paula one of her cards, which the woman looked at, before opening her phone wallet and placing the card inside. At that moment, Paula Simmons wasn't aware that she had information which could significantly assist the police inquiry. That realisation, when it struck her, would help to point the police in the right direction towards finding her mother's killer, but for now, the knowledge lay buried in the deepest confines of her memory.

CHAPTER 8
FIRST DESCRIPTION

Before the body of Betty Morton was removed from the scene, Police Constable Maggie Evans, the Family Liaison officer assigned to the case, arrived at the house, and was given a brief rundown of the events that had taken place by DS Church, who then showed her through to the living room, introducing her to Charlie Morton and Paula Simmons, leaving her to the job she was trained for.

Miles Booker and his Scenes of Crime team arrived and as soon as William Nugent gave the OK for the body to be removed and taken to the morgue, he and his people got to work, though, based on the first two murders, Miles wasn't particularly hopeful of finding anything helpful to Ross's investigation.

Ross, Drake, McLennan and Church retired to the kitchen, where McLennan took charge of the kettle and swiftly made drinks for them all. As the automatic kettle came to the boil, and clicked off, DCs Curtis and Sinclair arrived, having visited a number of nearby homes.

"Perfect timing, you two, tea or coffee?" McLennan greeted them.

"Coffee please Sarge," Sinclair said immediately.

"Same for me." Curtis echoed.

"Never mind drinks, have you managed to find me a witness or two?" Ross asked.

"We might have something, Boss," Curtis replied. "A Mrs Lisa Dale, three doors away, swears she saw a person following Mrs Morton as she passed her house on the way home."

Everyone's attention now focussed on Curtis.

"Did you get a description, Tony?"

"Sort of, Boss, but it's not that great. The person was dressed all in black, jogging pants, trainers, and a hoodie, the peak of a baseball cap showing under the hoodie. Mrs Dale remembers thinking it was odd that whoever it was had the hood up, what with it being a warm, sunny day. He or she was short, possibly about five foot two or three, she thinks, though she admits she could be wrong as she only saw this character through her front room window, for a couple of seconds. She's pretty adamant that this person was most likely a woman, though, Boss."

That really grabbed Ross's attention.

"What made her think that?" he wanted to know if this could be their first real lead.

"Lisa Dale is a physiotherapist," Curtis consulted his notebook, "and, as she said, in her own words, *I know the difference between a male and a female body. The body shape was all wrong for it to be a man. The hips, the backside, and just a hint of breasts under the baggy hoodie.* I think the lady knows what she's talking about."

"Don't forget the walk, Tony," Sinclair added.

"Yeah, I was coming to that. Mrs Dale added that the person had a funny walk."

"In what way, funny?" Drake asked.

"As if they were limping," Curtis replied.

"Or had something long and straight stuffed down her pants," said Sinclair.

"Something like a baseball bat!" Church knew where this was leading.

"Exactly," Curtis agreed.

"Did she manage to see any of this person's face, or hair colour?" Ross was hungry for more information.

"No, sir, I'm afraid not. The woman, if it was a woman, was only in her field of vision for a couple of seconds and as she said, she was virtually covered up by the hoodie."

"It's unusual enough to find a member of the public with the observational skills of this lady, Skip." Sinclair added.

"You're right Mitch," Ross agreed. "Anything else she could tell us?"

"That's all, Boss, but at least it's something," Curtis replied.

"It's something alright, Tony. If we take this woman's word for it, we know we're looking for a woman now."

"That cuts out about fifty percent of the population then," Curtis quipped.

"Tony!"

"Sorry, Boss, didn't mean to sound flippant."

"He's right though," Drake pointed out. "Thank God for a witness with a good brain for deducing the perp's gender."

"Now all we have to do is find a woman with a grudge against all three victims, and so far, we have nothing to link any of them together," McLennan, pointed out.

"Izzie, please, go and ask Charlie and his daughter if either of them has heard of the other two victims," Ross asked and Drake quickly rose, left the room, and returned within two minutes, shaking her head as she walked back into the kitchen.

"Neither of them has heard of the two previous victims," she stated, flatly, another avenue closed.

"Damn," Ross cursed. "Something, or someone, somewhere links them all together. We have to discover what it is before we can get a handle on who's doing this."

"Dare I risk theorising that the motive has to be linked to something sexual?" Derek McLennan suggested.

"I agree with you Derek," Ross nodded. "The nature of these killings can only point to an event in the past, definitely sexual in nature, but it could be almost anything."

"Maybe when we've delved further into the past lives of our victims, we might discover what this sexual mystery is," Church suggested.

"The thing is," Sinclair offered an opinion, "so far we have no idea whether our victims were angels or demons. You know, whatever this thing in the past is, they could have been on the side of good or the side of evil."

"That's a good way of putting it, Mitch," Ross was forced to agree with his newest team member. For all they knew, the three current victims could have been involved in perpetrating some kind of sex crime in the past or perhaps they'd been victims of such a crime. But he gave the opinion that if they'd been victims of a sex crime it would have been logical for their next of kin to be aware of it.

"So, that puts them on the side of the demons, then, Skip".

"We can't assume that as a fact, Mitch. We have to keep our minds open to anything at this time. Let's stick to the plan and find out everything we can about the past lives of each of our vics."

"Roger, Skip," Sinclair replied, further reinforcing Ross's view that his latest team member was definitely more Australian than British. He smiled inwardly before speaking again.

"And let's not forget that our killer has now struck three times in three days. I'm hoping against hope that he or she doesn't make it four out of four."

Izzie Drake had been thinking deeply while Ross was talking and now came up with an idea that might help them to track down their elusive killer, male or female.

"As it's obvious that this killer, I'll call her a woman, based on the one witness who's sure she saw a woman following

Betty Morton, has followed two of the three victims from the ferry to their homes, lying in wait for number two to return home, quickly dispatched them with a blitz attack, not giving them any warning or opportunity to defend themselves. Why don't we place people on the ferries with instructions to be on the lookout for anyone matching Mrs Dale's description. We'd need to borrow some bodies from Uniform division, putting them in plain clothes of course, because there aren't enough of us to cover every sailing."

Izzie stopped, waiting to hear what Ross and the others thought. Ross spoke first.

"That's a good idea, Izzie. I should be able to swing a few extra bods from Uniform, with Oscar's help."

"Should we be looking at sailings in both directions?" Church raised the point. "So far all the vics have crossed from south to north, but what if our killer suddenly follows their next target the other way."

"I'd say that's a valid point," McLennan joined in. "Can we get enough reinforcements to cover every ferry, from late afternoon to mid-evening, sailing in both directions?"

"It won't be easy, but I don't think we can ignore Izzie's idea," Ross responded to the various points. "Of course, we can't be sure our killer is going to strike again, maybe the three vics are the sum total of their targets."

"Or their next victim might not use the ferry, sir." Curtis added.

"That's right, Tony. Trust you to complicate things," Sam Gable said.

"He's right though," Ross had to agree with Curtis. "If this blighter strikes somewhere else in the city, we'll be back to square one."

"There's another way we could do it," Ginger Devenish now spoke up.

"Go on, Ginger, what's your idea."

DC Devenish had worked for the Port Police before being

recruited by Ross for his team, so when it came to anything to do with the Mersey, Ross was fully prepared to listen to his thoughts.

"We could enlist the help of the Ferry Company, Boss. If we circulate the description of this woman, if it is a woman, to the skippers of each ferry and they inform their crews to be on the lookout for anyone matching the description, with orders not to approach the person, but to report to the skipper, the captain can then contact us to let us know someone matching the wanted person is on their ship. We can then meet the ferry and either apprehend or follow the person matching the description. It might also help to reduce the number of uniforms we'd need to borrow. We can just have one man on each ferry who the captain can inform as well as phoning us."

"Brilliant idea, Ginger," Ross congratulated Devenish on his quick thinking. "If the ferry company will cooperate that could work. Get on to Mersey Travel, see if you can enlist their assistance. Stress the point that they'd be assisting with an important police investigation. As soon as the uniform bods arrive, we'll assign a couple to ferry duty, and they can get to work."

"Okay, Boss," Devenish replied, feeling quite pleased with himself for having thought of the idea. "I'll do it right away."

He immediately picked up his phone and proceeded with his plan.

Ross, meanwhile, quickly made his way to the office of Oscar Agostini, where the DCI readily agreed to his request for help from the uniform division and made a call there and then, with the result that a dozen officers would be reporting to the squad room, in civilian clothing, within the next two hours. Ross would be responsible for briefing them on their arrival.

"You can have them for two days, Andy. If you need any of them for longer than that, let me know and I'll see what I can do."

"Okay, thanks Oscar," Ross replied. "Can't hang about. I want to see if Devenish has managed to enlist the help of the ferry company in looking out for our suspect."

"Carry on then," said the DCI. "You can explain what you're talking about later."

Ross realised he hadn't told Agostini of Devenish's idea. He'd fill him in once he knew if the ferry people were on board. Giving Agostini a quick mixture of a wave and a salute, he swiftly made his way back to the squad room, where Devenish was happy to inform him that the Ferries Manager at Mersey Travel had agreed to his idea. If he could get copies of the description to the ferry terminal at the pier head as soon as possible, the on-site manager would ensure every ferry captain received a number of copies to ensure all their crews had an opportunity to memorise it before they sailed.

In Ross's brief absence, Devenish had run off plenty of copies of the description, in readiness for his plan to be put into motion.

"Well done, Ginge. I suppose you'd better get down to the Pier Head. The sooner those ferry captains get copies of the description and communicate it to their crews, the happier I'll be."

"Leave it to me, Boss. It won't take long, and I've arranged it that the Liverpool ferries will carry copies to be handed to the skippers of the ships berthed across the river too." and with that, Devenish grabbed his jacket from the back of his chair and was out of the squad room door in seconds.

"Impressive," Church said to Ross, referring to Devenish's idea and the speed with which he'd managed to put it into operation.

"If it's anything to do with ships and the Mersey, Ginger is definitely our go to guy."

"He used to be with the Port Police, didn't he? Bit of a change from Port Police to Specialist Murder Investigation."

"When I saw him at work with the Port Police when they

helped us with a particularly nasty case that involved a lot of work on the water, I knew he'd be an ideal member of the squad and I've never regretted the decision to steal him from the Port Police."

"You're quite single-minded when you set your mind of who you want on your team, aren't you?"

"No, Fee, I'm *very* single minded. Look up the file on the case we dubbed *A Mersey Mariner,* and you'll see what Devenish did to help us, and by the way, you're another example. I wanted you away from Cold Case, and I got you," Ross laughed.

"Yes, sir, I suppose you did," Church laughed with him.

While Ross left her and went across to talk with Paul Ferris and Kat Bellamy, Fenella Church was approached by Izzie Drake.

"How're you liking being on the team, Fee?" Drake inquired. "You seem to have slotted in perfectly while I was away."

"I love it Izzie. I understand you were partly responsible for the decision to bring me on to the team. I really owe you a big thank you."

"Don't be daft, you were the best person for the job, no brainer. Anyway, once the boss makes his choices, I've learned that nobody gets to change his mind. I know he gives the impression of being an easy-going type of guy, but when he wants to be, he can be a ruthless bastard, believe me."

"I've heard that," Church said. "Remind me not to fall foul of his dark side."

"You won't Fee. You're too professional."

"Thanks, Izzie," Church said, and the two women high-fived each other. A new, firm friendship had been born.

CHAPTER 9
THE TRIAL OF HOWARD BLAKE

William Nugent stood back from the autopsy table and sighed. The third such examination in three days had truly depressed him.

"Maybe ah'm getting too old for this job, Francis." He said to his faithful assistant.

"Not you, sir, you'll never be too old. There's nobody as good as you at this job anyway," Lees replied, surprised at his boss's outburst.

"Then tell me why I'm feeling like this. Three in three days, one evil bastard doing it, and ah cannae come up with anything to help Ross's people."

"That's not your fault," Lees stressed. "He's a very clever killer, leaving no clues or trace evidence. I daresay the forensics people are feeling exactly the same way."

Stripping his surgical gloves from his hands, Nugent angrily threw them across the room, for them to land closely together on the floor. Lees hurried to pick them up and dispose of them.

"Sorry, Francis," the pathologist said, wearily. "Ah should'nae be taking it out on you laddie."

Lees smiled inwardly. Despite the fact that he was in his

late thirties, his boss still occasionally referred to him as lad, or laddie, as if he were a young man still learning the ropes of the job.

"You're tired, that's all," Lees tried to mollify the senior pathologist for the entire area. "I'll go and make coffee, shall I?"

Nugent sighed and stretched his tired muscles.

"Aye, laddie, you do that, then we'll get this report together for Inspector Ross.

* * *

At about the same time, Miles Booker, Chief Scenes of Crime Officer was reporting directly to Andy Ross. Like Nugent, Booker was unable to deliver anything resembling good news to the DI.

"Sorry Andy, either this character is extremely clever, or just bloody lucky as hell. Three murders and not one iota of trace evidence to link him to the killings."

"Not your fault, Miles, if it was a simple case, it wouldn't have landed in my lap and, by the way, we seem to have a witness who believes she saw the killer following Betty Morton to her home and she's convinced the killer is a woman."

"How so?"

"The witness is a physio, and she says she can tell a person's gender by body shape, the way they walk, and so on."

"Clever lady, I'm impressed," Booker acknowledged.

Ross spent a few minutes bringing Booker up to date with the limited progress the team had managed to date, and just as Booker was about to take his leave, a quick knock on the office door was followed by the entry of Izzie Drake.

"Hi, Miles," she greeted Booker cheerfully before addressing Ross. Booker offered to leave but Izzie held a hand up, inviting him to hear what she was about to impart to the DI.

"You look pleased with yourself," Ross said, inviting Drake to sit down. She refused the seat, instead launching into the news she was anxious to present. "Come on then, out with it, before you burst," he knew when Izzie was about to say something important, and this was one of those times.

"We might have a lead," she began. "You remember I talked to Paula Simmons just after she arrived at her parents' house?"

Ross nodded and she continued.

"A few minutes ago, I received a call from Mrs Simmons. She was anxious to tell me that she'd remembered something that she thinks might be important."

"Now you've really got my attention," Ross waited for her to go on.

"Apparently when she spoke to her husband on the phone last night, he reminded her of something her mother often mentioned, something that she was involved in many years ago. She's been searching all over her mum's house and she's found what she was looking for and wants us to have it as she thinks it might be a big help to our investigation into her mother's murder."

"So, what is it, Izzie? Don't keep me on tenterhooks."

"It's a scrapbook, one from years ago. Her Mum used to keep it with details of all the big murders that took place. She was really interested in that sort of thing, and before you ask why I'm still here, Fee's already on her way to Knotty Ash. She volunteered to go and collect it as soon as I told her about it."

"And just how will this scrapbook help us to find her Mum's killer?"

"Apparently, Betty was somehow involved in one of the cases in the scrapbook."

"Bloody hell," Ross exclaimed. "We might be getting somewhere at last."

"Just how is your sergeant with the scar getting on, Andy?" Miles Booker suddenly asked to which Ross instantly replied.

"Bloody great, Miles. Fenella Church is a brilliant investigator, top marks for intuition and adaptability and to be honest none of us really notice her scars. She's a fully integrated part of the team now."

"That's great," Booker replied. "I know her story of course, and I must admit, she's a real looker, with or without the scar. Seems really professional on the couple of occasions I've met her."

"She most definitely is a total professional," Ross confirmed.

"Well on that piece of potentially good news, I'll leave you, and get back to work," Booker said, and, in a few seconds, he was gone.

"Well, Izzie, let's hope Fee gets back soon and we can see what's so important about Betty Morton's scrapbook," Ross said, as Drake eventually sat down in one of the visitors' chairs in his small office and the two of them waited patiently for Church's return.

* * *

Fenella Church had wasted no time in getting across the city to the Morton's home in Knotty Ash after Paula's call to Izzie Drake. On her arrival the door was opened to her by PC Maggie Evans, the Family Liaison Officer who had been at the house since soon after the mother's murder.

"Sergeant," PC Evans greeted her, before ushering her through to the kitchen, where Paula Simmons sat at the solid oak dining table with various papers plus what was obviously the scrapbook spread out in the centre. "DS Church is here to see you, Paula," Evans said, before withdrawing and returning to the sitting room, where she'd keep Paula's Dad company while she and DS Church spoke in private.

"DS Drake sends her apologies," Church began. "She's tied up with DI Ross, but I hope I'll do instead," and she flashed Paula a dazzling smile.

"Of course," Paula smiled in return. She'd seen this sergeant the previous day, though not in close-up, and she couldn't help the shocked look that the majority of people exhibited on seeing the terrible scars on Church's face. "Oh God, I'm so sorry, was I staring? I didn't mean to."

"Don't apologise," Church continued to smile. "Most people do it. It's difficult not to, I suppose. I was badly burned in a fire, while doing my job, Paula. I consider myself lucky to have survived so I think I can put up with a few stares now and then."

"Oh, how terrible for you, I'm so sorry," Paula said, sympathetically.

"Don't worry about it, I certainly don't, not anymore, anyway."

Church in typical fashion, omitted to mention the bravery she'd displayed and the fact that she'd been decorated as a result of her actions.

"Well, I must say I admire you going back to work after something like that. I don't know if I could have done it. I'd have probably hidden away from the world, for a while at least."

Church decided to get the conversation back on track. After all, she was investigating three murders, and discussing her own situation ranked fairly low on her list of current priorities.

"Can we get back to the scrapbook, please, Paula?"

"Yes of course, sorry. Let me explain. Mum was always interested in true crime stories and eventually, she began cutting out stories from the newspapers and keeping them in a scrap book, which is what you have in front of you, now."

"And how does the scrapbook relate to your Mum's

murder?" Church wished the woman would get to the point of this conversation.

"Well, about fifteen years ago, Mum was selected for jury service you see."

She now definitely had Church's attention.

"Go on, Paula, please."

"Have you ever head of Howard Blake, Sergeant Church?"

"No, I can't say that I have."

"Mum served on the jury at his trial. He was convicted of the rape and murder of three women, in and around Warrington. From the time of his arrest until his conviction, Blake constantly professed his innocence, but the case against him was a strong one. You can read about it in the scrapbook. A month ago, when Mum came to my house on her regular weekly visit, she was rather agitated, excited, a bit of both really."

"And the reason for her agitation had something to do with this man, Blake, I presume?"

"That's right. She said to me that she was pleased *that monster*, as she called him, was dead. I asked her what she meant, and she told me it happened a long time ago, and when she explained I remembered her being on jury service years ago when I was younger, though she didn't talk about it at the time. Why would she? It wasn't something a mother would discuss with her young daughter really."

Paula fell silent and passed a copy of the Warrington Guardian to Church opened at page three. Dated four weeks previously, a sub-headline on the page three read, *Notorious Rapist/Murderer Dies in Prison* and the accompanying article went on to relate the death, from a heart attack, in Manchester Prison, still colloquially known as Strangeways, of Howard Blake. Blake, it said, had always maintained his innocence, and had twice had pleas for parole rejected. His wife, Audrey had died two years previously and Blake was survived by his son, Darren and daughters Jacqueline and Gillian.

"And how do you think this refers to your mother's death?" she asked.

Paula hesitated for a mere fraction of a second, before she replied.

"Sergeant Church, my Mum was on the jury that convicted him. I bet if you check, you'll find that the other victims were too. You see, when he was convicted, the son apparently screamed at the jury that he was going to 'get them' for finding an innocent man guilty. Everything about the trial is in the scrapbook. His rant in court is included in one of the articles published after the guilty verdict was delivered."

Church picked up the scrapbook and flicked through it until she came to the pages carrying the story of the rapes and murders, and eventual trial of Howard Blake. The old newspaper report of the trial and verdict did indeed state that Darren Blake, aged twenty-three at the time, had threatened not only the members of the jury, but also the trial judge and prosecuting barrister. She now knew of a possible motive for the murder of Betty Morton, and if she could ascertain whether the prior victims were also jury members, they would also have a viable suspect.

"Is it alright if I take these back to headquarters with me?" she asked, indicating the scrapbook and accompanying papers on the table.

"Yes of course," Paula Simmons replied. "That's why I asked you to come here today. I knew there was something in Mum's past that might be helpful to you. If everything here proves to be true, it could explain a lot of things."

"You're absolutely right, Paula. Thanks so much for remembering your Mum's involvement with the case and for finding the scrapbook and everything else."

Church wasted no time in saying her goodbyes to Paula,

and then to her father and PC Evans, by popping her head round the door of the sitting room.

Evans quietly asked, "Everything alright, Sarge?"

"Couldn't be better, Constable. Everything ok here?"

Evans nodded in the affirmative, and Church made her way out of the front door, waved off by Paula Simmons. She drove as fast as the traffic and speed limit would allow and couldn't wait to impart what she'd learned to Andy Ross and the rest of the team.

CHAPTER 10
FERRY ACROSS THE MERSEY

DC Gary (Ginger) Devenish, having met with the Ferries Manager, and made the agreed arrangements decided to take a trip across the river, accompanied by PC Trevor Miller, who, as per instructions, met Devenish at the Pier Head dressed in plain clothes, in his case, scruffy blue jeans, and a well-worn sweatshirt bearing some sort of Knights Templar logo. Miller had reported to the ferry captain and been put in touch with Devenish who filled him in on what was expected of him.

"So, if I see this man or woman, I say nothing to them, make no approach, and inform the captain, who will inform the squad at headquarters?"

"That's right, Trevor. We don't want you radioing it in, as there's a chance the suspect might make you as a police officer if they should happen to see you talking into you r radio."

"Ah, I see," Miller replied. "I was wondering about that, you know, reporting any sightings to the ferry captain. I can see now that it makes sense."

"Just be sure to keep your eyes open," Devenish warned him. "This suspect, if we're correct, has killed three people in three days, and it's highly likely that they haven't finished their killing spree yet."

"Fucking hell. Three in three days!" Miller exclaimed.

"Yes, and every victim travelled on the ferry shortly before their murder," Devenish said, stressing the danger involved in potentially approaching the suspect. "Just stick to the rules, okay?"

"Okay," Miller agreed.

"I'll be coming back on another ferry, so once we get to the other side, you're on your own, so better keep your eyes peeled."

"Don't worry, I will," Miller replied.

Over the next two hours, each ferry captain received copies of the description of the suspect and there wouldn't be a crewman who wasn't aware of the person the police were looking for, on both the Liverpool and Birkenhead side of the Mersey.

Now, all the police could do was wait.

* * *

Meanwhile, back at police headquarters, Fenella Church had brought Ross, Drake and the others up to date on her visit to the Morton home. Ross had quickly perused Betty Morton's scrapbook, before passing it to Drake who likewise studied the contents. Soon, the whole team, including the newly returned Ishaan Singh, had been given a run down by Church on what she'd learned from Paula Simmons. Singh joined in the research into the past lives of the victims.

"But I thought you said the witness said the victim was a woman, sir," Singh pointed out.

"It still might be," Ross responded. "Darren Blake might have made the threats but that doesn't mean one or more of his sisters isn't guilty of putting those threats into action."

"You said one or both, Boss. Do you really think both sisters could be involved?" Curtis asked.

"Why not?" said Ross. "I've heard of stranger things in my time."

"We need to look into the brother and sisters, and quickly," Drake added. "Paul, can you start trying to trace these siblings through the computer?"

"I'm already on it," Ferris replied.

After falling silent for a minute as his mind worked on what they knew so far, Ross turned to Drake, who sensed that he'd had an idea.

"Come on, let's have it. I know when those grey cells of yours have hit on something," she invited him to say something.

"Mind reading again, Izzie? But yes, I've been thinking. It seems to me that, if what we've just learned is the truth, and I've no reason to think it isn't, then the root cause of what's happening now would appear to be the trial of this Howard Blake character, and/or the rapes and murders of his victims, which led to him being tried and convicted. Based on what we know, Blake never confessed to having committed the crimes he was convicted of, and in fact, he consistently pleaded his innocence right up to his death. So…"

Drake interrupted, "We need to go back in time and look at the original investigation and trial?"

"Precisely," Ross replied. "Plus, we need to see if we can find out exactly who served on the jury at the trial of Howard Blake."

"Do they actually record the names of jurors in the court records?"

"They must do, Izzie. People can only be summoned once for jury service, as far as I'm aware, so somewhere a record must exist. I don't really know much about such things."

"Another job for our Sergeant Ferris, I think."

"You're right, Izzie. Paul will know how to find out, that's for sure. But he's already searching for the Blake siblings. Kat can make a start on the court records."

With Ferris and Bellamy hard at work on the team's computers, Ross had to hope the rest of his team could begin to produce something that would help the investigation. Sure enough, as Ross crossed the squad room, he was called by DC Singh.

"What is it Ishaan?"

"I just got off the phone with Wanda Burnside's ex-husband, sir. At the time of the trial of Howard Blake they were still happily married. Roger Burnside remembers his wife being on the jury at the trial of Howard Blake. In fact, he says his wife was elected the jury foreman and she took the responsibly very seriously. She wasn't allowed to discuss the trial with family or friends while it was ongoing, but once it was all over, she told him something about her experiences on the jury. Apparently, it didn't take them long to reach a verdict as the evidence against Blake was so strong and they had no difficulty in reaching a guilty verdict."

"Well done, Ishaan. That possibly explains why Wanda Burnside was the first to die. As the jury foreman she'd have been the one to announce the verdict, so there's the killer's reason to eliminate her first."

"Thanks, sir," Singh said, feeling pleased with himself.

"It's a start," Ross cautioned him not to get carried away. "We have to locate the other jurors and possibly the rest of those involved in putting Blake behind bars."

"Of course, sir. What's next then?"

"I want the details of Blake's crimes. Sam's already working on it, but two heads are better than one. Go and work with her, Ishaan. We need to move fast before this bastard strikes again."

Singh was soon at work with Gable as the pair began delving into the past. Sam Gable couldn't help thinking that this was the kind of task that DS Church would once have been involved in during her time on the Cold Case Unit. She knew who to turn to for advice if she and Singh got bogged down in the minutiae of a historical investigation.

The next shadow to darken Ross's office door was that of DS Derek McLennan.

"Hey, Boss," he called as he knocked and entered, holding a large, wooden handled, vicious looking claw hammer in one hand.

Looking up, Ross saw the hammer and quipped, "Come to do me in have you, Derek?"

McLennan smiled, "Not with this Boss, but I was round at our Neil's earlier. He'd done some work on the car and I saw this ugly brute lying on his workbench. This could be the kind of thing our killer used. See how the handle is thicker at the end you hold? And the claw is just the sort of thing that could have caused the massive damage to the victims' genitals and led to the blood spatter in Betty Morton's murder. Neil said they don't make them like this anymore. It was his dad's previously."

Neil Simpson was McLennan's brother-in-law, and made his living restoring and selling vintage cars. He'd presented Derek and his sister Debbie with a beautifully restored Ford Zephyr 6 on their wedding day, and it was now Derek's pride and joy.

"What the heck does he use that for?" Ross asked. "It's not the kind of thing I'd have thought had a part to play in vehicle restoration."

"You'd be surprised, Boss," McLennan replied. "But what do you think?" he asked, waving the hammer around in a reasonable impersonation of the Marvel comic character, Thor.

"Okay, Derek, you've made your point, and yes, I agree. It looks more feasible than a narrower screwdriver handle, that's for sure. Put it to Doc Nugent and see if he agrees with you."

"I already did, and he agrees with my theory," McLennan grinned.

"Oh, does he now? Who told you, you could be a genius behind my back?" Ross laughed. "Good work, Derek, and don't forget to give Neil his hammer back. I don't want him coming charging in here accusing one of my sergeants of stealing his claw hammer."

"No danger of that, sir. I told him I was temporarily impounding it."

Ross shook his head. "Derek, since when do we impound somebody's claw hammer, for God's sake?"

McLennan laughed, "Since I just thought of it, actually."

"Oh, shut up and go and do some work, Derek."

"Will do, Boss," McLennan had a big grin on his face as he almost collided with the incoming Izzie Drake as he left the office.

As the working day drew towards a close, DC Devenish trudged wearily into the squad room. DS Church was the first to greet him on his return.

"How was your day on the river, Ginge? Did it bring back happy memories of your days with the Port Police?"

"It was pretty boring to be honest, Sarge. At least in the Port Police, I was busy most days, not just going back and forth across the river all day."

"And neither you nor any of the ferry crews saw anyone corresponding to the description?" she asked.

Devenish looked disconsolate as he replied, "Not even anyone remotely like our suspect. The ferry captains are at least all aware of who we're looking for and they've promised to make sure their crews continue to be vigilant."

Devenish was unaware that Ross had approached him from behind, as he spoke to Church, and Ross surprised him by saying,

"Don't worry, Ginger, it was still a good idea, and one which may yet bear fruit."

"Thanks, Boss. I really thought we might lay hands on the bastard today, though."

"We're going to get whoever it is, sooner or later, Ginge, you can count on it," Ross spoke determinedly, though Church countered with,

"We have to consider though, that the killer might still be planning to strike today. As you said earlier, there's no guarantee that all the jurors from fifteen years ago live in Liverpool. Some could have moved away and be living anywhere in the country."

"I know, Fee. That's been playing on my mind too, and to that effect, the chief has at my request circulated a flyer to all forces asking for us to be notified if they have any murders committed on their patch which might correspond to what's taken place here. Izzie's in charge of coordinating any responses we receive."

"Let's hope we can track down those Blake siblings before long too," Church said, knowing they were their strongest suspects at present, their only real suspects in fact.

As he eventually headed for home that evening, Ross felt that they were beginning to make some progress on the case, but he also hoped against hope that they could apprehend the killer, or killers, before they struck again.

CHAPTER 11
ROSS CONFESSES

Maria Ross knew there was something on her husband's mind. The previous evening, he'd arrived home late, and he'd seemed slightly distant, preoccupied even. Knowing how her husband took his cases very seriously, she'd assumed his mood to be work related and hadn't tried to get him to talk about it. Tonight, however, she'd had enough. Whatever was on his mind, he needed to get it out in the open.

"Andrew Ross," she only ever called him Andrew when she was mad or when she intended being deadly serious about something, "Whatever you have that's weighing your mind down, you'd better spit it out, because I'm not going to tolerate this heavy silence you're exhibiting for another evening. Is it work? This new case? What?"

"Kind of," was all he said.

"Kind of what, for God's sake. Come on, this is me you're talking to. Whatever's troubling you, you know you can tell me about it."

She fell silent, arms crossed like an angry headteacher, standing in front of him, barring his exit from the room,

Ross's face assumed what she called his 'stupid look,' a cross between a smile and a grimace.

"I'm waiting," she scolded him.

"Okay, okay," I should have told you last night, but didn't know where to begin."

Now she was worried and walked up to him, put her arms around his neck and quietly said, "Andy, talk to me, please."

After a few seconds, Ross confessed all to his beautiful, understanding and incredibly patient wife of over twenty years.

"What would you say if I told you that I'd not only taken on a large dose of added responsibility and accepted a promotion to DCI as well?"

"And you knew about this, when?"

"Er, yesterday."

"And you didn't tell me. Why on earth not?"

"Well, I've always said I wouldn't accept a promotion because I'd lose day to day operational control of the squad, and I thought you'd think I'd gone back on what I've always held firm on."

"But how long did you think you keep it to yourself, you daft twit?"

Ross adopted his 'little boy lost' look. It usually worked when he felt guilty about something.

"I thought you'd be mad at me for deserting my principles."

"Come here, you silly bugger," Maria said, pulling him into her arms, and hugging him tightly. "I just want you to be happy in your work and always knew you'd hate being behind a desk most of the day."

"Well, that's not going to happen," he replied as he relaxed and went on to explain to his wife exactly how the squad would operate in future.

When he finally fell silent, Maria walked to the drinks cabinet, poured them a drink each and passed a large Scotch to Ross and together they rather belatedly toasted his promotion, after which she took him by the hand and slowly and seductively led him up the stairs, saying, "Let's go and celebrate properly, Detective *Chief* Inspector Ross."

* * *

Ross woke the following morning feeling remarkably refreshed. He and Maria rose at 5.30 am as usual, showered and dressed and had just sat down to enjoy a quick breakfast together when Ross's mobile phone rang and began to vibrate its way across the kitchen table, seemingly imbued with a life of its own. Fearing the worst, Ross grabbed the phone and answered the call.

"Andy," came the voice of Oscar Agostini. "Sorry to catch you so early, but I have bad news, I'm afraid."

The DCIs last two words told Ross he wasn't going to like what Agostini was about to tell him.

"You're going to tell me we've had another one, aren't you?" Ross pre-empted Agostini's next statement.

"I'm afraid so," The DCI said, gravely. "The reason Ginger Devenish's ferry-watch yesterday failed to produce a result is because the bastard was probably on the road, preparing to commit his or her latest atrocity."

"Where?" was Ross's one-word reply.

"Fleetwood," Agostini replied likewise with the name of the coastal town, approximately sixty miles north of Liverpool, once home to one of the country's largest fishing fleets, now sadly declined. "I'll have all the details on your desk in the next five minutes. There's a local man, DI Macklin at the scene at present. He'll be waiting for you and your team to arrive. He sounds a good man. Soon as he saw the body, he remembered seeing our flyer and knew it was one of ours. He had his boss contact me right away."

"OK, Oscar, consider me on my way. It'll take me more than five bloody minutes to get to the office though."

"I know that, just get there soon, Andy. I'll save you some

time. Tell me who you want to head up to Fleetwood with you. I'll contact them and get them on their way."

"Drake can meet me at the office. You can send Church and McLennan up there for now. They'll be sufficient until I know what we're dealing with."

"I'll contact them and have them meet us at headquarters. It'll be best if you travel up together and arrive as a team, ready to get to grips with things."

"Okay, you're the boss," Ross agreed. "See you soon."

With that settled, Ross hurriedly gulped down his coffee, abandoning his boiled eggs and toast. He threw on his jacket and turned to give Maria a kiss. She kissed him back and then made him take his camel coat with him as well.

"You never know how cold it could get up there. Fleetwood's right on the edge of the Fylde Peninsular, really wild and open."

"How come you know so much about Fleetwood all of a sudden?"

"I don't know much, really, but I played golf there once with Dr Murray's wife, remember?"

"Oh yes, she was the one who tried to get you to learn the game."

"Unsuccessfully, of course. Anyway, the wind doesn't half come in strongly from the Irish Sea up there."

"Okay, I'll take the coat, just in case. I'd better go. See you later."

Ross drove as fast as he could and pulled up in the car park at headquarters just as Izzie Drake was getting out of her car. Together, they made their way to the squad room, where DCI Oscar Agostini was already there, waiting for their arrival.

"Sorry to drag you in like this," Agostini apologised, and both Ross and Drake waved his apology away.

"Just give us the details, Oscar, and we can get on our way," Ross said, anxious to get to work on the latest murder.

As the DCI was about to begin, the squad room doors opened, and Fenella Church entered the room. Ross couldn't help thinking that no matter what the time of day or the situation they were facing, the diminutive detective sergeant always looked immaculate. Probably because of what she'd suffered in the past and the partial disfigurement caused by the burns, she wanted to make sure she always presented herself in the best possible light. This morning, she'd donned a new wig, or at least one he hadn't seen before, turning her from the usual blonde she seemed to prefer, to a brunette, with wavy hair that stopped just short of her shoulders. Her make-up was subtly applied, and in short, Ross could only admire the woman for the way she'd fought back from her horrendous trauma and injuries. She wore a fawn-coloured jumper, teamed with a knee-length black skirt with a slight flare, and carried a black windcheater over her arm, ready to face the wind which they all expected to encounter at Fleetwood. Drake must have agreed with him, as she greeted Church with,

"You're looking great today, Fee. How do you do it at this time of the morning?"

Church laughed as she replied, "Thanks Izzie, you look good too. It's easy for me though. No kids, no husband to hog the bathroom and I don't exactly spend ages on my hair, do I?"

"That's true," Drake agreed. "It's bloody chaos at our place in the mornings. Funnily enough, it was easier this morning. Peter was still in bed and the baby was sleeping soundly, so I had time to make myself look decent, despite the early call out."

The brief feminine chit-chat ended as Derek McLennan made his entrance to the squad room, accompanied by Paul Ferris, always an early starter.

Agostini quickly brought them all up to date with the

Fleetwood murder. The victim had been identified as Mrs Vera Sims, aged 56, a widow who worked part-time in the club shop of the nearby golf club. The circumstances of her murder, according to the local police in Fleetwood, appeared to completely mirror the previous murders in Liverpool. DI Macklin and his people would remain at the site until Ross arrived. The local police doctor had visited the site and pronounced the victim dead, and then showing great initiative, had called William Nugent in Liverpool. Dr Nugent was already motoring northwards.

Ross left Paul Ferris in charge of the squad as he and the others prepared to leave for Fleetwood. Ferris had good news for him, before they left.

"Last thing last night, Kat and I succeeded in finding addresses for all three of Blake's offspring, and Kat has a list of the jurors at Blake's trial, based on what Sam and Ishaan discovered from the trial records. I've also got an address for Blake's ex-wife, Margaret."

"Yes!" Ross exclaimed. "Now we're getting somewhere."

"When they arrive, have Sam, Ginger, Tony and Mitch start by visiting the Blake offspring. Ishaan is in charge of finding out if the jurors are still alive, and if they are, we need current addresses for them."

"Okay, Boss, leave it with me. I'll get them organised. Better to send them in pairs, so one pair will have two calls to make. What about Blake's ex-wife?"

"The wife can wait. If they're divorced, I can't see her seeking revenge on the jurors that found him guilty. Are they all living locally, Paul?"

"The son, Darren, lives in Huyton, eldest daughter, Jacqueline is in Formby and Gillian, youngest of the three, is now married and living in Great Malvern in Worcestershire. I'll get Sam and Ginger to drive down to Malvern, while Tony and Mitch tackle Darren and Jacqueline."

"Good plan, Paul, we'll get someone to talk to the ex after

we see what the kids of the marriage have to say." Ross said as he and the others prepared to leave for the drive to Fleetwood. Less than ten minutes had elapsed since he and Drake had arrived in the squad room, and already he felt the case was assuming a whole new complexion.

CHAPTER 12
SIBLINGS

Within minutes of Ross and Drake leaving the building, the rest of the team began arriving in the squad room, surprised to find DS Ferris in sole command of the squad. Paul Ferris quickly brought everyone up to speed and dispatched the two pairs to their allotted destinations.

Sam Gable and Ginger Devenish, armed with Ferris's fact file on Howard Blake's youngest daughter, Gillian, now married and going under the name of Gillian Spalding, were soon heading south in a pool car. The drive to Great Malvern, nestled in the Malvern Hills of Worcestershire would take them around two and half hours, mostly on the M6 motorway. The journey gave them time to discuss the case and the way they intended to handle the meeting with the daughter of the now dead Howard Blake.

With Devenish at the wheel, Gable made the first comments on the case so far.

"D'you think we're on the right track, Ginge, with Blake's offspring I mean?"

"It looks like it, Sam. Who else would have a motive for murdering the members of the jury that convicted their father?"

"That's true. What d'you reckon? Is it one or all of them involved in the killings?"

"I don't know. Could be any of them, all of them or just two of them. With the distance we're travelling to talk to Gillian, I reckon she could be in the clear. Great Malvern to Liverpool and beyond is a bit too far to be commuting to commit murder, I think."

"Whoever it is that's carrying out the murders is being particularly brutal, Ginger. Surely, they could take their revenge without the excessive genital mutilations."

"I agree, Sam. It suggests to me that one or more of them has sadistic tendencies. Their father was convicted of rape and murder, so the mutilations are like a recreation of the rapes."

"Yes, but why use a bloody blunt object of some sort to penetrate the victims? Why not full-on rape, if the son is the killer?"

"It avoids any chance of DNA being transferred to the victims, that's one reason," Devenish suggested.

After a brief stop at a motorway services area for a quick coffee and a toilet break, they continued their journey, Gable taking over the driving. Their conversation continued as they gradually neared their destination.

"Ever been to Malvern, Sam?"

"No, never. Supposed to be an area of great beauty, lots of picturesque countryside, ideal for walkers," she replied. "I think it used to be a spa town back in Victorian times."

"That's probably why there's a Malvern Wells on the map as well as Great Malvern," Devenish observed, looking at the map he'd laid on his knees. "There's also a West Malvern and a Little Malvern".

"Thanks for the geography lesson, Ginge. Listen, when we get there, why don't you play bad cop and I'll be the good one, if it looks like she's getting rattled."

"Okay, but let's both be good cops to begin with. Maybe,

if she's not involved in the murders, she might not need too much persuading to cooperate with the investigation."

"Sounds good to me, Ginge," Gable agreed with her colleague.

They soon passed the city of Worcester and headed down through the Cotswolds towards the Malvern Hills, Sam slowing down as they entered the charming town of Great Malvern, which still retains many of its Victorian features, including its railway station, which once received thousands of visitors every year as the Victorian gentry arrived to 'take the waters' at the numerous spas in the area. The station is in fact a Grade 2 listed building, having been designed by the architect Edmund Emslie, and today is used by around half a million passengers a year.

Sam had used the station as a point of reference as Mr and Mrs Neville Spalding's address lay within a half mile of it. The woman who replied to Devenish's knock on the door of the obviously Victorian dwelling certainly wasn't what either Devenish or Gable was expecting. Gillian Spalding was small, some might say tiny, standing at no more than five feet tall, and dressed in the uniform of the Salvation Army.

"Mrs Gillian Spalding?" Gable asked.

"Yes. How can I help you?" the woman replied.

Gable and Devenish identified themselves and the reason for their visit. Gillian Spalding's face betrayed the horror with which she greeted the news that they were investigating a murder that may be connected to her father's trial and subsequent imprisonment. She invited the detectives into her home, led them into her neat and tidy sitting room, and inquired if either of them would like anything to drink. After both requested coffee, if available, she disappeared into her kitchen, returning a few minutes later with three cups on a tray. She took a seat in the armchair opposite the sofa where Gable and Devenish had seated themselves, but not before Sam Gable had taken a quick look around the room and commented to

Ginger Devenish that there appeared to be no family photographs on display. Both wondered if that might prove significant, a point proved a minute later when Gillian responded to their initial inquiry.

"I'm not sure I can be of much help," she said. "I've had very little contact with my brother and sister since my father was convicted and jailed."

"Did you attend his funeral?" Gable inquired.

"Yes, my husband and I travelled up for the service, but left soon afterwards. I barely spoke to Darren or Jackie."

"Can I ask what your husband does, Mrs Spalding?" Devenish asked.

Pointing to a photograph on the sideboard which stood against one wall of the room, she answered his question.

"Neville and I are both Captains in the Salvation Army, and we're co-pastors of the local corps. He's at Kingdom Hall at the moment, holding a prayer meeting."

"I see, and how long have you been a member of the Salvation Army?"

"Since soon after my father was convicted and imprisoned. I had to do something to come to terms with what he'd done, although he always maintained that he was innocent of the crimes he was charged with. Eventually, a friend invited me along to a service, which I attended and felt like I'd found somewhere I could belong. I met Neville soon after and we were married a year later."

"So, you didn't threaten revenge against the members of the jury who found your father guilty?" Gable asked her.

"No, that wasn't my way, Detective, though Darren and Jackie did make threats. I tried to tell them that as much as we might believe in our father's innocence, the jury could only return their verdict based on the evidence presented at his trial, and to be honest, the evidence was pretty damning. Oh, you don't mean these murders you mentioned have something to do with my brother and sister?"

Gable explained in full, exactly what had been taking place in Liverpool, mentioning also that their team was also attending another murder scene in Fleetwood at that very moment."

Gillian paled, the shock and horror on her face quite evident to both detectives.

"Please understand, my siblings' attitude towards those involved in Dad's trial were totally opposed to my own feelings and eventually, I'm afraid a rift developed between us, one which still exists today."

"But do you think one, or both of them, could have harboured their grievances all this time and then turned to murder after your father's death?" Gable asked, bluntly.

Gillian hesitated for a few seconds before replying.

"Nobody likes or wants to think their brother or sister could be capable of murder, but Darren has definitely got a temper, a bad one. That's why he's never been able to maintain a relationship."

"He's violent?" Devenish asked.

"I don't know about his recent past, but all I can truthfully say is that I know of three women who left him when he became violent and controlling."

Gable now asked something she'd been waiting to ask.

"Gillian, please tell me something, honestly."

The woman nodded.

"Do you believe your father was guilty of the rapes and murders of those women?"

This time there was no hesitation before the woman replied.

"No, detective, I don't. I know I said the evidence all pointed to him being guilty, and I could understand why the jury found him guilty, but they didn't know my father. A gentler, kinder man never lived. When we were children, he never raised a hand to any of us, he could be strict and he'd be angry if we misbehaved, naturally, but it was Mum who give us a smack if we needed one, never Dad. He brought us up to respect our elders and women especially, which is why I can't understand why my brother has such a violent streak. But, as I said, no, I don't believe my father could have committed those crimes and every day, I pray that someone will discover the truth and his name will be cleared."

"What happened to your mother? Is she still alive?"

"Mum divorced Dad five years after he was locked away. She remarried a couple of years later and she now lives in Barnstaple in Devon with her new husband.

"Did she believe he was innocent?

"No, she believed everything they said at the trial. Dad never got over her turning against him."

Finally, Devenish asked, "Can you tell us where you were for the last four evenings, Mrs Spalding. We have to ask, I'm sure you understand."

"Of course. Four nights ago, my husband and I held our regular service, three nights ago we were doing outreach work at the homeless centre here in town, two nights ago, I was sitting with a sick member of our congregation in hospital, and last night my husband and I spent a rare evening at home, just the two of us."

Before long, Gable and Devenish felt they'd learned all they could from Gillian Spalding, and having said their thanks and goodbyes, they were soon on the road, heading north once again.

"What d'you think, Ginge?" Gable asked as Devenish drove out of Great Malvern, heading for the motorway, and home.

"I don't she could have done it, that's for sure. She's not big enough to have overpowered the victims and dragged the bodies around. Then there's the Sally Army bit. I don't think her religion would allow her to commit cold-blooded murder, and she was honest about her brother and sister, as far as I could tell."

"The thing is, she remains steadfast in believing her father was innocent, despite the evidence. Have you looked at the original case, Ginge?"

"Not yet, Sam. Been too busy working on these murders. When I get time, I'll take a look. Do you think Blake could have been innocent?"

"No idea, mate. I haven't studied it either. Whether he was or not, it doesn't give his kids an excuse to start killing the jurors, just because their father died in prison."

"I agree. Let's hope the others have more luck with Darren and Jacqueline, or Jackie as Gillian called her."

* * *

Their journey continued as, back in Liverpool, DCs Tony Curtis and Mitch Sinclair had been busy interviewing the other offspring of the Blake family. They'd started with Jacqueline, now Mrs Elson, who lived nearest to headquarters, in Huyton. Arriving at the Eslon's home, Curtis rang the doorbell, hearing the sound of Westminster Chimes issuing forth from somewhere within the house. A female voice shouted, "Just a minute," from the interior of the house, and they waited for just over thirty seconds before they heard the sound of the front door being opened, a key turning in the lock before the door slowly opened.

They were both surprised when the woman who answered the door looked up them from her seat in a wheelchair. Both shared the thought that this woman couldn't possibly be the killer although she might possess information pertinent to the investigation. They looked quickly at one another, as if sharing those thoughts, as the woman spoke before either of them could speak.

"Hello, can I help you? I hope you're not selling anything."

Curtis spoke, realising the ramp that led up from the

garden path to the doorstep should have given them a clue as to the status of at least one resident of the house.

"Mrs Elson?"

"Yes?" the woman seemed surprised he knew her name.

"I'm Detective Constable Curtis, and this is DC Sinclair, Merseyside Police. We'd like to ask you a few questions if you don't mind."

"You'd better come in then," she replied, and she turned her chair around dexterously, and began wheeling herself along the hall, calling to the two detectives who trailed along in her wake. "Would one of you close the door please? Can't be too careful nowadays," and Curtis detected a hint of sarcasm in her voice. Sinclair closed the front door quietly.

They followed her through a doorway, which they could tell had been specially widened to facilitate easy wheelchair access. She stopped, spun round to face them and invited them to sit on the sofa, facing her.

"Now," she said, "Why do two of Liverpool's finest want to talk to me, I wonder?" almost as if she knew why they were there.

"I presume you've seen the news about the recent murders in the city?" Curtis asked.

"I've seen the news, and I recognised the name of one of the victims. Wanda Burnside was the jury foreman at my father's trial fifteen years ago. I presume that's why you're here."

The other victims were also on your father's jury, Mrs Elson. We want to talk about the threats you and your brother made against the jury after the verdict was announced," Sinclair informed her.

"Oh my God, after all this time," she laughed. "That was all said in the heat of the moment. You can't believe we seriously meant it."

"We have to investigate every possibility," Curtis told her.

"Listen, I was in a road traffic accident five years ago, and

I've been paralysed from the waist down, ever since, so I'm hardly in a fit state to murder anyone, and as for Darren, I know he's a bit of a hothead, but I think I'd know if he'd suddenly turned into a serial killer."

"See a lot of him, do you?" Sinclair asked.

"He comes to see me a couple of times a week, and sometimes my husband takes me to see him at the weekend."

"And he's never mentioned anything about his previous threats against the jurors?"

"Of course not. Darren wouldn't do anything like that, I just know it."

"We all think we know those closest to us, Mrs Elson, but we can be mistaken," Curtis added.

"When was the last time he called to see you?" Sinclair asked.

"About five days ago, I think. He's been busy recently, but he'll probably be round tonight or tomorrow."

I'll just bet he's been busy; the thought ran through Sinclair's mind.

The pair decided that they were unlikely to get much more from Jacqueline Elson and they thanked her and were soon in the car, heading for Formby, and the home of Darren Blake. Both detectives agreed that Jacqueline Elson couldn't have personally committed the murders, but that didn't mean she wasn't involved in helping her brother to plan the killings and possibly even now was helping him in plotting the next murder.

During the drive, Sinclair suddenly changed the subject of their conversation.

"What's Ishaan like, Tony?"

"Eh? How d'you mean?"

"He's the only member of the squad I don't know much about. Someone mentioned you know him well."

"Ishy's an old school mate of mine. We've known each

other a long time. He's a good bloke, trust me on that, and he's got a gorgeous sister too."

"Yeah?"

"Yeah. Her name's Mishka, about two years younger than him. I used to have a thing about her when we were teenagers. I used to spend a lot of time at his house, way back in our school days."

"You old dog you," Sinclair laughed.

"Shut up, you Aussie perv. It was just a teenage crush, nothing serious."

"Yeah, right, if you say so."

"Get your mind back on the case, Sinclair, and look where you're driving," Curtis warned him, as they narrowly missed stopping at a red light.

"Oops, yeah, Okay," Sinclair laughed again.

Darren Blake's latest girlfriend answered the knock on the door when they arrived at his home in Formby. Not knowing how close his relationship was, Curtis and Sinclair refused to tell her the reason for their visit when she told them he wasn't at home. She did, however, tell them he was working and gave them the address where they could find him.

"His sister phoned and said you'd be calling."

"And I suppose you've called him and told him we're looking for him?" Sinclair asked her.

"No, I bloody didn't," the girl, who identified herself as Sally James told them. "After he did this?"

She pulled up the left sleeve of her blue sweater to reveal bruising, as if someone, presumably Darren, had grabbed her arm with great force.

"He did this and then threw me on the bed and did what he wanted to me."

"So why are you still here?" Curtis said, with a degree of sympathy.

"Because the bastard told me I'd better be here when he

gets home, otherwise he'll come round to my place and beat the shit out of me, that's why."

"If you want to make a complaint against him, we can pick him up and have him charged with assault."

"You don't think that'll stop him, do you? He'll get bail and then come after me again."

"We'll leave you then and go and have a word with him at his work."

"Yeah, you do that, and I hope you're after him for something serious."

They left the house and made their way to Fuller's Woodyard.

After parking in the small customer car park, the two detectives approached the first worker they saw, and asked if Darren Blake was working that day. The man pointed them in the direction of a man some twenty yards away who was cutting planks of wood using a circular saw. The saw was very loud and the man they approached was wearing ear defenders and goggles so obviously didn't hear them when Curtis called his name in an attempt to get his attention.

Instead, he and Curtis walked around until they were facing the man, who stood at least six feet tall, with broad shoulders and muscular bare arms, and, having got his attention, Curtis made a gesture with his hand, which Blake took as a request to turn off the saw. He complied and removed his goggles and ear defenders before speaking.

"Something I can do for you, gents?" he asked.

"You can if you're Darren Blake," Curtis replied and Blake confirmed his identity, and in return asked them who they were and why they wanted to talk to him. They showed their warrant cards and proceeded to question the man, who, both detectives felt had assumed a furtive look as soon as he realised they were police officers.

Curtis and Sinclair, bearing in mind the witness who'd said she thought the killer was a woman, both wondered if the witness could have been mistaken, especially when Blake was unable to provide a satisfactory alibi for any of the murders, being unable to provide the names of anyone who could support his story of having been at home alone on each of the evenings in question, including the previous night when the Fleetwood murder had taken place.

"Have you ever been to Fleetwood, Mr Blake?" Sinclair asked.

"Yeah, a few times."

"What about yesterday?"

"You're joking, right? I was slaving away at this place till six o'clock, went home, got changed and was drinking in the pub till about ten o'clock. I called at my girlfriend's place, picked her up and took her back to mine and we spent the night together."

"And your girlfriend's name is…?"

"Sally James," Blake replied, and as his story appeared to coincide with that of his girlfriend so, lacking any concrete evidence to link him to the murders, they were forced to bring the interview to a close, but not before advising him that they may have more questions for him in the near future, and telling him not to leave town suddenly.

As they drove back to headquarters, Sinclair made an observation.

"You know, Tony, working in a place like that, Blake would have access to all kinds of tools, which could have been used in the murders."

"I'd thought of that, too, but what about the witness who seemed certain that the person following Betty Morton was a woman?"

"Yeah, that's puzzling, unless the person in the hoodie is nothing to do with the murders."

"But Blake seems to be out of the picture for last night's murder."

"True, but we don't know the details of what happened in

Fleetwood, yet. Maybe when the boss and Izzie Drake get back, we'll know more."

* * *

Curtis and Sinclair's arrival back at headquarters was perfectly timed to coincide with the return of Gable and Devenish, closely followed by the return of Ross and Drake from Fleetwood. Church and McLennan had remained behind to supervise the investigation into the Fleetwood murder.

Singh was still hard at work at his desk. He was busily talking to former members of the jury. Unfortunately, some of the addresses they'd found were out of date and he was also trying to track those individuals down. Those who lived locally were being informed of the possible danger they might be in and that the police would be keeping them under surveillance while the investigation continued. Singh was liaising with Ross's contact in the uniform branch, an Inspector Mike Duggan, to ensure that the appropriate action would be taken to watch over those at risk.

He was interrupted in his task by Ross, who now called the team together for an impromptu briefing and intelligence exchange session.

"Okay, people," he began as everyone waited for news of the latest murder. It looks like our killer has begun to stretch his legs, spread his wings, call it what you like. The latest victim is another woman, a Mrs Pauline Ashton, and this time, we definitely do have a credible witness."

A buzz circulated around the squad room at those words.

"For now, I won't bore you all with the physical details of the actual killing, as they are basically identical to the previous murders, rape, sodomy, no semen, and a single stab wound to the heart. However, this time the killer screwed up. As he or she exited the Ashton's home, the husband arrived home unexpectedly early from work. Seeing a stranger coming out of his garden gate, Mr Ashton stopped his car instantly and, throwing the door open he shouted a challenge to the black-clad stranger. Seeing and hearing the husband, the killer made a run for it, to use Mr Ashton's own words, *like a ferret up a drainpipe*. Ashton wasn't sure whether to give chase or run into the house to see if his wife was okay. He had to go and see his wife and gave up the chase. When he entered his house he found his wife, in the hall, much like the scene at Betty Morton's murder scene. His wife Pauline was already dead, and Ashton held it together long enough to call the police and his sister, before going into shock. When the police arrived, he was sitting on the front doorstep, rocking back and forth, and almost incapable of coherent speech, until his sister, Ruth arrived on the scene, and got him to answer the police's questions and he gave the description I've just given you. Oh yes, one thing that's important, like the Betty Morton witness, he said the figure running away from the house was short, no more than five-foot-two."

"So, it couldn't have been the brother, sir," Curtis said. "I can't say I liked the bloke, and he doesn't have an alibi worth its salt, but he's a big fella, definitely not as small as five-two."

Gable added, "And I think we can count Gillian out sir. She's got alibis for each killing.

"We can count the other sister. Jackie out, as well. She's paralysed from the waist down and spends her life in a wheelchair."

"So, who the hell is this character in black?" Ross asked in exasperation.

Before anyone could formulate a response, the telephone in his office could be heard ringing. Drake moved fastest to run across the squad room and answer it. She was gone for a couple of minutes with everyone left holding their collective breath, wondering what could be taking her so long. When she returned, she had news for them.

"That was Derek and Fee, she said," referring to McLennan and Church, who were still on the scene in Fleetwood. "Seems a couple of the Ashton's neighbours also saw the 'black hoodie' character running down the street after Mr Ashton shouted. They've confirmed his description, and one of them gave us a little more detail. The perp was wearing black cargo pants, not jogging pants, not that it tells us much. But while Derek was talking to DI Macklin, she took a walk down the street, knocked on a few doors, just to see if anyone saw or heard anything, and she got lucky. Two of the nearby residents looked out of their windows when they heard Mr Ashton shouting. One saw the black figure running but only got a rear view, but, and here we need to be thankful for raging teenage hormones, the second witness was a seventeen-year-old lad who swears the runner was a woman. She asked him how he could be so sure, and he replied, and I quote what Fee told me he said, *"because her fuckin' boobs were bouncing while she ran."*

At that, the whole team couldn't help themselves and the room filled with laughter. Murder was a serious business, but occasionally, moments of levity would creep into an investigation. Ross always said it helped keep them sane in the midst of madness.

"Did either of them see her face?" Sam Gable asked, as the laughter subsided.

"Not according to Fee," Drake responded, "but the young lad said he thought he saw blonde hair when the hoodie slipped a little as she ran, oh yes, he also said he thought she had a nice arse."

"Bless his little heart," Curtis joked, evoking another round of laughter.

"Alright, calm down, children, Anything else?" Ross hoped for more, and he got it.

"Yes, as it happens," Drake continued. "As she walked back towards the house, Fee made a note of the cars parked in the street. Most vehicles were parked on their owners' driveways, but there were half a dozen actually parked on the roadside. She put a call in and had the registration numbers checked and it turns out one of the cars, a blue Focus, was reported stolen last night from outside a house in Bootle."

"Now we're getting somewhere," Devenish exclaimed.

"Yes," Drake continued, "And Fee and Derek are going to call at the owner's address on their way back."

As the mood in the room calmed down once more, Ross quickly evaluated the information received from Church and McLennan.

"Right, people, if we now accept that our hormone fuelled young witness is correct in his assumption, it's a real step in the right direction, but of course it does tend to put Blake's offspring in the clear. In some ways it takes us back to square one but eliminating three suspects is a definite step forward."

"Yeah, Skip. Now all we've gotta do is conjure up a new suspect out of thin air," Sinclair said, rather disconsolately.

"Cheer up, Mitch, la', if it was that easy, you wouldn't be here with us, would you?" Curtis said, his face deadpan.

"True, but just where do we start looking for a new suspect, Skip?"

"We need to start thinking out of the box, Mitch. That's what we do at times like this. We need to look closely at Blake's life. Maybe he had a close friend who feels aggrieved that he was unjustly convicted, and with him dying behind bars, has decided to seek some sort of twisted revenge on his behalf," Ross postulated the first theory that came to mind.

Seconds ticked by, and then, Ross and Drake looked at each other, and in one of those well-known examples of their sharing virtually simultaneous thoughts, they both blurted out two words, "Prison visitors."

Sam Gable instantly caught on to their way of thinking.

"Of course, he could have had a lady friend visit him in jail. Let's face it, a lot of murderers attract women like bees to a honeypot. What if Blake had such a camp-follower who was prepared to do anything for him, even murder those she believes responsible for his death behind bars."

"Right-on, Samantha, spot-on you beaut." Sinclair enthused. He'd developed a habit of using her full name, which often irritated her, but she didn't have the heart to tell him that nobody called her Samantha.

"Yes, right, thanks, Mitch," was all she could say. The young Australian detective was just so enthusiastic, she hadn't the heart to potentially 'burst his bubble.'

"Don't forget, Boss, they have women prison officers too. Blake could have charmed his way into an officer's knickers and got her to do his dirty work, once he knew he was dying."

"Graphically put as always, Tony, but yes, a good point."

The team were beginning to re-evaluate their approach to the case, but before they could go much further, Ishaan Singh had a point to make.

"We've had four murders in four days. I know we've got surveillance on the homes of the jurors we have addresses for, but shouldn't we maybe make the uniform presence at their homes more visible? If our killer sees a police officer effectively camped out on the doorstep of their potential victim, it should deter her from going ahead with any attack."

"I think you're right Ishaan," Ross agreed. "I'll sort that out in a minute when we finish here. Meanwhile, Paul, can you get onto Manchester Prison, and see if we can get a list of all visitors Blake received in, say, the last two years leading up to his death? Also see if they'll tell you whether there were any female warders assigned to whatever wing he was kept on."

"Will do, sir," Ferris responded and immediately set to work on the computer.

CHAPTER 13
STRANGEWAYS

Citing the Data Protection Act, the Assistant Governor at Manchester Prison, refused to provide Ferris with the information he requested, murder inquiry or not. He told Ferris he'd be happy to allow the police access to the physical prison logs, which meant someone from Ross's team would have to drive over to Manchester in person.

Angry at the lack of cooperation from the prison, DS Izzie Drake took it upon herself to make the required prison visit. As she was preparing to leave, Ross suggested she take DC Sinclair along with her, saying the experience would do him good. So, as she breezed across the squad room she called out, "Mitch, you're with me, now!"

A shocked Mitch Sinclair virtually jumped up from his desk, grabbing his jacket off the back of his chair and as he left the room in Drake's wake, managed to call out, "Where're we going Sarge?"

As he drew level with her, Drake replied, "We're going to prison, Mitch."

Not until they were headed west on the M62 did she fill him in on the reason for their journey.

"Bloody ignorant, uncooperative drongo," Sinclair said, referring to the prison's Assistant Governor.

Drake suppressed a smile at Sinclair's colourful use of the Australian slang, and couldn't resist asking,

"I've heard the word used by Australians, Mitch, but what exactly is a drongo?"

Sinclair chuckled before replying.

"Technically speaking, Sarge, it's a bird. Well, a few birds really, there's a whole family of different kinds of drongos, but the word's used in Aussie slang to mean an idiot or stupid person."

"Right, thanks for the explanation and the ornithology lesson," Drake replied.

"Glad to help. Can I ask you a question now, Sarge?"

"Yeah, of course you can. Ask away."

"Well, some of the guys on the squad have been telling me that you and the Skipper, sorry, DI Ross, have a sort of telepathic thing going between you. Is that true?"

"I don't know what you'd call it, Mitch, but the DI and myself just seem to have a knack of knowing what each of us is thinking and often arrive at the same conclusions virtually simultaneously. It's just something we've developed over time in the years we've spent working together. I wouldn't say we're telepathic or have any kind of ESP going on between us. I really don't know how to explain it to you. All I know is, it's there and we'd be stupid not to make use of it, don't you think?"

"Sure do, Sarge. Thanks for explaining that for me. I wondered if it was true or whether the guys were just pulling my leg. So, how are we going to handle this when we see the drongo, sorry, the Assistant Governor at the prison?"

"We'll play it by ear, Mitch, but leave it to me to do the talking, at least to begin with,

"Sure thing, you're the boss," he replied.

On arrival in the city of Manchester, Drake followed the directions on the car's SatNav system and as parking at the prison was severely limited at the prison formerly known as Strangeways, now officially HMP Manchester, she parked a short distance away in the public car park on Park Place. Despite being almost a foot taller than Drake, Sinclair found himself struggling to match her pace as she determinedly strode along the street, and the pair arrived at the prison after less than ten minutes.

"Out of breath, Mitch?" Drake asked, smiling, as they waited to for admittance to the grim, fortress-like jail.

"You're one fit lady," he replied. "Guess I need a few sessions in the gym to be able to keep up with you."

After identifying themselves, and passing through the required security checks, they were eventually admitted to the office of Barry McArthur, the man who Drake had earlier spoken to on the phone.

She and Sinclair again flashed their warrant cards, identifying themselves to the Deputy Governor, who was accompanied by a middle-aged woman he introduced as Mrs Forester, his secretary. Drake wasn't in the mood to 'take prisoners' and she immediately launched onto the offensive.

"Mr McArthur, it is of vital importance that we are provided with the information I mentioned to you on the phone. Four people have been brutally murdered and mutilated by a killer we have to assume is on some sort of revenge mission associated with the death of Howard Blake."

"But Howard Blake died of purely natural causes," he replied.

"We know that, but someone is murdering the members of the jury that convicted him, someone who we think believes he was innocent of the crimes he was convicted of and who blames the jury members for him eventually dying in prison."

"But that's just appalling," McArthur replied, perhaps only now realising the true horror attached to the murders.

"I'm truly sorry I couldn't acquiesce to your telephone request, but you must understand…"

"Yes, we understand your position, but the question is, are you now prepared to provide us with the information we require, or do I need to waste vital time by obtaining a court order?"

To say Izzie Drake was forceful would be an understatement and Mitch Sinclair was privately impressed and in awe of the 'short of stature but big on cojones' as he admired her style. She had the man backed into a corner from which Sinclair knew he'd find it hard to wriggle out of.

"Yes, yes, of course, that's why I asked Mrs Forester to be here. She will of course provide you with whatever assistance you need, won't you, Mrs Forester."

"Of course," was the secretary's short reply.

"Perhaps you can take the detectives through to your office and arrange to provide them with the information they require."

Mrs Forester rose from her seat and invited Drake and Sinclair to follow her. Drake turned to McArthur before leaving his office and delivered a terse, "Thank you for your cooperation."

McArthur merely nodded in acknowledgement.

Once in her own domain, Mrs Forester appeared to undergo a personality transformation, as she invited the detectives to take a seat and smiled before asking them exactly what they were looking for. Drake explained their needs and Mrs Forester, who asked them to call her Wendy, apologised for her boss's dour personality, "It kind of goes with the job, you know," and immediately set to work.

She began by locating the records of Howard Blake's visitors for the two years prior to his death, the period Ross thought most likely to contain any females who might have become besotted with the convicted rapist/killer. It didn't take her long to provide the necessary information. Apart from visits from his children and his solicitor, the only 'outsider' to have visited Blake was a woman, who'd visited him on a number of occasions in the relevant time period.

"We might have something here, Mitch," Drake said, when Mrs Forester finished speaking and passed the relevant page of the visitors log across her desk.

"Would anyone here at the prison know anything about this Angela Ryan?" Sinclair directed his question to Mrs Forester.

"It's possible some of the warders who were on visitor supervision might know something that might be helpful to you," she replied.

"Can you find out who would have been on supervision duty on the relevant dates, Mrs Forester?" he now asked.

"It's possible," she replied. "I'd have to check the staff work records for those dates, and we may need the senior officer of the day in order to find out who was assigned to the visiting room."

"Will it take long, Mrs Forester?" Sinclair pulled his 'little boy lost' look, known to melt the hearts of middle-aged and elderly ladies wherever he went.

"Oh, please call me Wendy, and no, let me make a phone call and I'll see what I can do for you."

Drake gave Sinclair a look of her own, which he rightly translated to mean, *You creep*. He grinned in return.

A few minutes after Wendy Forester ended her phone call, a knock on her door was followed by the entrance of a burly, balding prison officer who she introduced as Officer Thomas Brooke, carrying a large black book under his arm.

Forester introduced the detectives and informed Brooke what they were looking for, also explaining exactly why the information was important.

"I don't even need to refer to the book," Brooke said, immediately. "Blake and the Ryan woman were thick as thieves, a right pair of lovebirds," he told them. "I must have been on duty at least three times during her visits. A quick check in here," he tapped the book under his arm, "shows that she visited him six times in the last year. I think she was one of those women who were attracted to violent criminals. You should have her details on record in the files of visiting orders, Mrs F," he said, and Wendy Forester nodded.

Drake and Sinclair now felt they were making progress, but Drake now knew she had to ask a rather more delicate question.

"Tell me something, Officer Brooke. In the time Howard Blake was here, would there have been any female prison officers on his wing?"

"I wouldn't know that, Sergeant," he quickly responded. "Mrs Forester will have all the staff assignments in her files, though."

Wendy Forester immediately acknowledged that she would indeed have the information and after delving into her computer records, she came up with a result.

"In the last year, both Officer Parsons and Officer Merson worked on the wing, with Merson working there in the three months prior to Blake's death."

"You don't seriously think one of our officers might have become involved with the prisoner, surely?" Brooke looked aghast at the implication.

"We're not making any accusations," Drake told him, "But we have to look at all possibilities. I'd appreciate it if you don't say anything to the two officers before we speak to them."

"I won't say a word, I promise," Brooke replied.

"Are either of them in work today?" Drake inquired, hoping to take the opportunity to speak to them immediately."

It turned out that both female officers were present at work at that very moment, so Drake had Wendy Forester contact their immediate supervisor, and after thanking Officer Brooke for his help, she and Drake waited in Forester's office for the two officers to arrive.

Maggie Parsons was the first to arrive, quickly followed by Tracy Merson. Merson was asked to wait in the outer office while the detectives spoke with Parsons, who was quick to dispel any thoughts that she might have been romantically involved with Blake. Following their line of questioning, she admitted having been in contact with Blake through her job, but as for anything else, she pulled a small wallet from her back pocket and produced a photograph which she passed to Drake. It showed her in what could only be called a 'loving clinch' with another woman.

"That's Sharon, my partner, Sergeant. We're getting married next month, by the way. I'm not interested in men at all, at least, not in the way you're suggesting."

"But did Blake every try coming on to you?" Sinclair asked.

"Never," she responded emphatically. "As far as I knew he had a girlfriend anyway, some woman who used to visit him regularly."

Satisfied that Parsons wasn't involved with Blake, Drake allowed her to go after thanking her for her time and called Tracy Merson into the room. Merson was very different to her colleague. Where Parsons had been quite tall with short, brunette hair cut in a fashionable bob, Merson was short, standing around five foot three, with blonde hair that was obviously quite long, tied in a bun to keep it clear of her face.

As soon as Drake made it clear what her line of questioning was, Merson was quickly at pains to deny any personal involvement with Blake.

"Howard Blake was a model prisoner, never gave us any trouble on the wing. He always maintained his innocence of course to anyone who'd listen, but he was definitely not my type of man, Sergeant. I don't go for older men in the first place, and he was old enough to be my father, and I definitely wouldn't risk my job by having a relationship with an inmate. On top of that, I have a boyfriend I think the world of, so no way would I have allowed such a thing to happen, and don't forget, he had a girlfriend who visited him regularly."

"I see," Drake responded. "Did he ever mention his trial to you, or anything about the jury that convicted him?"

"No, but it's like I said, I don't get involved with prisoners on any kind of personal level. I wouldn't have spoken to him about his trial. If he'd tried to discuss it with me, I'd have told him to save it for his solicitor, it was nothing to do with me."

Drake knew she was unlikely to learn anything of use from Merson and she allowed the officer to go back to work. She and Sinclair had learned all they could from their visit to the prison, and after a quick final call on the Assistant Governor to pass on their thanks, they thanked Wendy Forester for her cooperation, and were about to leave when Sinclair thought of one last question.

"Was Blake close to any other prisoners, a cell-mate perhaps, someone who might have been recently released?"

"I don't know, but I can ask around," the secretary replied.

"We'd appreciate that, Wendy," he smiled, and Wendy smiled in return.

Drake knew that Sinclair's charm had definitely worked on the secretary, who she was sure would get in touch if she discovered anything that she thought could help them.

The two detectives left the prison, armed with the address of Howard Blake's supposed girlfriend, Angela Ryan, sure as they could be that neither of the two female prison officers who'd been employed on Blake's wing were involved, and looking forward to hearing from Wendy Patterson who Sinclair was certain would call him with the names of any special friends Blake had made during his imprisonment. As they motored back along the M62, Drake couldn't help commenting on Sinclair's way with the ladies.

"Are you always like that with older women, Mitch? You virtually charmed the pants off Mrs Forester back there."

"Ha," he laughed. "I just seem to have a way with ladies of a certain age."

"You can say that again. Poor woman was virtually undressing you with her eyes."

"Hey, what is it you ladies say? If you've got it, flaunt it, and if it helps us with our investigation, don't knock it, eh, Sarge?"

Drake joined him in laughing.

"At least we're getting somewhere," she said, as she pulled out to overtake the slower moving traffic in the central lane of the motorway. "Let's get back and see what we can find out about this Angela Ryan woman."

CHAPTER 14
THE BOOTLE CONNECTION

Fenella Church and Derek McLennan, after working the murder site in Fleetwood, had returned to headquarters and were quick to report their findings to Ross.

"The abandoned car was stolen in Bootle, a blue Ford Focus belonging to a Mrs Patricia Heath. She'd left it parked on her drive, right outside her house. She admits she may have forgotten to lock it, as she'd only recently arrived home with her shopping and had taken it all indoors and it took her a while to unpack her bags, put the frozen food in the freezer etc. She admits she's often gone out to her car to find she's left it unlocked," Church said.

"I think she'll be a little more diligent about locking her car in future," McLennan added. "Apparently, her husband was furious when she told him the car was gone, and that she'd left it unlocked. We didn't speak to him, as he was at work when we called."

"Does Mrs Heath work?" Ross asked.

"No," McLennan replied. "She doesn't need to, according to her. Her husband is a chartered accountant and makes enough to keep them both. The Focus was his birthday present to her just three months ago."

"Where's the car now?" was Ross's next question. Church provided the response he was hoping to hear.

"On the back of a trailer heading for Liverpool for full forensic examination. DI Macklin's people conducted a basic examination on the spot, checked for fingerprints etc before allowing us to take charge of it. Miles Booker's people should be crawling all over it in no time."

"That's what I wanted to hear," Ross said. "If the killer did in fact use that car, and intended to return to it after the murder, they didn't expect to be seen and chased away, so there's a chance Miles might find some trace evidence when he and his people carry out a detailed forensic examination of the vehicle."

Ross felt they were now on the verge of a potential breakthrough. If the forensic team could unearth evidence to link the killer to the car, there might just be an opportunity to put a name to the so far anonymous, unidentified subject.

* * *

As luck would have it, just as Church and McLennan finished delivering their report, the squad room door opened to admit DS Drake and DC Sinclair, newly returned from their visit to Manchester. Having welcomed the pair back, Ross was eager to discover what, if anything they'd learned.

He and the others listened carefully as Drake and Sinclair jointly delivered their findings. When Drake mentioned one fact, everyone realised they'd made a potentially important connection.

"Bootle?" Ross knew straight away what the address of Blake's girlfriend implied. "You don't know yet, but Fenella ran a check on a car, left on the street after the Fleetwood attack. I'll fill you in with the details shortly, but for now, let's just say it was stolen in Bootle, the night before this latest murder."

"Strewth, Skipper, maybe we're onto something with this Angela Ryan, eh?" Sinclair exclaimed, excitedly.

"We just might be, Mitch," Ross concurred. "Paul, see if you can find anything out about Angela Ryan before we go and talk to her," he instructed Paul Ferris. "Just in case she is the killer, pre-warned is pre-armed. I want to know as much as possible about her, as fast as possible. She could be planning her latest kill even as we speak."

"I'm on it Boss," Ferris replied, as his fingers immediately began dancing across his keyboard.

It transpired that Angela Ryan, aged 35, lived only two streets away from Patricia Heath, the owner of the stolen Focus, and was employed in a local gymnasium as a fitness and mixed martial arts instructor. She was in everyone's opinion, a prime candidate for their number one suspect. She lived alone and was currently serving a two-year driving disqualification for numerous accumulated driving offences. Bearing in mind that she may, at that very moment be preparing to commit her next murder, Ross decided they should waste no time in paying her a visit.

"Are we going in heavy, Boss?" Curtis asked.

"We are Tony. I want the house surrounded as far as is possible. Izzie, let the uniform boys know we're mounting an operation on their patch. I don't want her being scared off by the sight of police uniforms in the street before we arrive."

Drake nodded and picked up the nearest phone. Ross continued.

"I don't want to take any chances with this woman. She's already killed four times, so I doubt she'd be averse to adding any of us to her tally in an attempt to avoid arrest and capture. The team will consist of me, Izzie, Fenella, Derek, Tony, Ginger and Mitch. Sam and Ishaan, I want you on stand-by with the cars, in case she manages to evade us and makes a run for it. If that happens, it'll be your job to try and bring her down, by whatever means you see fit."

Gradually, Ross and Drake put the plan together, wanting the whole operation to go smoothly, with military-like precision. Ferris had pulled up a plan of the area where Ryan lived and it was agreed that Ross and Drake would knock on the door while Derek McLennan, Mitch Sinclair and Tony Curtis would keep watch from the street. Fenella Church and Ginger Devenish would be ready at the rear of the property in case the woman attempted to evade Ross and Drake that way. Sam Gable and Ishaan Singh already knew their part in the operation.

"Are we taking firearms, Skip?" Sinclair asked.

"No Mitch," Ross replied. "We've no indication that this woman may be armed, dangerous, yes, but so far not a hint of a firearm. I want to avoid making a bad situation worse if at all possible."

Singh was the next to ask a question.

"What do we do if we all descend on her house and she's not in?"

"That's a good question, Ishaan and the truth is we won't know until we get there. As the murders have all been committed either late afternoon or early evening, so if she's not at work, it's reasonable to assume she'll be at home."

"Unless she's already en route to her next kill," Church joined the conversation.

"You're a real prophet of doom Fee, d'you know that?" McLennan responded with a wry grin.

"Sorry, I'm just saying," she replied.

"Actually, she has a good point," Drake added. "And while we're playing Devil's Advocate, we should remember that we may have the wrong suspect altogether, though I admit that's unlikely."

"Okay, if we've all finished being negative, can we please get back to the operation to take this woman down?" Ross brought the conversation back on track, ending the current debate.

***

Ross and Drake approached the front door of Seaton Road, the rest of the team in their pre-arranged positions. They couldn't help noticing an old, blue and white good condition Citroen 2CV6 parked on the drive.

"Why steal a car if she has one of her own?" Drake spoke softly.

"Well, that thing would be rather easy to identify, wouldn't it?" Ross instantly replied.

"Yeah, I suppose you're right." Drake conceded.

Ross knocked loudly on the door, ignoring the ornate brass door knocker. Mere seconds passed before they could make out the figure approaching the door, through the frosted upper panel of the door. They were poised, like snakes about to strike, as the door opened, and they were confronted by a woman who didn't quite match with their expectations. To begin with, the tall, young brunette who smiled benignly at the detectives had the wrong colour hair, and secondly, she had her right arm in a sling. Their confusion was alleviated moments later when they identified themselves and asked the woman if she was Angela Ryan.

"I'm sorry, but Angie's not at home right now," the woman replied.

"And you are?" Drake asked.

"I'm Belle, Isobel Garside."

"Do you live here with Miss Ryan?" Drake inquired next.

"Yes, but not *with* her, if you know what I mean. I'm a student at the university and rent a room here from Angie."

"What happened to your arm, Miss Garside?" Ross asked her.

"I fell badly during a hockey match and broke it," she replied.

The plaster cast on her arm certainly led them to believe she was telling the truth.

"Do you know where Angie is, Belle?" Drake felt instinctively that the girl was guileless and truthful.

"No idea, sorry. She doesn't confide in me about her movements. She's just my landlady," Belle replied.

"What are you studying?" Drake asked next.

"Oh," the girl seemed surprised to be asked. "English literature. I'm in my second year."

"So, you don't know much about Miss Ryan?"

"Not really. She spends a lot of time lately going out. I just presumed she'd got a new boyfriend or something."

"Did she go out last night?"

"Yes, she did, and she didn't get back till quite late. But listen, what are you asking all these questions for? Has Angie done something wrong?"

"Let's just say she may be able to help us with our inquiries," Ross replied.

"Do you have any idea when she's likely to be home?" Drake probed a little more.

"No, sorry. She was already out when I came home an hour ago."

"How long have you lived here, Belle?" was Ross's next question.

"Not long, maybe six or seven weeks," the girl replied.

"And you really don't know much about Angie's daily routine?" Ross inquired, sensing they weren't going to learn much from Isobel Garside.

"Nothing at all really," she responded, shaking her head. For some reason she felt disappointed at not being able to help the two police detectives. "She has been spending a lot of time going out in the time I've been here, and there's been a few nights when she hasn't come home at all until the next day, but I couldn't honestly say whether that's normal behaviour for her or not."

"That's okay, I understand," Ross said, frustrated at not finding Ryan at home. "We'll leave you now, Belle," he said, "but my officers will be keeping a watch out for Miss Ryan arriving home, so please don't attempt to interfere if they attempt to speak to her if she does come home."

"This sounds serious, Inspector. Should I be worried, or am I in any danger?"

"I'm sorry if this has caused you to worry," Ross said, "I suggest, if there's somewhere else you can stay for a couple of days, you might think about doing so."

"Oh God, right, it is serious then. I do have friends I could stay with for a few days if it's that important."

"Do it, then, Belle," Drake said. "Give us your mobile number if you have one, and we'll let you know if and when it's safe to return."

Belle was clearly shaken by this sudden turn of events, and her face became etched with worry lines.

"Where does Miss Ryan work?" Drake next inquired and Belle gave them the name of the local fitness centre where apparently, Ryan worked on a part-time basis three times a week."

Disappointed, Ross and Drake left the house leaving Belle to pack a bag and, at least temporarily, move out to stay with her friend until they could resolve the situation. Gathering the rest of the team together at the end of the road, Ross filled them in on the result of their conversation with young Belle.

"What now, then, Boss?" Curtis asked.

"Sam and Ishaan, I want the two of you to stay here and keep the house under surveillance in case Ryan returns. If necessary, I'll have you relieved in four hours. In the meantime, the rest of us are going to visit the fitness centre, in case Ryan's working there. Her lodger knows nothing about Ryan's private life so she might be there, or she could be elsewhere, setting up her latest kill for all we know."

Twenty minutes later, a rather dispirited Ross and his team

departed from the fitness and leisure centre where they'd hoped to find Angela Ryan. Pieter Van Cleef, the tall, blonde-haired manager of the centre, greeted them warmly on their arrival. The Dutchman was as helpful as he could be, and Ross learned from him that Ryan hadn't been working at the centre for almost three months. Ross quickly put two and two together by realising she'd probably not been at work since the time of Howard Blake's death or thereabouts.

"She used to be a happy and popular instructor," Van Cleef told the DI. "Shortly before she stopped coming however, she appeared to have had something of a personality change. She became sullen and smiled very little. I asked her if everything was alright on a couple of occasions, but she always told me everything was fine."

"Did she give a reason for leaving?" Ross asked.

"That's the thing, Inspector, she did not even inform me she was leaving. She just stopped coming. I phoned her a few times, but she never answered her phone. Is Angela in some kind of trouble?"

"That's very interesting, Mr Van Cleef, and yes, she could be in some sort of trouble. If she contacts you, please let us know. In the meantime, thank you for your help. We'll be going now."

They'd left a rather mystified Pieter Van Cleef staring after them as they departed and soon reassembled back at headquarters. The first thing Ross did was to check in with Gable and Singh, who reported that all was quiet at the house. Isobel Garside had left in her old Citroen soon after Ross and Drake had spoken to her, and the place now had that certain deserted feel about it.

Next, Ross asked for volunteers to watch the house through the remaining hours of the day and the coming night. Every hand went up of course and he soon had a rota in place, just in case Ryan returned during the hours of darkness.

"The downside of this is that we have to assume Angela

Ryan is probably on another revenge kill mission," he announced to the team, "and we're bloody blind and impotent without a clue where the hell she's going to strike next."

"At least we have surveillance on the jurors' homes," Devenish stated, but Ross countered with,

"Trouble is, Ginger, there are a couple that we don't have addresses for. What if she strikes at one of them?"

"Shit, I never thought of that," said the red-haired detective constable.

For the time being, Ross knew that all they could do was wait, and hope.

* * *

Taking advantage of a few hours at home, Fenella Church showered and changed, knowing she'd be on surveillance duty with DC Curtis later that night. Sitting in front of her dressing table, she was trying on two new wigs she'd bought recently, one blonde, one auburn. She liked them both, and decided she'd wear the shoulder-length auburn one that night. She applied her usual minimal make-up, colours teamed to go with her new auburn look. Satisfied with her appearance, she was about to go downstairs to fix herself a quick meal, when her mobile phone ringtone sounded. Not recognising the number of the caller, she answered formally,

"DS Church."

"Detective Sergeant Church," a vaguely familiar male voice spoke. "It's Alan Deal."

Doctor Alan Deal was a Manchester-based psychiatrist who had been of help to the team on one of their recent cases (* as told in A Liverpool Lullaby). Given the name, Church realised who the man was.

"Doctor Deal? To what do I owe this honour?"

"I hope you don't mind me calling you, Sergeant Church, but you gave me your card with your mobile number when we last spoke, and, well, it's taken me a few months to pluck up the courage to call you like this."

Church recalled the psychiatrist had told her how he'd lost his wife, who'd been badly burned, similarly to herself, in a fire following an automobile accident. Despite a number of skin grafts, the poor woman had eventually succumbed to her injuries. Deal had somehow felt a degree of empathy with the detective, and now, it appeared he wanted to talk to her about something.

"How can I help you, Doctor?" Church was intrigued by this surprise call from Deal.

"Please call me Alan," he said. "Actually the reason I'm calling you is that since we met during your inquiries into the Adamson case, I haven't been able to get you out of my mind, and like I said, it's taken me months to gather enough courage to…to…oh hell, Fenella, I would like very much if you'd allow me to take you out for dinner one night. There, I've said it. Please tell me to get lost if you want. I'll understand if you're not interested."

"I don't know what to say," Church replied. "You've certainly taken me by surprise."

She remembered Deal as being a handsome man, around fortyish, tall and with well-groomed brown hair, and he'd been immaculately dressed. She'd sensed at the time of their original meeting that he felt attracted to her but hadn't thought any more about it after the case under investigation had been concluded. Clearly, Alan Deal hadn't forgotten her and had probably been wrestling with his thoughts for a long time before making this call.

"I know, I'm sorry, if you're not interested, I'll go. I'm sorry for bothering you."

"No, it's not that, er, Alan. It's just that I'm getting ready to head out on a surveillance operation, and you've really taken me by surprise."

"Oh, I'm sorry," Deal replied. "I'll just go then. Sorry to have bothered you."

"No, wait," Church quickly interjected, before he could hang up. On an impulse, based on what she knew of Deal, and realising how much effort it must have taken him to call her after all this time, she went on,

"I haven't said 'no' have I? Let me get work out of the way and I'll call you. Is that alright with you."

She could almost hear the sigh of relief Deal must have expended at hearing her words.

"Yes, of course it's alright. You don't mind me calling you out of the blue like this, then?"

"As I said, Alan. You've taken me by surprise, a nice surprise, I must say. A girl does like to feel wanted after all. Now, I really must go and get ready for work. I promise I'll call you. I'll be on duty all night, so it'll be some time tomorrow before I can call you back."

"That'll be great, whenever it's good for you, and Fenella, thank you."

The original hesitation had gone from Deal's voice, as he clearly relaxed, and a sense of optimism crept into his voice.

"Bye for now, Alan," she said, and he reciprocated her words before they both hung up their respective phones.

Fenella Church now looked at her reflection in her dressing table mirror, smiling to herself as she spoke to the face that looked back at her from the mirror.

"Well, girl, looks like you've still got it. Who'd have thought it, after all these months?"

Using the pastel pink lipstick which she'd just used on herself, she leaned forward, reached across her dressing table and wrote on the mirror, *Phone Alan Deal.*

"There, you won't forget to make that call." She spoke to her reflection again, tossed her head back to test the fitting of her wig, which behaved perfectly naturally, and laughed. Maybe her social life had just taken a turn for the better.

CHAPTER 15
LOVE, LIFE AND EVERYTHING

Just before midnight, Church and Curtis, having met at headquarters, arrived to relieve Sinclair and Devenish, who'd earlier replaced Singh and Gable, in keeping watch on Angela Ryan's house. Devenish reported to Church that all had been quiet, with no sign of their suspect arriving home from wherever she might be.

"I just hope she isn't carrying out another out-of-town murder, Sarge," Sinclair had said, and Church agreed, before sending him and Devenish home to get some rest.

"Well, Tony, this could be a long night," she said, as she and Curtis settled down in the car, positioned far enough away, but still close enough to see if Ryan or anyone else arrived and tried to enter the property.

"You could be right, Sarge," he replied, to which she countered,

"You can drop the 'sarge' while we're out on the job, Tony. Fee will do."

"Great, thanks," he smiled. "You seem to be in a good mood, tonight. Anything you want to tell me?"

"Is it that obvious?"

"Is what that obvious?" he teased.

"Give over, Curtis," she grinned. "Yes, alright, as it happens, I got a dinner invitation earlier, the first one in quite a while."

"Hey, that's great. Good for you, sar…I mean Fee."

Curtis was pleased for her, though inwardly slightly jealous. He couldn't help it if he found Fenella Church drop dead gorgeous, while at the same time he knew that as shew was his superior officer, he didn't stand a chance with her.

"Anyone I know?"

"No, I don't think so. He was someone who provided us with background information on 'The Doctor' murders a while ago."

"Let me guess. Either the solicitor or the psychiatrist. Bearing in mind the solicitor was older and married, I'd guess at the psychiatrist."

"Bloody hell, Tony. Anyone tell you, you'd make a bloody good detective?" she grinned. "Yes, it's the psychiatrist, but how did you work that out? You never met either of them during the inquiry."

"No, I didn't but I read every file and report on the case, and I remember everything about that damn case. It led to Nick's death after all, and I'm hardly likely to ever forget every detail of it."

'The Doctor', aka Peter Adamson had been responsible for a series of rapes and murders, and the eventual murder of DC Nick Dodds, Curtis's long-time friend and regular partner on the squad's inquiries for almost eight years.

"I don't think any of us will, Tony," she replied, placing a consoling hand on his left arm,

"I know," he said, quietly as he allowed his thoughts to linger on memories of his friend.

They sat there, peacefully for a while, their minds on the past, but with their eyes firmly fixed on the target's house. As time ticked by, Curtis reached into the back of the car and pulled a holdall into the front from which he removed a vacuum flask, two mugs and two packs of sandwiches. Long hours on surveillance could drag, and he knew the benefits of refreshments while on such a stakeout.

"Good thinking, Tony. Thanks," said Church, accepting a mug of strong coffee and a pack of cheese salad sandwiches.

"I wasn't sure what your tastes in meat were, so I stuck to cheese," he said as she bit into a sandwich.

"That was very thoughtful," she replied, "but you needn't have worried. I'm not a vegetarian or vegan. I'll eat any meat, but I'm a bit picky when it comes to fish and shellfish."

"How so?"

"I like tuna in a sandwich, but I'm not keen on anything else, apart from prawns."

"I'll remember that for the future."

"God, isn't it boring, the things we find to talk about on an all-night surveillance job?" Church quietly laughed.

"Yes, it is. You wouldn't believe some of the things me and Nick used to talk about when we shared a car in the dead of night."

"I don't think I want to hear about that, thanks, Tony," Church was pleased, however, to hear him mention Nick Dodds in a general conversation, without referring to his friend's death. "Anyway, what about you? No girlfriend waiting for you at the end of a shift?"

"No, afraid not. I've had girlfriends in the past, but they never seem to last. I did have one, her name was Pippa, who lasted about six months, but in the end, she was like the others, and got sick of the job coming first for me, you know the scenario, cancelled dates, having to dash off in the middle of something."

"Not much different to how it is for married officers, really," Church commented.

"You're right, Fee. Anyway, me and Nick used to go out together a lot, had some great times, and if we managed to pull a couple of good-looking girls, we often ended up going out as a foursome for a few weeks until the girls got fed up with us."

"Never mind, Tony, you never know, you might meet the right girl one day, someone who'll take you as you are, job and all."

"Yeah, maybe," he replied as he fell silent, thinking to himself that Fenella Church would be the ideal woman for him if it wasn't for her rank. He recalled how she'd taken his hand to give him support as he'd almost choked as he prepared to deliver his eulogy to his friend at Dodds's funeral, later taking his arm and guiding him from the church in tears at the end of the service. She'd definitely showed her empathic side on that awful day, though he was mature enough to know that that was all it had been, a show of empathy with a colleague in his hour of need. *Damn it, why does she have to be so bloody good looking?* Quickly pulling his thoughts back to the job, he asked Church a question.

"Do you think this Ryan woman is definitely our killer?"

"It looks increasingly like it. I'm just concerned that she may be anywhere in the country right now, taking revenge out on another of the jurors, while we sit here, twiddling our thumbs."

"I've been thinking the same thing, to be honest," Curtis said as he finished his sandwich and then drained his coffee mug.

They shared an amicable silence for a few minutes and then Church spoke once again.

"You got any brothers or sisters, Tony?"

"No, I'm an only child. Me Mum and Dad probably took one look at my ugly mug when I was born and decided one like me was more than enough for any family."

Church laughed as she replied, "Surely not. After all, the squad don't call you Tony for nothing do they? You do bear a remarkable resemblance to Tony Curtis the film star, you know."

"I know, though I only realised it when our former DCI, Harry Porteous gave me the nickname when I first joined the squad. Me being a sad bugger started watching all the old Tony Curtis movies and that TV series he did with Roger Moore, *The Persuaders*. Once he called me Tony, it stuck and most everyone calls me Tony nowadays."

"I remember that show. It's often repeated on some of the more obscure channels on Freeview. What was your favourite Tony Curtis film, then?"

"There's a couple. He was great in *The Vikings*, with Kirk Douglas, and played a great comic role in the *Great Race*. Did you know, his real name was Bernard Schwartz?"

"I didn't know that. Doesn't have quite the same ring to it does it?" she laughed quietly. "I've seen *The Vikings* but not the other one. I suppose you've become a bit of an afficionado of his movies since being compared with him?"

"I suppose I have," he smiled.

With that, silence descended upon the car again, the only activity in the street being a couple of cars that drove along the road without stopping and just before they were due to be relieved Curtis said,

"Listen, do you hear that?"

"Yes, it's the bloody milkman," she observed, and sure enough an old-fashioned style electrically powered milk float passed them before stopping, as the milkman got out, and commenced to deliver two pints of milk to the house next door to Ryan's.

"There can't be many dairies still using those things," Curtis commented.

"They're very eco-friendly though. Maybe they're making a comeback."

"If we weren't stuck here, I'd go and ask him," Curtis said, at the same moment as they both went instantly on high alert as they saw headlights approaching and slowing down as they approached the house.

The car drew to a halt right outside Angela Ryan's home and a few seconds later a figure alighted from the black cab, dressed in jeans and a green fleece jacket, a black holdall in one hand, paused to lean in and speak to the driver, handing over what was probably the fare and then watched for a couple of seconds as the taxi drove away before heading up the garden path towards the front door.

"That's got to be her," Curtis almost whispered, as though the woman might hear him in the still of the night.

"She fits the description, as far as I can make out in the dark," Church replied.

The detectives had to go by the description they had of Angela Ryan, bearing in mind they hadn't seen a photograph of the woman up to that point in their investigation.

"Are we going to take her down then, Sarge?" Curtis asked, formality in his request.

"Not without back-up. She could be very dangerous once she's cornered," Church responded.

Church instantly got on the radio and was soon in touch with Izzie Drake. Together, Drake and McLennan were at headquarters, getting ready to set off to relieve Church and Curtis for the last few hours of the night.

"Don't do anything until we get there, Fee," Drake said. "Just keep watch on the house, but if she tries to leave you might have to make a move to detain her. Derek and I will be with you as soon as possible. We're leaving right now. I'll call the boss while we're on the way and let him know what's going down."

"Roger that," Church responded, and she and Curtis, their senses now honed and at their sharpest, impatiently waited in the car, poised to move as soon as Drake and McLennan arrived.

CHAPTER 16
ANGELA RYAN

Angela Ryan, known to most people as Angie, had just showered and changed into a pink nightdress and her warm, fluffy matching dressing gown, and had made her way downstairs to the kitchen and was about to make herself a cup of tea, when there was a loud knock on her front door. There was certainly no mistaking the loud voice that immediately followed the knocking.

"Miss Ryan, we're from Merseyside Police. Please open the door," called the voice of Derek McLennan.

"Shite," she exclaimed aloud, realising that the police had probably somehow pieced things together and identified her as their prime suspect. Dressed as she was, in her nightwear, she knew she wouldn't get far even if she could get past the police at her door, plus she was unaware of how many police officers were out there. She correctly guessed there'd be more than one, and quickly came to a decision.

"I'm coming," she shouted as she approached her front door. She slowly unlocked the door and opened it slowly, revealing the figures of McLennan, and Drake on her doorstep, with two more officers visible in the car parked outside her front gate. She realised any attempt to make a run for it would be cut off by the two officers in that second car. Such was the design of the house that the back door was actually on the side of the house towards the rear, and she surmised, wrongly as it turned out, that the police would have that exit covered too. Her mind worked fast, and she took the only action she saw possible for the immediate future.

Looking as innocent as she could, she tried to appear surprised to see the police on her doorstep and said, simply,

"Yes? How can I help you?"

Drake responded, "Are you Angela Ryan?"

"Yes, I am."

"Could we come in please?"

"Why? What's this about?"

"We'd rather discuss this indoors, if you don't mind," Drake said forcefully, giving Ryan no opportunity to refuse.

"Well, you'd better come in then," Ryan replied, still trying to look innocent and unable to understand the police presence at her home at such an unearthly hour. Leading them into the lounge, Ryan sat down in one of the two armchairs in the room, where she crossed her legs, leaned back in the chair and waited for the detectives to speak.

Realising they had an extremely cool customer in front of them, the two detectives looked at each other, and Drake gave an almost imperceptible nod, signalling for McLennan to speak first.

"Strange time to be coming home, isn't it? Mind telling us where you've been until this time in the morning?"

"I slept with a friend, a man, if that's any of your business."

"I suppose he'll verify that if we were to ask him?"

"I suppose he would," she smirked in reply.

She fully expected McLennan to ask her to name her male friend, but instead, Drake asked,

"Can you account for your whereabouts for the last four days, particularly the late afternoons and early evening time?"

"Why should I have to?"

"Because we're asking, that's why."

"And how did you get back from Fleetwood?"

That really took her by surprise.

"Eh? What? What's Fleetwood got to do with anything?"

"I think you know exactly what Sergeant Drake means," McLennan now added.

Drake and McLennan were cleverly skipping from one aspect of their questioning to another, hoping their quick-fire tactics would force Ryan to trip herself up. They were both aware that, as yet, they had no concrete evidence that could be used to justify arresting her on the spot.

Ryan had fallen silent a Drake then said, "You were seen you know, in Fleetwood."

"When was this? I haven't been to Fleetwood for years."

McLennan now changed tack again,

"This man you spent last night with. Does he have a name?"

"I don't see that's any of your business," Ryan responded.

"Does this mean you've forgotten about poor old Howard?" Drake added.

"Howard? Who's Howard?"

"Your boyfriend Howard Blake, recently deceased," Drake responded.

"Never heard of him," Ryan hesitated slightly before replying.

"Really?" Drake fired back at the woman. "Strange then, that the records at Strangeways show that you visited Howard Blake on numerous occasions in the last year."

Ryan fell silent. Drake had definitely unsettled her.

McLennan sought to further upset her equilibrium.

"What's his name, this man you spent the night with? Where does he live?"

"Eh? What? Why should I tell you?"

"Suit yourself," Drake now took the interview a stage

further. "I'm afraid we're going to have to ask you to accompany us to police headquarters, to assist us with our inquiries."

"What bloody inquiries?" there was panic in Ryan's voice now.

"Murder of course, Miss Ryan."

"Get lost," Ryan snapped. "If you had any proof of that you'd be arresting me."

Drake had picked up on the fact that Ryan hadn't asked what murder they were investigating, a sure sign of guilt in the sergeant's mind.

"Are you going to accompany us to the station or do we have to formally arrest you. You'll just be assisting us with our inquiries after all. We're not placing you under arrest," *Yet*, thought Drake.

Ryan looked like a rabbit caught in a car's headlights. She was silent and merely nodded to confirm that she understood the words of the caution. Ryan's mind was working quickly as she sought a way out of her current predicament and finally, she asked.

"Can I at least get dressed, unless you want to take me to the police station in my nightie?"

"Of course," Drake replied, "But I'll have to accompany you to your room while you get dressed."

"Whatever you say," Ryan muttered, so Drake and McLennan had to strain to hear her words. She rose, and walked from the room, followed by Drake, and made her way upstairs.

Ryan's bedroom was neat relatively tidy, considering the fact she'd recently arrived home, showered and changed into her nightwear. Drake assumed she'd placed her clothes in the large Ali Baba clothes basket that stood in one corner of the room. She desperately wanted to look in the holdall that Ryan had walked into the house with but there was no sign of it. She knew she needed a search warrant for the house, and fast.

Downstairs, Derek McLennan was equally frustrated. As

much as they felt certain that Angela Ryan was the killer they sought, her refusal to give straight answers to their questions and the lack of physical evidence was so far proving a real barrier to closing the case. While Drake was upstairs with Ryan, he quietly took a look around the downstairs area of the house, but again, could find nothing that directly linked her to the murders. While Drake was upstairs, he put in a call to headquarters, requesting a car with two uniform officers be sent to pick up Angela Ryan and transport her to headquarters for questioning. He was informed the car would arrive at his location within 15 minutes. McLennan was being cautious. The unmarked car he and Drake had arrived in didn't have a security screen between the front and rear of the vehicle and he didn't want to have Ryan unattended in the back seat, or have either Drake or himself seated beside her in the back, if indeed she was the killer they were after. Who knew what tricks she might pull on either of them in the enclosed space of a car's rear compartment?

In the bedroom, Angela Ryan took her time getting dressed, her mind continuing to work on a means of escape. With her back towards Drake, she took a pair of flesh-coloured tights, black panties and a black bra from the set of drawers that stood beside her wardrobe, put them on and then opened the wardrobe doors. From the other side of the room, Drake could see that the wardrobe was well-stocked with blouses, skirts, dresses and on the shelf above the hanging rail, a number of sweaters and more than one set of track suit trousers and sweatshirts, neatly folded and stacked, but, significantly, no hoodies.

Ryan seemed to take a veritable age in selecting what to wear, finally deciding on a pink cotton blouse and a short, straight black skirt. She turned as though parading herself in front of Drake, walked around the bed and said, "Excuse me," and as Drake stepped aside, she sat on the dressing table stool and proceeded to select the make-up she intended to apply.

"We haven't got all day to wait while you tart yourself up," Drake informed her, as her patience ran thin.

"I've got the right to look decent, haven't I?" Ryan replied. "Anyway, I want to look my best when I talk to your boss. I presume he'll be talking to me, and you and your pal downstairs are just his messenger boy and girl, right?"

Drake remained tight-lipped, saying nothing. A couple of minutes later, Drake had had just about enough of Ryan's delaying tactics.

"That's it, time's up Miss Ryan. Let's go, now," she said, firmly.

"Alright, alright, don't get your knickers in a twist," Ryan said as she leaned forward under the dressing table, Drake immediately standing back slightly, wondering if the woman was reaching for a weapon of some kind. Ryan emerged holding a pair of black leather, wedge-heeled shoes, which she proceeded to put on, finally standing up, giving Drake a particularly cheeky 'catwalk' twirl, and saying "Ready when you are, Sergeant."

Within minutes, they handed Angela Ryan over to the two uniformed constables, who swiftly and unceremoniously assisted her into the rear of their patrol car.

"Get her to headquarters as fast as you can," Drake instructed them. "DI Ross is waiting to talk to her, so don't waste any time in getting her there, got it?"

"Got it, Sarge," PC Thomas replied, as he and his partner, PC Wallis prepared to drive away. With Ryan safely on her way to headquarters, McLennan and Drake stood on the pavement and sighed as they were joined by Church and Curtis.

Seeing their sighs, and reading their body language, Church spoke quietly,

"Looks like you're both relieved to see the back of her."

"You can say that again," Drake replied. "There's something about Angela bloody Ryan that gave me the creeps."

"Me too," McLennan added. "She was too cool for my liking and managed to avoid giving direct answers to most of our questions."

"She's as slippery as an eel," Drake added.

"Well, let's hope the boss can get a confession out of her," Curtis added.

"I don't know," McLennan looked worried. "It's just a feeling, but I don't think things will be as easy as we hope."

He didn't know at that moment just how prophetic his words would prove to be.

CHAPTER 17
A BOLT HOLE

"Escaped? How in the name of God could she escape from the back of a locked police patrol car?" Ross's fury was more than evident as his voice could be heard not just in his office and the adjoining squad room, but virtually everywhere on the fifth floor of police headquarters, where the Specialist Murder Investigation Team was based.

Facing the full force of his temper, as he stood by the window of his office, were PCs Thomas and Willis, from whose car Angela Ryan had made a sudden and unexpected escape as the car was held up in traffic by a red light at roadworks on Dale Street. Standing behind the two PCs was Izzie Drake who couldn't help but feel a little sorry for the two officers, who were both young and she thought, perhaps inexperienced.

"Well, I'm waiting," Ross thundered. "Come on, one of you tell me what happened."

The two constables looked at each other and after a slight hesitation, Willis spoke.

"We're really sorry, sir. We were told the woman wasn't under arrest and was being brought in to assist with inquiries. And, when we drew the car from the car pool we assumed everything was ready and working. We didn't know the rear door locks hadn't been activated."

"For God's sake man, didn't either of you think to check things out for yourself?"

"No sir. Sorry sir. I was the one who put her in the car, so I take full responsibility."

"That's not right sir. We were both responsible," PC Thomas spoke up, in an accent which immediately identified him as being of Irish parentage, refusing to allow his colleague to take the blame by himself.

"Just tell me exactly what happened," Ross demanded, and Willis responded.

"Well sir, we were proceeding along Dale Street, and there were some roadworks ahead, with temporary light controls. The lights turned red, and we were forced to stop, in a line of traffic. As we were stationary, and before we knew what was happening, the back door flew open and Miss Ryan leaped out and took off running back the way we came and, well, she's not very tall, sir, and even though we leaped out of the car right away, she'd simply disappeared into thin air. She could have gone anywhere, and we couldn't just abandon the car, so we returned to it and radioed in with a report on what had taken place."

Ross shook his head, unable to believe they'd had Ryan in their grasp and somehow allowed her to escape. He also knew that the two PCs couldn't really carry too much blame, as Ryan hadn't been under arrest or in handcuffs which would have made escape far less likely. Before he could respond to Willis's words, there was a knock on his office door, followed by the entry of Sergeant Paul Ferris, who walked up to Ross's position by the window, and spoke in a virtual whisper to the DI.

"Sorry to interrupt, Boss, but I thought you'd want to know, I've had the mechanics in the garage do an urgent check on the car Ryan was travelling in and it was given a full service only three days ago, so should have been in tip-top condition. But, though the switches for the child-proof rear door locks were in the 'lock' position, there was a fault, and the doors could be opened with them in that locked position."

"Thank you, Paul," Ross said out loud, and then looked at the two constables.

"It looks like you two are partially off the hook. Seems there was a fault in your patrol car's locking system. Though the switch was set to the locked position the doors could still be opened from the inside. So, it looks like Ryan tried the door and got lucky. It remains a fact that if either of you had checked the doors when you placed her in the car, you could have identified the fault before setting off, but I realise that's not something most of you lads would do as a matter of routine, though perhaps from now on, you should do. In fact, it's a suggestion I'll make to higher authority. It might prevent a similar cock-up happening in the future. Now, the two of you had better bugger off before I change my mind, and make sure you both learn a valuable lesson from today. Go on, get out and get back to work.

"Yes, sir, sorry, sir, thank you, sir, it won't happen again sir," the two PCs jointly responded with relief showing all over their faces, as Izzie Drake held the door open for them and they beat a hasty retreat, anxious to put as much distance between themselves and the furious Detective Inspector, in as short a time as possible.

When they'd departed, Ross finally moved away from the window and sat down in his chair. Drake and Ferris waited for him to say something.

"Do you think I was too hard on them?" he asked the two sergeants.

Drake blew her cheeks out before saying, "Bloody hell. I thought you were about to turn blue with rage. Those lads must have been wetting themselves, or at the very least quaking in their boots."

Ferris added, "I don't think I've ever seen you so livid in all the years we've worked together. I think you were what they call incandescent with rage."

"To be honest, we should have cuffed her and placed her under arrest. So, in a way, you should blame me and Derek."

"You couldn't arrest her, Izzie. We didn't have any evidence on which to base an arrest. If you'd done that, she'd have come in here, refused to say a word, and demanded a brief, who'd have had her out of here by teatime. Then she'd have done a runner and left us with the task of hunting her down, much the same situation as we're in now."

"Yeah, but…"

"No buts, at least the fact that she's on the run proves we were right to suspect her and now I think the DCI will find a way to get us a search warrant for her house. If we can find one iota of evidence the arrest warrant will be issued in double-quick time. Now, please, will you go and find us some coffee."

* * *

Angela (Angie) Ryan leaned against the bronze figure of John Lennon one of the statues of The Beatles on Liverpool's Pier Head. She was slightly out of breath after her unplanned but fortuitous escape from the police patrol car. As the car waited at the road works, for the traffic light to turn green, she'd placed her hand on the door handle, and suddenly realised the handle would work, opening the door. She looked at the two officers in front, and saw they were engaged in a conversation about football, an ever-popular subject in the city. Without really thinking about what she intended to do, Ryan opened the door, as quietly as she could, and as soon as her feet hit the pavement, she began running back in the direction from which they'd come, and the police car couldn't turn around, Dale Street being a one-way street, to chase her. Turning down the first side street she came to, she paused long enough to take a rubber band which she wore around her wrist, and used it to tie her hair up, providing her with a makeshift disguise from the constables who would be looking for a woman with shoulder length, free flowing hair. She spent the next ten minutes weaving from street to street, easily losing herself in the crowds of shoppers and tourists that thronged the city streets, eventually reaching the Pier Head. Checking that there was no sign of pursuit, she took a few seconds to formulate a makeshift plan. The sound of ship's hooter sounded, giving her an idea. It was the ferry, and she now realised that if she could board the next ferry, she could reach the other side of the Mersey and if she could make it to Birkenhead, she knew a friend there who could be trusted to provide her with a temporary refuge, but first, she had to get there. An hour later, after an uneventful ferry crossing and walking at a leisurely pace, making herself as inconspicuous as possible she finally knocked on the door of a house on Violet Road, near Birkenhead Park.

"Angie!" shouted the excited voice of her friend, Eloise Parker as she threw her arms around Ryan's neck in an ecstatic greeting. "I haven't seen you for ages. What brings you to my door? I haven't seen you for months."

"Elly, please can I come in? I'll explain everything to you, but I need to get off the street."

"Yes, yes, of course," Eloise replied, taking hold of Ryan's right hand and virtually dragging her into the house, not stopping until they reached her kitchen, where she finally released the hand. Eloise looked at her friend and couldn't help noticing the panic in her eyes. "For God's sake, Angie, what's wrong. You look as if the hounds of hell are after you."

"Elly, listen, the police are looking for me and I need to get away from Liverpool for a few days." She'd decided that in order to be convincing in eliciting her friend's help, she'd stick as close to the truth as she dared, without revealing everything, of course.

"The police? What the hell have you got yourself mixed up in?"

"You might have heard on the news about the murders that have been committed in the last few days?"

"Yes, I have, but what have they got to do with you, Angie?"

"For some reason, the bizzies seem to think I'm involved somehow," Ryan replied, using the local slang word for the police.

"Please tell me they've got it all wrong," Elly looked horrified, as she wondered just what trouble her friend might be bringing to her door,

"Of course they have. You don't seriously think I'd kill anyone, do you?"

"No, no, of course not, but why do they think you're involved?"

"Elly, I know I've been pretty stupid, but I got involved with a man, who was in jail for crimes he didn't commit. Don't ask me how I met him, it's too complicated to explain. Anyway, a while ago, he died in prison, and since then, someone's been killing members of the jury that convicted him."

"And the police think you're the killer?"

"Yes, they do. Can you believe it Elly? I mean, me, a murderer, for God's sake?"

"They must have got it seriously wrong, Angie. The whole idea is just preposterous. Can't you just explain to them that they've got it all wrong?"

"I've tried that," Ryan did her best to look like a victim, rather than a criminal. "They wouldn't believe me. They were actually taking me to the police station when I managed to escape from the car taking me there at some traffic lights. I managed to shake them off, thought of you, hopped on a ferry, and well, here I am. Please say I can stay here for a day or two? I won't get in your way, and I'll be gone as soon as possible, I promise."

The forlorn, pleading look on Ryan's face did the trick and Eloise Parker soon acquiesced to Ryan's request, agreeing she could stay under her roof, "As long as it's not for too long," she responded.

Ryan, in a show of gratitude, threw her arms around her friend, hugged her and thanked her profusely. For now, she had a bolt hole that she was certain the police would never find. She now set her mind to trying to devise a way out of her current predicament.

CHAPTER 18

THE ROAD TO WIGAN PIER

"The Chief Super's not a happy bunny, Andy. Knowing we had Ryan and let her get away from us like she did hasn't gone down well with the DCS," Detective Chief Inspector Oscar Agostini said, as Ross stood fidgeting from a mixture of anger and embarrassment. "Before you say anything, I know it was a case of unfortunate circumstances that led to Ryan slipping through our fingers, but Hollingsworth is still fizzing mad."

"Ha-ha, I wouldn't have thought fizzing was quite the right word to describe her mood," Ross retorted, unable to suppress a grin as they discussed their overall boss, Detective Chief Superintendent Sarah Hollingsworth.

"I was trying to be polite," Agostini replied. "Seriously though, Andy, she was mad as a box of frogs when I told her what had happened with Ryan, and before you say anything, I told her it was nobody's fault, but I'm glad those two uniformed lads weren't within range while she was ranting."

"It still shouldn't have happened," Ross turned deadly serious. "But our hands were tied. We didn't even have enough to hold her on suspicion, and we had no grounds for an arrest, so the uniform lads couldn't even cuff her while transporting her."

"I'm sure your team all feel bad about it, Andy, but the important thing now is to move heaven and earth to find this Ryan woman, and there's something else I think you should consider."

"Go on," Ross replied, wondering what Agostini might be about to reveal to him.

"We're all pretty much agreed that this Ryan woman is the killer, yes?"

"Yes of course, so what are you leading up to?"

"Just this," Agostini spoke quietly as he made his next point. "Angela Ryan may be a vicious and sadistic murderer, but have you considered the fact that she may not be working on her own?"

"Funny you should mention that Oscar, but a germ of an idea along those lines has been niggling away at the back of my mind for a day or two, but with nothing to back up the thought I haven't been able to do much about it."

"Andy, I seriously think you should give some credence to that thought. Listen to this theory, let me finish and then give me your thoughts."

Ross nodded and sat waiting for the DCI to proffer his theory.

"Angela Ryan was quite clearly involved with Howard Blake, in some romantic fashion, and it's likely she believed him when he continuously told her he was innocent and the murders are her way of getting back at those she feels responsible for his unjust incarceration, agreed?"

"Agreed," Ross nodded.

"Well, even if we accept that premise, it's okay to see her as a cold-blooded killer, knowing her skills in martial arts, but, and it's a big but, she's a personal trainer or whatever she calls it, and has no known legal connection, so, there's a big question coming here, Andy, how the hell did she find out who was on the jury that convicted Blake?"

"Bloody hell, Oscar, that's it. That's what I couldn't put a finger on. I must be getting old or something. There has to be someone else involved in the murders, someone who's feeding her the information on the victims."

"Exactly. You can't just go along to your local library and look up the names and addresses of jury members for any given trial, so whoever's helping her has to be someone connected with the Blake trial."

"Of course it does. Oscar, you're a fucking genius."

"I know that," Agostini smiled. "So, you know what you need to do next."

"Right. We need to look at the original trial records and find someone involved in the proceedings who had access to all the sensitive information, and who may have maintained some form of contact with Blake since the end of his trial."

"As well as trying to find Ryan as soon as possible, before she tries to hit anyone else," Agostini concluded. "We got lucky in Fleetwood; we may not be so lucky in preventing her next attack."

"We're doing everything we can," Ross replied, "but I think we need to take a big step and inform the public we're seeking her in connection with the murders."

"I agree, Andy. I'll get George Thompson to come and see you and put an announcement together and we'll plaster the bitch's name and face all over the media. I presume you do have a photo of her that George can use?"

"Actually, no we don't, but I know where we can get one. Apparently, all the instructors at the fitness centre where she works have profiles on a notice board with their photos and personal qualifications listed."

"Then get someone down there fast and get that photo."

Within minutes of returning to his office, Ross had despatched Ishaan Singh on the errand to obtain a usable photo of Angela Ryan, as he filled in the rest of his team on the results of his meeting with the DCI, in advance of the arrival of George Thompson, the force's Press Liaison Officer.

The highly experienced PLO would know just how to word the public appeal for information on Angela Ryan.

"Ryan just wouldn't have had the access needed for her to locate the members of the Blake trial, "Ross reiterated to his team, which means that she must have an accomplice, someone who was closely connected to the trial," he stated, bluntly, as the gathered detectives nodded in agreement.

Izzie Drake was the first to speak.

"Why didn't we think of that before?"

"Because we've all been too focussed on apprehending the actual killer," Derek McLennan responded, and Ross agreed.

"That's right, Derek. Somehow, we kind of dropped the ball along the way with this one. I should have realised, as soon as we figured out the connection to the Blake jurors, that someone had to be feeding the killer with the information she needed to locate her victims."

"In other words, Boss, Angela Ryan is just the weapon, someone else is the one who's pulling the trigger," Tony Curtis summed up, rather eloquently.

"That's about the truth of it, Tony," Ross agreed.

"Strewth, all these genius detectives, and not one of us thought of it before now," Mitch Sinclair added, and silence descended, every eye in the room staring almost malevolently at the newest member of the team. Recognising the silence, Sinclair realised he might have 'put his foot in it' and quickly tried to extricate himself from the situation.

"What?" he asked. "Was it something I said? It was just an observation, folks."

"Don't worry about it," Ross defused the tension that had instantly gathered in the room. "Let's just say your Antipodean bluntness can be rather unsettling sometimes, Mitch."

"Oh, right, Skip. I get it. Sort of, be a bit more diplomatic in how I put things? Or just, watch your big mouth, Sinclair."

"Something like that, Mitch," and Ross just couldn't avoid the slight grin that found its way to his face.

Thankfully, at that moment, thoughts of Sinclair's 'big mouth' were forgotten as the door to the squad room swung open as the figure of George Thompson, the force's PLO walked into the room. Now in his early sixties, Thompson had known Ross and the long-serving members of his team for years, having been the Press Liaison Officer for as long as any of them could remember. As always, he was immaculately dressed in a navy-blue, pin-striped suit, white shirt, and regimental tie, having once served as an intelligence officer in the Royal Air Force in his younger days. He retained a full head of dark brown hair, despite his age and his black shoes were polished until they shone like mirrors.

"Morning all," he said by way of introducing his arrival.

"Good morning, George," Ross replied. "It's good to see you."

A couple of Ross's detectives joined Ross in greeting the PLO, who went on to ask how he could help. Ross quickly filled him in on the case and his immediate requirement for a press release that would engage the public in the hunt for Angela Ryan, without of course inciting panic in the local population. Thompson promised to have something suitable composed within an hour, appreciating the urgency of getting a press release out to all local, and perhaps national media outlets as soon as possible.

"A photo of the woman would be helpful, Andy," he suggested.

"DC Singh is working on that as we speak. By the time you've created a suitable release, he should have returned with a fairly recent photo of Angela Ryan."

Having made sufficient notes to enable him to do his job, Thompson took his leave of the squad room, returning to his own office to create the required press release. Well aware of Thompson's professionalism, Ross was now confident that by the end of the day, Angela Ryan's face would be featured in the local press and on the regional TV news programmes. He hoped it would help in engendering a positive public response, and that it wouldn't be long before someone, somewhere, reported a sighting of the fugitive woman. Sure enough, DC Ishaan Singh returned half an hour after Thompson's visit to the squad room, eagerly clutching the required photograph.

"I've got the original, Boss," he reported to Ross. "I told them a copy wouldn't be suitable but had to promise to return it when we've finished with it."

"Good lad," Ross replied. "Get that straight down to the PLO's office and make sure you put it in George Thompson's hand yourself. He's waiting for it so he can produce a suitable press release that we can get out to the media today."

"Okay, Boss," Singh responded, quickly turning on his heels and exiting the squad room no sooner than he'd entered, bound for Thompson's office.

* * *

Next on Ross's agenda was the subject of the potential accessory to Ryan's crimes.

"Okay, listen carefully. I take full responsibility for not thinking of it sooner, but as the DCI correctly pointed out, Ryan just couldn't have obtained confidential information and court documents be herself. She just doesn't have the skills or the authorisation to have accessed the necessary information. So, we need to delve deep into anyone who did have that sort of access and who might have been sympathetic to Blake's version of events."

"There can't be many people who fall into that category," Izzie Drake pointed out.

"I agree with Izzie," Fenella Church said, and her agreement was very quickly followed by equal words of agreement from the rest of the team.

"Okay, let's hear your thoughts," Ross invited his team to comment.

Derek McLennan was the first to speak up.

"Right, sir. In my opinion it's easier to first eliminate those we feel we safely discount from having any involvement on Blake's behalf."

"Go on, Derek. Such as?" Ross urged him on.

"Okay, starting at the top of the ladder, so to say, we can forget the judge, who sentenced him, and similarly, let's eliminate the prosecuting counsel and their team."

"Not necessarily, Derek," Fenella Church interrupted. "It would be nice to assume what you say is true, but what if, having seen all the evidence and the trial documentation, someone on that prosecution team felt strongly enough to not only believe in Blake's innocence, but was prepared to do something about it, acting outside the law?"

"I take your point, Fenella," Ross responded, "but I tend to err on the side of Derek's theory. Whoever's involved in supporting Ryan is far more likely to be someone involved in his defence. God alone knows there must have been a fair amount of people in both his solicitor's and barrister's offices who had access to the court papers, and who maybe agreed with his assertions of innocence."

"But Boss," Curtis now added. "Why would anyone put their entire career and possible their freedom at risk, for the sake of a convicted murderer?"

"I know, Tony. It doesn't appear to make much sense, but our best chance at present does seem to point to someone who had unlimited access to all the information surrounding the trial and conviction of Howard Blake."

Turning to Paul Ferris, Ross now instructed his computer specialist, together with Admin Assistant, Kat Bellamy, to 'dig deep; into the original trial, find out who represented Howard Blake, and if possible, obtain a list of employees at the time of his trial.

"If there's anything to find, Boss, we'll find it, never fear," the detective sergeant replied. Without another word, both he and Kat Bellamy turned around, and in seconds the pair set to work at their computers.

"What about tracking down, Angela Ryan?" Ginger Devenish posed the question.

"I know, Ginge," Ross replied. "We still need to prioritise the search for that damned woman. The entire force is on the lookout for her. Ishaan, can you get copies of that photograph of Ryan circulated to every police station in our area, please. It would help if the uniform guys knew exactly what the fugitive looks like," Ross said to Ishaan Singh.

"No problem," Singh responded.

"Try her work again, see if they know the names of any of her friends. Who's looking into her family background?"

"That's me, sir," Sam Gable replied to his question. "So far, I've come up with a mother who lives in Stalybridge, and a father, divorced from the mother who died two years ago. She has a younger brother, Joseph, who lives in Wigan."

"The brother sounds our best bet, Sam," maybe you should pay him a visit.

"Okay, sir," she replied.

"Take Mitch with you, in case she's holed up with her brother. Let's not take any chances, we all know how dangerous she is."

"Sinclair immediately rose from his desk and walked across to join Gable.

"Ready when you are, Sam," the young half-Australian smiled at her.

"Okay, Mitch, let's go. Want to drive?"

"Nah, you drive, Samantha. I've never been to Wigan. I can admire the scenery."

"Scenery? Wigan?" Gable joked. "You won't see much scenery on the M58, mate. Are you seriously telling me you've never had to go to Wigan on any previous cases, before you joined us?"

"Scout's honour, Samantha, never once. I wouldn't mind going to watch a rugby match there, though. They've got a top-notch Rugby League team from what I've read and seen on the telly. I even know about a book by George Orwell called The Road to *Wigan Pier*. Looked it up once and thought it sounded a bit downbeat and depressing."

"Don't tell me you were a boy scout too?" She ignored his rugby reference, as she knew nothing about the game. "Do you read a lot?"

"Nah, just a phrase, and yes, I read a great deal, Samantha."

"Okay, come on, let's go," Gable said, just pausing to ask Paul Ferris, "Got an address in Wigan for this bloke, Sarge?"

It was Kat Bellamy who picked up a sheet of paper from her desk and passed it to Gable. It contained an address in Ince-in-Makerfield, usually just known as Ince, a small town that forms part of the borough of Wigan.

"Probably take us about an hour to find the place," Gable pronounced to Sinclair. "Let's go."

"Lead on, Samantha," Sinclair said, faithfully following Gable from the room.

"That bloke is irrepressible," Devenish commented as the squad room door closed behind the pair of detectives.

"That's a good word for Mitch Sinclair," Fenella Church said. "Bloody irrepressible is right."

"Better than being maudlin and depressing," Ross said with a smile.

"I think you're getting used to his constant cheerfulness," Izzie Drake grinned.

"You think so? God, I must be getting old," Ross laughed.

* * *

Just over an hour later, Sam Gable brought the unmarked police Peugeot to a halt outside a neat semi-detached home on Jubilee Terrace in the small community of Ince. She was pleased to exit the car, as her colleague, the irrepressible DC Mitch Sinclair had barely paused for breath from the time they left Liverpool until she turned the ignition key to turn the engine off. She sighed, and Sinclair turned to her and said, "You alright, Samantha?"

"I'm fine, thanks," she replied, "but, boy, I thought I could talk a lot. Do you realise you've barely drawn breath since we set off?"

"Oh, sorry, Samantha. You should have told me to button it. I was just interested in the sights along the road, that's all."

"That's ok," Gable smiled at him, "but honestly, I couldn't see what was so interesting about some of the stuff you were talking about, like…a power station cooling tower?"

"Hey, like I said, people don't realise the incredible science behind the whole concept of the shape of those cooling towers, how they're designed to…"

"Okay, okay, I surrender to your superior knowledge of the design of cooling towers. Now, please can we go talk to this brother of Angela Ryan?"

Sinclair grinned and walking side by side with Gable, said, "I promise to keep my mouth shut on the way home, unless it's work related, deal?"

"Deal," Gable grinned back at him.

*　*　*

Joseph (Joe) Ryan was at home, fortunately for the detectives. He didn't seem too surprised to find a pair of police officers on his doorstep, as he ushered them into the kitchen of his home, explaining he was in the middle of preparing the ingredients for an apple pie. Ryan stood just under six feet tall, with short light brown hair and penetrating brown eyes that looked very much like those of his sister.

"I suppose this is about our Angela?" he said as they sat around the kitchen table with cups of coffee that had seemed to appear as if by magic before them.

"Are you married Mr Ryan?" Gable inquired, before answering his question.

"I am, but Julie's at work. She works in a bank in town. And please, call me Joe, I hate being called Joseph."

"And what do you do for a living, Joe?" Sinclair asked.

"I'm a chef, hence you see me up to my elbows in cookery ingredients. I don't start work till later this evening, so I'm making Julie an apple pie, her favourite. Now, what's our Angela been up to, and how can I help you?"

"First question, Joe," Gable began, "Is do you know where your sister is? And why did you automatically think we were here about your sister?"

"Honest answer, Detective, is no, I've no idea. Look, before we go on, let me tell you something. It's an open secret that Angela and I don't get along, never have since we were kids. And I guessed you had to be here about her because I've done nothing wrong, and Angela has always been headstrong, and it wouldn't surprise me if she got herself involved in something she shouldn't have done."

"And why's that? I mean, why don't you get along with each other?"

"Truthfully, I don't really know. We could just never agree on anything, whether it was what games we should play, or if Mum was going to take us to the cinema, we'd fight over which film we wanted to see, that kind of thing. As we got older, we both disagreed with each other's views on just about anything, politics, sport, you name it, we could always find a reason to disagree."

"So," Sinclair interrupted, "You'd probably be the last person she'd turn to if she was on the run from the police?"

"Yes, that's right, but, on the run? What is it that crazy sister of mine has done now?"

"Let's just say we need to speak to her urgently in connection with a case we're investigating" Gable stated, not wanting to bring the word 'murder' into the conversation, not yet anyway. "Would you know any of her friends, Joe? Any special mates, she might go to if she needed help?"

Joe Ryan sort of screwed his face up, his brow furrowed as he thought about Gable's last question. Eventually, he cleared his throat, held two fingers up and responded.

"I can think of two girls, they'd be women now of course, that she was very close to in her teens. One was named Imogen something or other, let me think, oh yes, Garside, that was it, Imogen Garside and the other was a rather weird girl called Parker, Eloise Parker."

"Why do you say she was weird?" Sinclair asked.

"Well, I suppose it was a childish thing, really. Being called Parker, it was inevitable she'd end up being called Nosey Parker, but thing is she really was a nosey little sod. She seemed to know everything their little gang of girls were up to, and I swear, even at that early age, she was blackmailing her friends. Not for money, we're talking things like sweets or later on, clothes, make-up and so on."

"And your sister told you all this, even though you didn't get along?"

"I know I said we never got along, but that was really only ninety percent of the time. Angela would tell me these things because she wanted me to be on her side, I suppose, or maybe she thought I'd go and beat Eloise up or something. I'd never have done that because I was brought up to respect women, both of us were."

"Do you have any idea if she's still in contact with either, or both of those close friends?" Gable pitched in with a question.

"No idea, sorry. I'm afraid I can't help you."

"Any idea where they might be living?"

"None at all. You need to remember, it's years since we were all kids, then teenagers at the same time, when we lived at home in Norris Green."

Gable pushed a little further.

"Have you seen any of them recently, maybe in the last few months?"

Joe Ryan fell silent, thinking for a few seconds before replying.

"Yeah, I did see Imogen about three months ago. I didn't recognise her at first, but she called out to me in the street one day, and I remember being surprised she'd recognised me after all this time. She'd changed a lot since our teenage days, if you know what I mean."

"You mean she'd grown into a woman, not a kid anymore," Sinclair interjected as a statement, rather than a question.

"That's right," Joe replied. "She'd filled out a lot up here," he said, indicating his chest, and her hair was a different colour from what I remembered. Anyway, she knew me alright, said I'd barely changed at all. She asked how I was, and asked about Angela, said she hadn't seen her for years."

"Did she say where she worked?" Sinclair asked.

"Yeah, she told me she's a bus driver, for Mersey Travel. Thought it a bit strange as she was a bit of an intellectual at school and thought she'd end up doing something like being a solicitor or doctor. Anyway, she seemed happy enough."

"And she told you she hadn't seen your sister for years?"

"That's right."

"And you've never seen the other girl, Eloise?"

"I told you, no, and I've no idea where she might be living, either. Just what do you want my sister so badly for?" he asked again.

Both detectives ignored his question and quickly came to the conclusion they were getting nowhere, with Gable adding.

"We appreciate you answering our questions, Joe, and if you do see your sister, please give us a call."

"But what the hell has she done?" Ryan asked again.

Sam Gable looked at Mitch Sinclair who nodded to her and she replied to Joe Ryan.

"Joe, we suspect your sister of being involved in a string of violent murders. She could be desperate and dangerous to anyone close to her, even you or a close friend. You must inform us immediately if you hear from her,"

Joe Ryan looked aghast at her, then at Sinclair, as if questioning the seriousness of Gable's words.

"You've got to be joking, right? Our Angie, a murder suspect, pull the other one, guys, really."

"I'm afraid we're deadly serious," Sinclair responded, and Joe Ryan knew from the tone of his voice that the police were indeed considering his sister as a serious murder suspect.

"Oh, Jesus Christ," was all Ryan could say.

"One last question," Gable said quickly. "Did you sister have any close male friends that you know of in recent years?"

"Not as far as I know. Like I said we haven't really been in touch much in recent years. I'm sorry, I can't help you."

Deciding they weren't going to learn anything helpful from Joe Ryan, the detectives thanked him and headed back to headquarters, where, they found a stranger in the squad room, involved in a conversation with DI Ross and DS Drake.

CHAPTER 19
DAVY GRANT

As soon as Gable and Sinclair entered the squad room, DS Church beckoned them over to her desk.

"You'll meet him soon enough, but in case you're wondering, the well-dressed man with the DI and Izzie is the first of the new personnel to be assigned to our new expanded team, a DC Davy Grant. He's Scottish, but not too difficult to understand. He'll be working with DS Ferris and Kat on the computer side of the team. He's apparently something of a cyber-genius from Computer Services and the brass decided he should start right away to allow him to learn everything about the way we work before they bring in any additional new people.

Save your questions for when you meet him. In the meantime, how did you get on in Wigan?"

"Not very well," Gable replied. "The brother barely has anything to do with her, hasn't really been close to her since they were kids. He gave us the names of a couple of her school friends, but neither of them sounds like they have anything to do with the case."

"Check them out anyway," Church ordered them. "We need to tick every box in the search for Angela Ryan."

"Okay, Sarge," Sinclair acknowledged. "Come on, Samantha, let's see if we can find those old girlfriends of hers."

The pair wandered over to Gable's desk, where they quickly typed up a report of their visit to Wigan and the interview with Joe Ryan, and then began their search to locate the current addresses of Imogen Garside and Eloise Parker.

Meanwhile, after his initial briefing from Ross and Drake, Detective Constable Davy Grant was taken around the squad room by DS Paul Ferris to meet the other members of the squad. Grant had already met Ferris and Admin Assistant Kat Ferris with whom he'd be working closely together. Standing no more than five feet ten, Grant wasn't tall, but even through his pale grey self-striped two-piece suit, it was evident that he was well-built, muscular and not one to be easily bested in a confrontation. He'd begun his career as a uniformed constable walking a beat in the Fazakerley area of the city, eventually making his way up to detective constable, worked for three years in CID and after attending a number of courses, his skill with computers was soon noticed and he eventually ended up working in the Force's Computer Services Division, from where Ross had 'poached' him as an addition to add to his team's growing need for extra computer savvy personnel as the team was about to grown in numbers.

"Bit of a surprise to see you suddenly appear," Tony Curtis said as he shook hands with the new man.

"I was told to keep it quiet until my appointment was confirmed," Grant replied. "I received a call from my superintendent this morning and was told to get over here as soon as possible. Seems it was all signed, sealed and delivered. Bit of a shock, I must say."

"Good to have you with us, anyway," DS Church responded.

"It'll be good not to feel like the new kid on the block

anymore," Ishaan Singh added, also shaking hands with Grant.

"So, you're here for good from today?" Ginger Devenish asked.

"Yes, he is," Ferris interrupted. "Now, if you all don't mind, I need to help Davy settle in, give him an insight into what we do here and what we expect from him."

Introductions over for the time being, it was back to work for the team. They still had a murderer, possibly two, to apprehend. DI Ross called the team around him, and they all listened as he laid out the next step in their search for the possible accomplice to Ryan's brutal murders.

"We're pretty sure Ryan wasn't operating alone. So, while we need to track her down and bring her into custody as soon as possible, to prevent her striking anyone else, it's imperative we find her accomplice."

"You're sure there's an accomplice out there, Skip?" Sinclair queried.

"There has to be, Mitch. Angela Ryan just doesn't have the inside knowledge of Howard's trial that would provide her with the names and addresses of the jurors who convicted him. There has to be someone on the inside helping her, maybe even orchestrating the whole thing, using her as a puppet to fulfil his or her own warped sense of justice," Ross replied.

"Strewth, I hadn't thought of it in that context," Sinclair looked shocked.

"By inside, you're focussing on those responsible for his defence, right sir?" Devenish asked, for confirmation.

"That's right Ginger," Izzie Drake replied to the question. "The solicitors who handled his case were a firm called Metcalfe and Dunn, and the barrister who represented him at his trial was a QC called Ambrose Machin, from a highly reputable firm called Machin, Sanders and Hall. Knowing how difficult it might be to get these various legal eagles to open up to us, DCI Agostini took our request to question these people to DCS Hollingsworth, and she herself has made some calls and got both firms to agree to talk to us."

Ross once again took up the narrative. So, Izzie and I will be going to talk to Howard's barrister, Ambrose Machin, while Fenella and Tony, I want you to go and talk to the people at Metcalfe and Dunn. Your first point of contact will be Adrian Metcalfe, who was the instructing solicitor in Howard's case."

"And the rest of us, sir?" Derek McLennan asked.

"You, Derek, are in charge of co-ordinating the search for Angela Ryan. She can't have got far. Use every resource at your disposal. I suspect she's lying low somewhere, probably not too far away. Her escape was a spur of the moment thing, unplanned, so she won't have made any plans on where to go, or how to stay out of sight."

"Right boss," McLennan replied. "She's probably panicking right now, wondering what the hell to do next. It's possible she'll make a mistake and walk right into our hands, if we get lucky."

* * *

Eloise Parker arrived home from her four-hour shift at the local care home where she worked part-time as a care assistant, four days a week. Angela Ryan was sitting at the kitchen table as Eloise walked into the room and literally threw that evening's issue of the Liverpool Echo on to the table in front of her. Ryan's face crumpled and her stomach lurched as she saw her own face staring out at her from the paper, under a headline that stated, POLICE SEEK LOCAL WOMAN IN CONNECTION WITH MURDERS.

The accompanying article went on to name Ryan and warned the public not to approach her if seen as she was considered to be potentially dangerous to anyone attempting to apprehend her. Anyone seeing her was advised to call the police immediately.

"What the fuck is all this, Angie? It sure doesn't sound like a case of mistaken identity to me. Just what the hell have you done, for God's sake?"

Ryan had been unprepared for her friend's verbal onslaught and sat staring at Eloise, without speaking for what seemed to her friend to be interminable seconds.

"Well? Say something, for Christ's sake, Angie," Eloise shouted at Ryan.

Eventually, Ryan pulled herself together and managed to stutter, "Elly, I'm sorry, really sorry."

"Sorry? You're sorry! Just how deeply are you involved in these murders, Angie? No, don't answer that. I don't want to know, but I want you out of my house. You can't stay here any longer."

"But where am I supposed to go, Elly?"

"I don't know, and I don't really care. You're wanted by the police and if they find you here, I'm likely to be arrested as an accessory or something. If you think anything of our friendship, please, just go."

"If I leave now, I'll probably be picked up within an hour or so. Can't I please stay until it's dark? I'll have a better chance of getting away in darkness. Please, Elly?"

Eloise thought for a few seconds before replying.

"Okay, you can stay until it's dark, but I want you out by ten o'clock, Angie. No later, okay?"

"Okay Elly, and thanks, for everything."

"You can thank me by leaving."

"I'll be gone by ten o'clock, I promise."

"I'm going for a shower," Eloise said as she left Ryan sitting at the kitchen table.

Left alone, Ryan began thinking of her next move. For a few seconds, she contemplated disposing of her friend, and using her home as a long term hide out, but quickly discarded the idea. First of all, she concluded, Eloise had a part-time job, and if she suddenly failed to appear for work, and her boss and possibly workmates would start calling her phone if she hadn't reported in sick. Without a reply, they'd quite probably send someone round to find out why she hadn't gone to work. Second, dead bodies had a very bad habit of beginning to decompose quite rapidly, especially in a warm environment such as they were in at present. She was pretty certain she would be unable to contend with the smell of decomposition once it set in. Third, if the police were on the ball, and she had no hesitation in believing they weren't, a bit of digging around in her past would likely reveal Eloise to have been a close friend of hers in their younger days and it wouldn't take them long to find out where she lived and send someone to question her on any possible contact with Ryan. If they found Elly's dead body, she'd have little to no chance of beating a murder charge. Leaving her friend dead would be as good as broadcasting the fact that she was the killer.

No, she told her friend nothing that could be used to incriminate her. She'd admitted nothing and in fact she'd basically denied everything to Eloise, and if she ended up testifying, what could Eloise say about her? Nothing at all that could connect her to the murders. No, she decided, she'd leave as she'd agreed when darkness fell, but first, she needed to make a couple of phone calls.

* * *

Ross and Drake were shown into the office of Ambrose Machin QC by his immaculately dressed secretary, identified by her name badge as Mary Allan. She was aged around fifty, Ross guessed, dressed in a two-piece black skirt suit, a white blouse with a self-attached black neck scarf, and glistening black patent leather high heels that Izzie Drake just knew she'd have a problem standing up in, aside from walking in.

"Thank you, Mary," Machin said, as she introduced the two detectives to her boss. "Can I offer you tea or coffee," he asked. Machin looked to be about sixty to sixty-five and had clearly been involved in the law practice for a number of years, bearing in mind the length of time that had passed since Howard Blake's trial.

Ross and Drake both asked for coffee and Machin simply nodded to his secretary, who would doubtless return in a short time with the required drinks. Ross quickly laid out the reason for their visit, after thanking the barrister for taking the time to see them.

"Your Chief Superintendent stressed that it was both urgent and important," Machin said without preamble. "I'm sure you understand I'm unable to discuss matters that might fall under client confidentiality, Detective Inspector," he addressed Ross.

"As I said, it's not actually your client we wish to discuss," Ross began. "It's more a matter of, and this is not an accusation, of the possibility of one of your employees having been sympathetic to the cause of Howard Blake."

Machin appeared genuinely shocked, but being an experienced trail barrister, he quickly assumed a calm and assured exterior. Before he could respond, a knock on the door preceded the entry of Mary Allan, carrying a tray containing a cafetière of hot coffee, three cups and saucers, milk and sugar and three teaspoons. Machin thanked his secretary who withdrew from the office with a barely perceptible nod to her boss. She'd made no attempt or offer to pour drinks, clearly Machin liked to do some things for himself. In fact, he poured coffee for all three of them, leaving the detectives to add their own milk and sugar if required.

"Well, detectives, I must say you do surprise me. I have a rather good memory for all my cases, but the Howard Blake case stood out as being one of the most open and shut affairs I can remember."

"You remember it that well?" Drake asked.

"Yes, Sergeant, I do. The evidence against Mr Blake was overwhelmingly in favour of a guilty verdict, but the man insisted he was innocent, and of course, I had to abide by his wishes and proceed with a not guilty plea. I did the best I could for him, but the guilty verdict was virtually inevitable from the start."

"I see," Ross said, thoughtfully. "But was there a chance that any of your legal staff or secretaries etc, might have believed in his innocence and thought his conviction to be unsound?"

"Inspector Ross, you need to realise that I'm not trying to be unhelpful, but please understand you're talking about a trial that took place over fifteen years ago. Apart from our chief clerk, Mr Purvis, my secretary, Mrs Allan and one or two others, our staff has undergone many changes in personnel since then. Moreover, I think if any of our employees harboured any thoughts of Mr Blake's innocence, they would in all likelihood have kept such thoughts to themselves, unless they were directly involved in the trial, like my assistant on the case, Cordelia Walters, and I can assure you, she was as convinced of his guilt as I was."

"Is Cordelia Walters still employed by your firm?" Drake inquired.

"I'm afraid not," Machin's face underwent something of a transformation. "Soon after the Blake trail I proposed to Cordelia and much to my surprise, she accepted."

"So, she's your wife now?"

"No sergeant, she isn't. A few months after we got engaged Cordelia was diagnosed with skin cancer and six months later, she was dead and gone."

"Oh God, I'm so sorry," Drake said, looking shocked at Machin's words.

Machin just nodded an acknowledgement and spoke again.

"As I said, Cordelia and the members of my staff involved in that case, although we were defending Mr Blake, were all convinced of his guilt. My defence strategy was really one of damage limitation, which was made harder by Mr Blake's constant denial of being involved in the murders. Because of that stance, I couldn't even put forward a mitigating defence of him never having meant to kill anyone, the deaths were accidental, and the charges should be reduced to manslaughter."

"I understand," Ross replied. "He insisted he was innocent so any such defence would have been moot."

"That's correct, Inspector," Machin fell silent, indicating that there was little else to say on the subject. "Look, I understand what you're looking for, but I honestly don't think you're looking in the right place," the barrister said, tellingly, and Ross instantly realised that Machin might have something else to say.

"Then, where do you suggest we should be looking?" Ross asked immediately.

"I don't believe I'm breaking any confidences by telling you this," Machin said, and after a short hesitation, he continued. "Inspector Ross, at the time of Mr Blake's trial we were of course acting under instructions from his solicitors," he paused to look at the file, "Metcalfe and Dunn, that was the name of the firm. I recall now that Mr Blake was represented by the senior partner, Adrian Metcalfe. I must admit, Metcalfe was quite vociferous when he first approached me with a view to me taking the case at trial."

"Really? Do you know why that was?" Drake inquired.

"Oh, yes, Sergeant. Adrian Metcalfe was a hundred percent sure of Mr Blake's innocence and did a great job of convincing me I should take the case. It wasn't till I'd accepted the brief and conducted a number of interviews with my new client that I began to seriously question Metcalfe's opinion, and indeed Mr Blake's assertions of innocence."

"But surely, it's quite normal for a solicitor to believe in his client's innocence?" Ross asked.

"Yes, there's nothing ostensibly wrong with that," Machin responded, "But not to the extent that Adrian Metcalfe did in the Blake case."

"Can you elaborate on that assertion?" Ross asked, feeling that Machin was possibly holding something back.

"It was just a feeling I had that steadily grew as the case developed. Adrian Metcalfe was wholly convinced of his client's innocence and when I began to raise doubts about the potential outcome of the trial, he seemed horrified at possibility of a guilty verdict."

"Have you any idea why he would have reacted like that?"

"Sorry, Inspector, I have to answer in the negative. I had no idea then, and certainly have no idea now, why Adrian Metcalfe was so adamant in his belief of his client's innocence. The wildest possibility I can ascribe to his belief, and I admit it is wild, is that Metcalfe either knew Mr Blake was definitely innocent because a) he knew who real murderer/rapist was, or b) Adrian Metcalfe knew Mr Blake was innocent because he himself was the killer!"

If the barrister was expecting a reaction to his final words, he certainly received one.

"Good God!" Drake exclaimed, as Ross couldn't help swearing, "Bloody Hell, Mr Machin. That's a hell of a supposition to make. What made you think like that?"

"Like I said, I know it's a bit wild, but I had occasion to speak with Metcalfe's clerk once or twice, and he also spoke as if there could be no doubt about Mr Blake's innocence, and that despite the evidence which was accumulating against their client, as far as he was concerned, if his boss believed he was innocent, then he was innocent."

Ross's mind tried to assimilate the inferred suggestion from Machin.

"Are you seriously suggesting that Blake's solicitor could have been in any way complicit in his crimes?" he asked.

Machin seemed to hesitate before replying.

"Perhaps I shouldn't have said that, Inspector Ross. I have no proof to back up my words, I apologise shouldn't have voiced what were really just my thoughts."

"Don't apologise," Ross replied. "You'd be surprised how often someone's random thoughts can lead to a breakthrough in difficult cases. From what you've just told us, my immediate thought is that your first suggestion may have been accurate and that Howard Blake, if he was innocent, may have known or suspected who the real perpetrator was and shared that knowledge with his solicitor."

"Hmmm," the barrister was thoughtful. "Yes, that could be a possibility. But if Mr Blake possessed such knowledge, which clearly could have helped with his defence, why didn't he allow Adrian Metcalfe to use that information in his defence?"

Drake provided him with the obvious answer.

"To protect someone, Mr Machin. It wouldn't be the first time an innocent man had allowed himself to go to prison in order to protect someone else from prosecution."

"Yes, Sergeant Drake is correct," Ross added.

Realising he'd set in motion a new train of thought in the detectives' minds, Ambrose Machin now appeared pensive as he tried to think of anything else that might assist the police inquiry. He quickly flicked through the rest of the documents in the Howard Blake trial folder before pausing on one particular page, where he began tapping the page with index finger of his right hand, his head slowly nodding as he did so.

"Something you've remembered, Mr Machin?" Ross had instantly noticed the barrister's actions on seeing something that might be significant in the file.

Machin held a hand up for a moment, as he picked up his phone and pressed a button.

"Would you mind stepping in here for a moment, please, Mary?" he said, summoning his secretary. "I think Mary might be able to help with something," he said, as a single knock on the office door was followed by the reappearance of Mary Allan.

"Mary, the Detective Inspector and Sergeant Drake need our help with an active case of theirs. I hope your memory's in good working order, because this concerns a case I took to trial over fifteen years ago."

"Oh, I'll try to help if you think I can," the secretary replied with a smile.

"Please, take a look at the annotation you made here on one of the pre-trial depositions and try to remember exactly what thoughts were going through your head when you wrote it."

Mary Allan had by now walked around to stand beside Machin, as he sat in his plush leather office chair. She bent over to look at a page in the file on his desk, where he continued to tap a section of it with his finger. Ross and Drake waited quietly while Mary Allan did as her boss requested. Mary read the words she'd typed all those years ago, allowing herself to recall exactly why she'd had those thoughts. After a minute she straightened up, nodded and spoke, directing her words to Ross and Drake.

"Oh yes, I remember it well. I just took me a minute to dredge it out of my memory. I typed, *this man and his entire team appear to be wholly on board with the belief that their client is innocent, almost to the point of obsession.*

"Can you tell us why you came to write that note, Mrs Allan?" Ross asked.

"Yes, Inspector. Mr Machin had been due to hold a meeting, here in the conference room, but his brother, Anthony, was involved in a road traffic accident that morning, and was seriously injured."

"Yes, I remember it well," Machin nodded as she spoke.

"Anthony almost died, Inspector. He had multiple fractures, a ruptured spleen and a punctured lung. He was on the critical list in intensive care. I cancelled all my appointments for the first two days, so I could be there to help his wife, Helen and their two children. Our mother was also in something of a state, as you can imagine, so I had her to look after as well. My Father had passed away some years prior to this so you can imagine it was a stressful time for the whole family. I asked Mary to stand in for me that first day, by holding whatever meetings she could, making relevant notes and rearranging important meetings where appropriate."

"And that's what I was doing in this particular case," Mary carried on. "The solicitor Mr Metcalfe was accompanied to the meeting by his chief clerk, his name's here somewhere, yes, a Mr Clive Evandon. I felt I had to write this insert because Clive Evandon was a really awful type of character. Most solicitor's clerks are well-educated, polite and deferential, particularly in their dealings with a QC and his staff. Not Mr Evandon, oh no, Inspector. Not only did he have what I could only describe as a 'superior' attitude, but at times it felt like he was the one in charge and Mr Metcalfe the assistant. He spoke in a way that made me think he was telling Mr Metcalfe how to instruct Mr Machin. I reminded him that I was Mr Machin's personal secretary and that this was not the case meeting, merely me meeting them as a curtesy in the absence of Mr Machin. He was a most unsavoury character, and I was relieved when they left the office. My final note on the visit states; *Two of the most weak and despicable representatives of the legal profession it has been my displeasure to meet.*"

"I take it that such behaviour is hardly commonplace in your profession?" Ross directed his question to Machin.

"Certainly not," the barrister replied, his voice firm and uncompromising. "I made the decision there and then after speaking to Mary, that in future we would accept no further referrals from Metcalfe and Dunn. I called a meeting with the partners, and it was unanimously agreed, once they were made aware of the circumstances."

Soon afterwards, Ross and Drake took their leave of Ambrose Machin and Mary Allan and headed back to headquarters.

"What did you make of that, Izzie?" Ross asked as he drove the unmarked police Peugeot.

"Bloody hell, the way Mary Allan described that meeting with them, they sound like the solicitors from hell, and that Evandon guy came across as having an undue influence over the senior partner. All a bit strange if you ask me."

"I agree. I can understand Machin, Sanders and Hall wanting nothing further to do with them. I also think we can eliminate Machin and his people as being potential proponents of Howard Blake's innocence, either before, during or after the trial."

"God knows what Fee and Tony are likely to come up with, assuming they've managed to speak to anyone at Metcalfe and Dunn."

"That's always assuming the people who were involved in Blake's case are still engaged by the firm," Drake mused.

* * *

DS Fenella Church and DC Tony Curtis's visit to the firm of Metcalfe and Dunn, carried out almost simultaneously with Ross and Drake's interview with Ambrose Machin had proved to be almost pointless. Five minutes after Ross and Drake had departed from headquarters, Church made a call to the number listed in the court papers for the firm of Metcalfe and Dunn, only to be met with an 'unobtainable' tone.

"Damn," Church exclaimed, her outburst overheard by the new computer tech, DC Davy Grant.

"Problem, Sarge?"

"Seems the solicitor I want to see has an unobtainable number."

"Give it here," he said, and Church wrote the number on a yellow post-it and passed it to him. "Give me two minutes," he smiled as he turned to his keyboard.

Sure enough, in slightly less than two minutes he swivelled his chair to face Church and Curtis.

"Interesting," he said. "Metcalfe and Dunn went out of business eight years ago."

"Shit," Curtis said.

"Never fear, Davy's here," Grant smiled. "A quick trace of the Law Society records shows that, of the two partners in the firm, Adrian Metcalfe passed away ten years ago, but Gerald Dunn is still alive, retired and I have his current phone number for you."

He passed the yellow post-it back to Church, with the number written below the one she'd written.

"Well done, Davy," she thanked the new detective, and walked to her desk and picked up the phone.

Curtis stood chatting with Grant while she spoke on the phone. As she concluded the call, he looked expectantly at the DS, who said without hesitation.

"Come on, Tony, we're going to West Derby. Mr Dunn says he'll be happy to talk to us."

Thirty minutes later, Church and Curtis found themselves seated comfortably on a large brown leather sofa in the spacious lounge of a well-appointed three-bedroomed detached bungalow situated in a leafy cul-de-sac in West Derby, with immaculate gardens and an almost new gleaming bronze Bentley parked on the drive, in front a large, double-fronted garage.

"Cor, look at that, Sarge. Bet that doesn't get many miles to a gallon."

"If you need to worry about the price of petrol, you don't buy a car like that, Tony," Church responded.

"I suppose you're right. Just shows there's big money to be made out of other people's misery, eh? You know, charging the earth for sorting out the less fortunate's legal problems."

"I won't argue with that," Church agreed. Gerald Dunn's Bentley clearly indicated that the man had made a good living in his years as a solicitor.

Dunn himself answered their ring on his doorbell, and after they'd identified themselves, he led them through the house and into a large conservatory, before inviting them to sit down, but not before asking his wife, Beatrice, to bring tea and coffee out to them as they spoke.

After Church explained the reason for their visit, Dunn sat, thinking for a minute before, after clearing his throat, he did the best he could to assist the detectives.

"I really don't know much about the case you're talking about," Dunn began, although I can tell you that it was the case that signalled the beginning of the end for Metcalfe and Dunn."

"Can you explain that remark, please Mr Dunn?" Church asked.

"I'll try and make it short, shall I? I remember the Howard Blake case of course, though it was my partner who was the instructing solicitor. What I can tell you is that Adrian became totally obsessed with the case, to the exclusion of any other cases on our books."

"So his work, his professionalism began to suffer?" Church pressed further.

"That's correct Sergeant, but I had no idea at the time that Adrian was already showing the early symptoms of the illness that would eventually kill him. We'd been friends for years and set up the firm of Metcalfe and Dunn together although Adrian was senior partner owing to him having the larger investment in the set up. It was around the time of the Blake case that I first noticed certain changes in his behaviour and attitudes."

"In what way?" Church was extremely interested in what Dunn had begun to reveal.

"How should I put this?" Dunn mused for a few seconds. "Let me just say, Adrian's decision making began to be erratic, illogical at times. I spoke to him about it, obviously but he refused to acknowledge the fact that he might have a problem. The trouble became worse as Adrian had always inspired great loyalty in those who worked with, and for him. As a result of that misplaced loyalty some of his staff not only failed to see what I saw and suspected, but they actually encouraged him as he proceeded to either take on cases we had little chance of winning, or when faced with a potentially open and shut case, like Howard Blake's trial. If only I'd realised how sick my old friend was, got him to seek medical help, maybe things wouldn't have turned out as they did."

"What exactly was wrong with him, Mr Dunn?" Curtis asked, suspecting already what the answer might be.

"Adrian Metcalfe was eventually diagnosed with a malignant brain tumour, but not before his decisions and mishandling of a number of cases led to a disastrous drop-off in business for the firm. Putting it bluntly, other solicitors, barristers, court officials decided that Metcalfe and Dunn had lost all credibility and the work dried up. By the time Adrian sought medical help after collapsing during a Crown Court case one fateful day, it was too late to save either the firm, or my old friend's life."

"I'm so sorry," Church.

"I thought you were going to say that" Curtis added, with a certain sympathy in his tone of voice. "I had an uncle who suffered from the same thing. He was a draughtsman, but he died at the age of forty-five. It was sad to see him slowly deteriorate, so I do understand why and how it kind of crept upon him, and on you and your staff."

"Did Mr Metcalfe have any family?" Church inquired.

"Not close family," Dunn replied. "His parents had passed

away some years prior to him becoming ill and he had a brother, Terence, who lived in Australia. He flew over here for the funeral, where I met him for the first and only time. He was quite candid in telling me that he and Adrian were close as children but once he, Terence I mean, met and married his wife, Joyce and moved to Australia, the two brothers just slowly drifted apart. There was no falling out or anything like that. Their lives just diverged and followed different paths."

"What did Terence do for a living?" Church delved a little deeper, thinking that despite outward appearances, there may have been something that held the fabric of a familial relationship together.

"He was a professional diver, who apparently organised tours along the Great Barrier Reef. Nothing at all like his brother."

Church and Curtis could see there was little to be gained by looking further into the brother of the deceased solicitor. Next, they made inquiries about the staff of the now defunct firm.

"You mentioned the fact that some of the staff were fiercely loyal to your partner," Church began. "Was there anyone in particular who might have blindly followed him, even once he seemed to have veered away from what you might have seen as ethical procedures?"

Gerald Dunn didn't hesitate before replying.

"There certainly was, Sergeant. We had a chief clerk by the name of Evandon, Clive Evandon. That man had an almost sycophantic relationship with Adrian. Whatever Adrian said, you could be sure Evandon would agree with, and then there was a young solicitor called Graeme McCain, who Adrian hired. He assisted Adrian on some of his cases, including, I believe, the Blake case. Even when we started losing business and I attempted to talk some sense into him, to tell him he was hurting his own career by blindly following Adrian and his methods, the poor young fool just refused to listen and when Adrian found himself being cut adrift by most of our clients, young McCain ended up going the same way. Last I heard, he was working as a legal representative for a charity of some sort."

"What happened to that Evandon chap?" Curtis asked.

"I've no idea, Detective," Dunn shook his head. "To be honest, once Adrian had become incapacitated by virtue of his illness, I wasted no time in dismissing Evandon from his employment with us. There was a lot of rancour at the time, with Evandon trying to tell me I couldn't get rid of him, but I did, and I've no idea, or interest in knowing what became of the man."

* * *

By the time Eloise had finished taking her shower and had calmed down sufficiently to return downstairs, Angela Ryan had formulated the next stage of her escape plan. It all depended on the one person she felt could help her.

"Elly, I promised I'd be gone by tonight and I will be. I just need your help in a couple of things."

"I told you Angie, I won't get involved in anything illegal, even for a friend."

"I'm not asking you to do anything like that, honest," Ryan assured her. I just need to make a phone call, and I want to borrow a change of clothes from you. If I can change my appearance, it'll make me harder to spot. That's all I ask, oh, and some hair dye if you have any."

With a great deal of reluctance, Eloise agreed, feeling it was the only way to rid herself of her unwanted house guest. Together, the two women scoured Eloise's wardrobe until, despite her being quite a bit shorter in height than Ryan, they found a dark navy skirt and white polo neck top that succeeded in transforming Ryan's appearance. Eloise managed to find an old, unused bottle of hair colouring she'd bought on a whim during a visit to a local supermarket, and in no time, Angela Ryan was transformed into a blonde, her change of clothes making her appear to be one of thousands of average looking working girls who populated the city.

While Eloise busied herself in the kitchen, Ryan made her way into the hallway, where Eloise's landline telephone was situated. Her escape plan now hinged very much on the result of the call she was now making. After punching in the numbers on the telephone keypad, she waited anxiously for what seemed an age for a reply. Suddenly, her heart appeared to miss a beat as the ring tone ceased and a familiar voice answered her desperate call.

Over the next five minutes she did her best to elicit the help she required from her final hope of getting away from the city as the police net inevitably closed in on her. At last, her contact agreed to help her to flee the city.

"Can you make it to the ferry terminal in time for the 6.20 sailing?" the voice asked.

"I think so."

"If, as you say, you've managed to change your appearance you'd better tell me what you'll look like, what you're wearing. If you see me as you board the ferry, do not, under any circumstances acknowledge me, do you understand?"

"Yes, I understand. How are you going to get me away?"

"Just leave that to me. I'll explain when I see you. The important thing is to get you out of the country, do you agree?"

"Oh, yes. That would be the best thing to do."

"Okay, it'll take me a little time to organise things, but I'll have a plan in place by the time I see you."

"Thank you so much," she said, with relief in her voice. I knew I could count on you."

"Yes, well, better hang up now, and I'll see you on the ferry later."

"Okay, great, see you later then," she said, but the line had already gone dead.

"Everything sorted then," Eloise asked, as Ryan re-entered the kitchen.

"Yes, I'll be gone soon, Elly. I can't thank you enough, really I can't."

"Don't thank me. I'll just be glad when you're gone, and I don't have to worry about the police coming and knocking my door down in the middle of the night."

Eloise herself felt relief wash over her at the prospect of Angie Ryan being out of the way. She just wasn't the type of person to get involved in things like this. She looked at her watch. *Not long now*, she thought to herself, making yet another coffee for the pair of them, in the hope it would help the time pass a little quicker.

CHAPTER 20
THE LEAVING OF LIVERPOOL?

The morning briefing was a chance for Ross and his team to pool whatever intelligence they'd gathered from the previous day's investigations and interrogations. So far, despite the entire uniform branch being on high alert and armed with the photograph of Angela Ryan, there hadn't been a single confirmed sighting of the fugitive. Admittedly, there'd been a couple of reported sightings of women supposedly fitting her description, but they'd proved to be nothing but dead ends, false alarms.

DCI Oscar Agostini had decided to sit in on the briefing, to keep himself completely updated with the progress of the investigation. He decided to say a few words before Ross got things going.

"Good morning ladies and gents, I'm only here to see what's we've got so far. I know this is a bastard of an investigation, but let's be positive. We're reasonably sure we know who the killer is, right?"

"Right sir," Ross agreed, and the DCI continued.

"It was damned unfortunate that we had this Ryan woman in our hands, and then lost her to a combination of bad luck and unfortunate circumstances."

In response to a half-heard comment from the back of the room, Agostini said,

"Is there something you wish to add DC Curtis?"

"I just said, bloody woodentops, sir. Those uniform lads let her get away from them like water from a leaky watering can."

"The uniform lads have already been spoken to and the matter dealt with. It wasn't entirely their fault. Seems there was a fault with the central locking system, so let's hear no more about it, okay?"

"Okay sir, sorry," Curtis apologised, though Agostini could understand the detective's frustration, which he shared.

"Forget it now, Curtis. Andy, what do we have so far?" the DCI stood to one side, allowing Ross to take over the briefing.

"Thanks, sir," Ross began. "I think we can definitely say that Ryan is our killer, for the simple reason that since we identified her, the daily killings have ceased. She's obviously gone into hiding since her escape and it's now a priority that we locate her and get her behind bars as soon as possible. Having said that, the other side of the coin, so to speak, is that we now firmly believe Ryan isn't working alone on these murders. Someone with access to the court records pertaining to those who made up the jury for Blake's trial has to have been feeding her with the names and addresses of the jurors."

He nodded at Izzie Drake, who took over from that point.

"We've had some of you looking into the legal firms connected with Blake's defence, on the basis that someone involved in his defence is most likely to be the one who's helping her, or may in fact be the main player in all this, the driving force behind the murders, with Angela Ryan his or her pawn, setup to take the blame for the crimes, based on her romantic connection to Howard Blake. The boss and I went to talk with the barrister, Ambrose Machin and he gave us some very interesting information, not about his own firm, but relating to the solicitor who represented Blake, Adrian Metcalfe, and his chief clerk a man named Evandon."

"That would be Clive Evandon, I take it," Church interrupted.

"That's right, Fee. I take it his name came up with your inquiries into Metcalfe and Dunn?"

"You might say that" Church responded, taking it as her cue to deliver the information she and Curtis had gleaned from their talk with Gerald Dunn. Ross and Drake were surprised to learn that Metcalfe and Dunn was no longer in existence, and even more surprised at the reasons Gerald Dunn had given them for the firm's closure.

"So, Metcalfe had a brain tumour that was affecting his ability to do his job, losing his ability to think rationally, I can understand that, but how does Clive Evandon fit into all this?" Agostini queried.

"Evandon appears to have been some kind of sycophantic believer in everything Metcalfe told him," Ross replied. "From what Ambrose Machin told me and Izzie, and from what Fee and Tony have learned, he somehow managed to follow Metcalfe's beliefs and instructions, not only in the Blake case, but also subsequent ones, until clients turned away from the company, which eventually saw its cases dry up and they were forced out of business."

"Yes, that's right sir. We heard exactly the same kind of narrative from Gerald Dunn," Church confirmed. "As soon as Metcalfe passed away, Dunn lost no time in dispensing with Evandon's services."

"And where is this Evandon chap, now?" Agostini probed further.

"Nobody seems to know, sir," Church replied.

"There's one man who might know," Curtis suggested. "Remember, Sarge, Dunn told us about a junior solicitor with the firm, Graeme McCain, works for some find of charity now he said."

"That's right," Church agreed. "He was another who was

close to Metcalfe. Perhaps, as Tony suggests, he might have kept in touch with Evandon over the years."

"Then let's track McCain down and see if he can help us to locate Evandon's current whereabouts," Agostini suggested. "From what you've all learned so far, this Clive Evandon has suddenly shot to the top of the 'most wanted' list, to my way of thinking."

"My thoughts exactly," Ross agreed with the DCI. "Fee, get back in touch with Mr Dunn and try and find out if he has any knowledge of this charity that McCain works for, and if he has anything else that might help us find Evandon. He told you he's no idea what happened to him but if pushed, he might remember something that could give us a clue to his whereabouts."

"Right you are, sir," Church replied. "Tony, while I phone Gerald Dunn, you can make some inquiries, see if Clive Evandon has ever been picked up for any minor offences, maybe traffic violations and so on. If he has, there'd have to be a record of his address."

"Okay, Sarge," Curtis responded, immediately, "Though if he does have anything recorded against him there's no guarantee he'll still be at the address he gave, if it was a few years ago."

"And then again, it might have been last year, last month, we won't know unless we delve deep, will we?"

"Don't worry, Sarge, I'll leave no stone unturned. If Evandon has had any contact with our side of the law in the last fifteen years, I'll find it."

"Good lad, now go, start delving," Church smiled as she spoke, and DC Curtis grinned back at her as he positioned himself at his desk and fired up his computer.

Ross now turned his attention back to the search for Angela Ryan, speaking first to Derek McLennan.

"Any leads in the search for the Ryan woman yet, Derek?"

"Well, Boss, from what we've been able to learn so far, it

seems she doesn't have any close friends. We know the names of a couple of her friends from her younger days. It's probably worth following up on them. Her brother told us he'd met one of them recently and she told him she hasn't seen her in years, though it's always possible she was lying of course.

"Make it a priority to get someone to trace those old mates of hers, Derek. Get someone to visit them asap. Someone, somewhere must have an idea where we can find her, unless she's found a damn good place to hide out, a place nobody knows about where she feels safe".

"Or someone's keeping her hidden in their home," Devenish joined in with a suggestion, which was as close to the reality as anyone had unwittingly come, up to that point.

"Sounds a bit weird if you ask me," Mitch Sinclair added his thoughts to the exchange of views.

"How so, Mitch?" Ross was interested to hear Sinclair's ideas.

"She's a relatively young woman, right? But, according to her family members and the guy who runs the fitness centre where she works, she hardly has any friends, which is what I find a bit 'off' in this day and age."

"Good point Mitch," Ross agreed, "so what would you suggest we do?"

"Well, Skip, I'd hit that fitness centre again and talk to everyone who came into contact with her, especially the staff and her regular clients. There's a chance that someone might know something that might be useful to us."

"OK, good idea, if you can spare them, Derek, why not let Mitch and Ishaan go and do just as he suggests?" Ross, having put McLennan in charge of that side of the investigation, diplomatically allowed him to make the final decision.

"Yes, definitely, sir. The fitness centre is all yours, Mitch, Ishaan," McLennan instructed Sinclair and Singh, who wasted no time in exiting the squad room.

"We have to consider the possibility that if she's been

helped by someone connected with the old Metcalfe and Dunn law firm, that person could now be helping her by providing her with a hiding place or maybe a way to get out of the country," Ross intimated, thinking on his feet, in the lack of any solid proof. "I want to know who the hell is behind all this. The more I think about it, the more I'm sure that Ryan is nothing but a pawn in someone else's Machiavellian scheme."

Fenella Church had been quiet for a few minutes, seemingly lost in thought, and now held a hand up to gain Ross's attention.

"Yes, Fee, what is it?"

"I'm not sure, sir, but it's just that when this bloody case kicked off, we were working on the principle of find the killer, close the case, agreed?"

"That's right, Fee, but why do I get the feeling you've just come up with an idea that might suggest we've overlooked something back in the beginning."

"It's nothing concrete, sir, but I've been trying to think back, working on the premise that now we know we're looking for someone else in connection with the murders, Ryan's enabler for want of a better term, well…" she hesitated, and Ross urged her on, "Come on Fee, out with it. It's not like you to hold back if you have a workable theory."

"Okay," she recommenced, "I think it might be worth us revisiting the Blake siblings. We thought we'd cleared them of any involvement in the murders, but can we honestly say they're in the clear as far as possibly being the brains behind the whole thing?"

"That's a good theory, one we haven't considered," Ross agreed. "Okay, Fee, I'm putting you in charge of looking deeper into that possibility."

Church nodded and began to plan how to approach this new side to the investigation.

Oscar Agostini, pleased that things were beginning to

move forward, albeit slowly, decided to leave Ross and the team to get on with things, after first checking with Ross that young DC Grant was settling in with the squad satisfactorily, and soon withdrew and took his leave of the team, returning to his office, where he'd soon be on the phone, bringing DCI Hollingsworth up to date with the investigation's progress.

* * *

Meanwhile, across the Mersey in Birkenhead, Angela Ryan said her goodbyes to her friend Eloise, picked up her bag, containing the clothes she'd arrived in and a few items of cosmetics that Eloise had given her to tide her over until she could buy some of her own.

"Thanks Elly, for everything. I really appreciate your help."

"Angie, whatever it is you've got yourself mixed up in, I just hope this friend of yours manages to help you to sort it out."

"I'm sure my friend will have me out of the country by this time tomorrow. Once I'm gone, hopefully the police will concentrate on finding the real killer. Don't worry, I'll be okay, and if the police do somehow come here looking for me, just tell them the truth, that I told you I'm innocent and I've gone away until they find the real killer."

Eloise Parker breathed a sigh of relief as her friend finally took her leave of her home. She couldn't escape the feeling that her old friend, Angie had been somewhat economical with the truth about her involvement with the series of murders that had recently become front page news, in the local paper, radio and TV news too. In truth she suspected Angela was much more deeply involved in the murders than she'd first suspected when she'd arrived begging for a place to hide out for a day or two. She watched Angie as she walked confidently away from the house, bag in hand, heading for the ferry terminal, her changed appearance definitely making her difficult to recognise from the photo that had been reproduced in the news outlets. For the sake of their old friendship, she hoped Ryan's unnamed friend could successfully help her to leave the country until the case was resolved, and Ryan's name was cleared.

Angela Ryan was soon on board the ferry which pulled out into the waters of the mighty River Mersey. It wouldn't be long before she was back in the city of Liverpool, though not for long. Her contact's plan as explained to her would only require her to be in the city overnight, after which she'd quickly be heading out of the country and staying away as long as necessary. Anything, she knew, would be better than being locked in a prison cell for years, as would be her fate if the police were to apprehend her.

As instructed, she made her way to the stern of the ferry, and stood quietly looking over the stern rail, watching the frothing waters of the river, as they were churned up by the ship's propellers. The sight was almost hypnotic, as she allowed her mind to wander, remembering every detail of every one of her 'missions' of murder. She became so engrossed in the memories that she failed to hear or sense the arrival of her contact, who stepped up quietly behind her. As the effect of the undulating waves held her in their thrall, she was totally unprepared for what happened next.

CHAPTER 21
GOOD NEWS, BAD NEWS

The team having been sent home as evening dawned, Derek McLennan and his wife Debbie had enjoyed a visit from Debbie's parents and her brother, who spent most of the evening talking to Derek about the performance of the classic Ford Zephyr 6, that had been a wedding present to the couple. After their visitors had departed around ten pm, Derek and Debbie worked together clearing away the dishes, putting them in their recently acquired dishwasher, locked up the house and before they knew it, it was bedtime for the weary pair.

Apart from Derek's job, which Debbie knew was stressful and tiring, her job as a trauma nurse could leave her in a state of exhaustion after a busy day at the hospital. Today had been no exception, and as he turned the key in the front door, she turned to her husband and said,

"I'm going up, Derek, just need a quick shower before we turn in."

"Okay, Honey," he said as he called up after her retreating figure as she reached the top of the stairs. "Won't be long, I'll probably be in bed by the time you've finished."

Sure enough, Debbie spent no more than ten minutes in

the bathroom, and made her way to the bedroom, where she found her husband, flat out on top of the bedcovers, still fully clothed, gently snoring.

Debbie shook him, not too hard, just enough to bring him out of his slumbers.

"Hey, you," she grinned at him. "Thought you were waiting for me, before going to sleep."

"Sorry," he quietly mumbled. "I guess I was more tired than I thought."

Opening his eyes fully, he suddenly noticed his wife was wearing a short, red satin nightie, which left very little to the imagination.

"Wow!" he exclaimed. "Is it a special occasion? To what do I owe this honour?"

Debbie laughed, then bent over him where he lay on the bed, and gently kissed him fully on the lips.

"What would you say if I told you I had something very special to announce to you, Detective Sergeant McLennan?"

Derek, still sleepy, didn't quite grasp what his wife was attempting to convey to him at first.

"Come on Debbie. I'm too tired for guessing games. You'll have to give me a clue but hurry up because that nightie is suggesting things to my brain that I won't be able to control much longer," he replied, with a big grin on his face.

"Do you mean to tell me that the great detective can't work out what his little wife is trying to tell him?"

"I haven't a clue. I give up. Tell me, and hurry up, please."

As she began to slowly undo the buttons of his shirt, Debbie continued smiling, then took hold of his right hand and gently placed it on her midriff.

"Come on now, Detective, think hard. I'm giving you a nice big clue right here."

Now fully awake, Derek McLennan slowly ran his hands up and down Debbie's satin-clad body, as his own body began to react to the sensuous feel of the red fabric.

She reached down, taking hold of both of his hands, holding them in place as they lingered over her midriff.

"If I told you I'd visited Dr Bradbury earlier today, and came away feeling extremely happy, do you think you can work it out?"

Now wide awake, Derek finally realised what she'd been trying to tell him.

"Debbie McLennan, you're bloody pregnant!" Derek suddenly caught on, his senses now fully in gear.

"Yes, you great nitwit. Took you long enough, didn't it? You're going to be a dad, my darling."

"And you're going to be a mum," he almost shouted, gleefully. "I love you, you know that don't you?"

"Of course I know it, or I wouldn't be having your baby, now, would I?"

Ecstatic at his wife's news, and now knowing exactly why she'd donned his favourite sexy nightie, Derek drew her down till she was on top of him, and all his love for his beautiful, and very sexy wife poured out in one long, lingering kiss, which inevitably led to a few more intimate celebrations before an hour later the pair fell into a deep and loving sleep, his arm around her, as her head rested on his shoulder. Beside the bed, the red satin nightie lay, crumpled on the floor, its job done.

* * *

Just after dawn the following day, the Liverpool Port Police received a disquieting phone call. Sergeant Daniel McNichol and Constable Phillip Hewitt were the first responders on the scene and what they found was enough for McNichol to place an immediate phone call to the Port Police's duty CID officer, Detective Constable Ralph Todd who, after examining the crime scene, wasted no time in contacting the liaison officer with Merseyside Police, Chief Inspector Rod Howes.

The Port Police is a non-Home Office ports police force which bears responsibility for Liverpool, Bootle, Birkenhead, Ellesmere Port and Eastham Dock Estates and Freeports, as well as the Manchester Ship Canal area. Its authority covers the docks themselves and anything within one mile of the docks. Although a separate entity, the force works and liaises closely with their colleagues of the much larger Merseyside Police Force. Before transferring to the Merseyside Force, DC Gary (Ginger) Devonshire had been a member of the Port Police, who had impressed Ross greatly during a case in which the two forces worked together. It was Ross who'd been instrumental in obtaining the services of the DC for his team.

So, while all the above communications may appear long and drawn out, the various phone calls took little more than ten minutes. The next link in the chain was completed when Chief Inspector Howes, having ascertained certain information, made a call to Detective Chief Inspector Oscar Agostini of the Merseyside Police, Specialist Murder Investigation Team.

Having thanked Howes for the information, Agostini made his way down to the Specialist Murder Team's Rooms on the fourth floor, where he knew Ross and Drake would definitely be in work early as usual, preparing the morning briefing. Agostini knew he was about to open a whole new can of worms for his team, and on entering the squad room, he saw that in addition to Ross and Drake, Detective Sergeants McLennan and Church, and Detective Constables Gable and Devonshire were also present, a great example of the team's professionalism. He guessed correctly that it would only be a matter of minutes before the others arrived, and sure enough, no sooner had he beckoned Ross and Drake to join him in Ross's office, and closed the door, giving them a modicum of privacy from the squad room, than DS Ferris, DCs Singh, Curtis and Sinclair, and Admin Assistant Kat Bellamy wandered in to join the others.

Of course, as soon as Agostini closed Ross's office door the team gathered in the squad room and began to speculate on why the DCI needed to hold a behind closed doors meeting with Ross and Drake. They didn't have long to wait. Less than five minutes passed before Agostini led a grim-faced Ross and Drake from the office, back into the squad room. The DCI called the room to attention, flanked on either side by Ross and Drake.

"Ladies and gents, I have received some disquieting news within the last half hour. Chief Inspector Howes, who is the force's liaison officer with the Port Police, called to inform me that earlier this morning, at first light, a body was pulled from the Mersey, about a half mile from shore, by the crew of the Manx ferry, *Manxman*, inbound from Douglas. The body was that of a young woman and the reason for Howes's call to me was that the body was quickly identified as that of Angela Ryan."

A series of audible gasps went up around the room, together with a couple of comments, "Shit," from McLennan, "Strewth," from Sinclair, and "Fuckin' Hell, Sir," from Curtis.

Ross allowed a few seconds for the shocking news to sink into his team and took over from the Detective Chief Inspector.

"As you've probably guessed, DCI Agostini has just briefed Izzie and me on what's known so far, which to be honest, isn't a lot."

"Apart from," Drake interjected, "Ryan's death was not accidental."

More rumblings could be heard from the assembled team of detectives.

"Izzie's right," Ross confirmed. "It appears, at first glance, according to Chief Inspector Howes, that he has spoken to the officers who were called to the scene, a Sergeant McNichol and Constable Hewitt, who informed him that the body exhibited signs of a stab wound to the back."

"Bloody Hell, someone's done her in then, Boss," Sam Gable piped up.

"Looks like it, Sam," Ross replied.

Agostini now spoke again.

"I immediately requested that Doctor Nugent be allocated the case, and he should be there by the time you arrive," he said, referring to William Nugent, the city's leading pathologist and chief medical examiner.

"Where exactly is the body?" Ross inquired of Agostini.

"Aboard the *Manxman*, as far as I know," Agostini replied. "I asked that the body be left untouched until our people and the ME arrived on the scene. The ship has now docked so you can get down there and start the investigation right away, Andy."

Ross took Agostini's words as his cue to make a move and he quickly organised the team's next move.

"Right, Izzie and I will get down to the Pier Head. We'll talk to the ship's skipper and crew. We need to speak specifically to whoever first saw the body in the water, and to those who took part in recovering it from the water. Fenella, Derek, Tony and Mitch can join us, I don't know how big the crew of the ship is so we might need some help talking to them all. Ginger, I want you with us too. You might be able to help in talking with the Port Police lads. Do you recognise any of the names mentioned?"

"Yes, sir. Dan McNichol was a constable when I was with the Port Police. He was a clever lad back then, so I'm not surprised he made sergeant. I don't know the other lad. He probably joined after I left to join the team here."

"Good, your previous experience with McNichol could be helpful."

"It might have been a passenger who first saw the body, sir," Church commented, having had a sudden thought.

"That's true, and if that's the case, I hope the skipper requested that person to wait on board to speak to us instead of allowing them to leave after the ship docked. For now, everyone else continue with our previous threads of the inquiry. Sergeant Ferris will be in operational control of the office until we get back, okay Paul?"

"Okay, Boss," Ferris replied.

A few minutes later, with most of the team heading for the docks, the squad room assumed an almost tranquil air as the remaining detectives took the opportunity to discuss the latest shocking development in their case. For the time being Derek McLennan had decided it would be prudent to keep his good news to himself. This was not the time to make a happy announcement.

"I never expected that," Sam Gable said, beginning the conversation.

"Probably the last thing any of us saw coming," Ishaan Singh agreed.

"Obviously, the person behind Angela Ryan, whoever was pushing her buttons, decided she was too much of a liability once it became known we were on to her, and took what they considered to be the necessary steps to eliminate her to prevent us getting hold of her and the possibility she'd give him or her up to us," Paul Ferris summed the situation up quite succinctly.

"And we still haven't the faintest idea who that might be," Davy Grant added, pessimistically.

"But we do have some leads, Davy," Gable responded to his negative comment.

"Yes, we do, Sam," Ferris agreed, "and we need to get to work looking into the backgrounds of our potential suspects, while the boss and the others are getting some fresh air."

"Good way of putting it, Sarge, a bit of fresh air," Grant chuckled.

"Well, they are, Davy, and we're here pounding the keyboards like good little keyboard warriors."

"I've never thought of myself as a warrior," a smiling admin assistant, Kat Bellamy chimed in.

"Ah, but you are, Kat," Ferris assured her. "You fight for the side of good versus evil. You might not be on the force, but in the time you've worked with us you've helped to put a fair few bad guys away, and that's the truth."

"Thanks for the compliment," she replied. "It's nice to feel appreciated."

"My God, girl, if you don't know by now, how important you are to this team, you'll never know." Sam Gable assured her.

"Okay, everyone, mutual admiration society is now closed," Ferris also smiled as he spoke. "Let's get back to work. We still have a killer to identify and apprehend."

"Except now we're looking for the killer of a killer," Singh thought it wise to mention.

"Too right, Ishaan, so let's get down to it people, okay?"

CHAPTER 22
POLAR STAR

"It's bigger than I thought it would be," Izzie Drake said to Ross as the pair approached the RO-RO ferry, *Polar Star*, its black hull and white upperworks, and large red and black funnel appearing to tower over them as it sat at anchor beside the quay. The company owner's crest was clearly emblazoned on the main body of the superstructure. In short, it was a highly impressive vessel.

"It's certainly a good size for a ferry," Ross agreed.

Having parked close by, Church, McLennan, Curtis, Sinclair and Devenish joined them, and the party made their way aboard the ship.

"Nice boat," Sinclair commented as he followed Curtis on to the deck.

"It's a ship, actually," Devenish corrected him.

"Right, I stand corrected," Sinclair smiled back at him.

In fact the *Polar Star* was just over 400 feet in length with a beam of 77 feet, powered by two diesel engines with twin propellers and twin bow thrusters, with a maximum speed of just under 20 knots, and could carry over 600 passengers and a total of 275 cars, all of which they learned from the ship's first officer, Ben Ford, soon after setting foot on the deck of the ferry, as he led them to the sick bay where, he informed them, Doctor Nugent and his assistant, Francis Lees were already in attendance, plus, as he put it, a couple of uniformed police officers. Guessing that the ship's sick bay would probably be quite small, Ross expected to find a cramped, perhaps chaotic scene. He was soon proved wrong, however.

Ford led them into a surprisingly large, well-lit and spacious area, which, he explained, was a state-of-the-art sick bay/hospital. With the number of passengers and crew the ship carried, the owners had made sure that any sickness, whether a minor ailment or something more serious, could be dealt with quickly and efficiently by the ship's two doctors and four nurses.

Officer Ford led them towards an area that had been curtained off. Just outside a young crewman sat, waiting, accompanied by a fresh-faced constable who Ross correctly assumed to be PC Hewitt. Ford introduced the crewman as Seaman Clark, who'd been the first to report the sighting of the body and who'd helped retrieve the woman from the water.

"Don't go away, young man," Ross instructed him, and the man, who appeared pale and perhaps in a state of shock, nodded his acquiescence. Ross called Devenish to come and talk to Clark and learn what he could from PC Hewitt. Ford pulled the curtain aside to admit Ross and Drake, while the rest of the detectives took advantage of the seats in the waiting area to wait for their next instructions, as Ford had been asked to set them up with an area where they were tasked with talking with the rest of the ship's officers and crew, if any of them had anything of use to the investigation.

Beyond the curtain, the body of the young woman lay on an examination table, with Doctor William Nugent the medical examiner and Francis Lees, his assistant, already at work. Three other men stood to one side, who Ford quickly introduced as Captain Woodley, and Ship's Senior Medical

Officer, Doctor Winstanley plus Sergeant McNichol of the Port Police.

"Ah, here you are, Inspector," Nugent greeted Ross and Drake who looked upon the body on the examination table, the blonde streaked hair, wet and plastered to the head, clothes lying neatly beside her, blue jeans, a pale-yellow polo neck sweater and a green fleece jacket, all very different from what she'd last been seen wearing.

"Morning, Doc," Ross replied, as Drake nodded a greeting to the doctor. "Anything to tell us yet?"

"Aye, as it happens, I have. Poor lassie was killed by a single stab wound to the back, which penetrated her right lung. She basically drowned in her own blood. From the look of these marks on the front of her legs, the killer came up behind her and pushed her hard, probably causing her to fall forward over a ship's railing, which likely also caused the blunt force injury I've found on the lassie's head, which I suspect cracked her skull. I'll know more when I perform the autopsy. Maybe she was on a launch or one of the Mersey Ferries, but that's your department of course."

"Thanks, Doc, we'll talk again in a few minutes," Ross responded, thinking that there might be yet another connection with the Mersey Ferries, as Francis Lees moved around the room, photographing the body from every possible angle. Leaving the pair to continue their work, he and Drake moved to speak to the captain, the doctor, and Sergeant McNichol.

After shaking hands with the three men, Ross began by speaking to Captain Woodley, while Drake spoke with Sergeant McNichol.

"Anything you can tell me that might be useful, Captain?" Ross asked the smartly dressed skipper of the vessel.

"Sadly no, Detective Inspector," Woodley replied. He handed the ship's log to Ross, who perused it as the captain spoke. "As you can see, the poor woman's body was first spotted by Seaman Clark who notified the bridge, where I was ready to bring the ship in to port. I immediately ordered the engines to go to full reverse and brought the vessel to a halt. Clark, and two other crewmen maintained visual contact with the body, and as soon as it was safe to do so, I ordered a boat to be lowered and we recovered the body and removed it to sick bay. Doctor Winstanley pronounced the woman to be deceased and he also informed me that the woman had been the victim of foul play, due to the obvious presence of a stab wound to the back. At that point, I ordered the doctor to take no further action as I would need to contact the police. I did just that of course with a call to the Port Police and, well, here we are."

"Okay, Captain. Thanks for that, and thanks for stopping to recover the body. I dare say not every skipper would have stopped, and some would have called the police and left it to us to find and recover the body."

"I'm old-fashioned, Inspector. I believe in doing things the right way," Woodley replied.

"One more question, Captain. At the time you discovered the body, were there any other vessels in close proximity to you?"

"No, nothing. We'd seen a small container vessel heading out to sea about twenty minutes earlier, but there wasn't a lot of traffic on the water at such an early hour."

There was little else Captain Woodley could report so Ross left it at that.

Drake, meanwhile, had been in conversation with Sergeant McNichol.

"Is it okay to call you Dan?" she began, "I'm Izzie. We have an old friend of yours with us, by the way."

"Yes, of course it is, and you must be talking about Gary Devenish. I was still a PC when your gaffer nicked him from us to join up with your mob," he replied with a smile.

"Yes, it is. He's out there talking to your constable and the guy who spotted the body."

"He's a good man, is Gary," McNichol said, praising his former colleague. "I bet he's fitted in perfectly with your team. I always knew he'd make a good detective."

"Yes, he is a good man and a very good detective, but please, tell me what you found when you arrived on board."

"There's not a lot to tell, to be honest, Izzie. We got the call and young Hewitt and I got here as soon as we could. The crew had retrieved the body from the river and Doctor Winstanley had conducted an examination, determining that the woman was dead, and that she'd likely been killed by a stab wound to the back."

"What made you realise she was the woman we were seeking in connection with our case? She's managed to change her appearance, hair colour etc, so she doesn't exactly look like the photo we sent out to all stations in the area?"

"That was easy," McNichol smiled a knowing smile. He bent down and picked up a soggy black holdall that had been placed on a rubber mat under the examination table. Reaching inside, he slowly extracted a slim wallet, which, when opened, contained a driving licence in the name of Angela Ryan, which he passed to Drake.

"How the hell did that thing stay with the body after she hit the water?" Drake was puzzled.

"The lads who pulled her from the water told us that the holdall was worn diagonally, over the shoulder, so it remained in place easily when she went into the river. It also helped her maintain buoyancy, so she floated easily."

"So, that makes me think whoever killed her was definitely an amateur," Izzie concluded. "A pro would have made sure she sank to the bottom and stayed there, at least for a few days, until the body's gasses caused it to rise to the surface."

"I agree with you. An astute observation. This was a hurried and opportunistic murder if you ask me. Anyway, once we knew who the victim was, we got on the blower to

Chief Inspector Howes and he contacted you guys, and well, here we all are," the sergeant concluded.

"Of course, it gives us another headache to solve now," Izzie politely used a single finger to scratch her head.

"I can see that," McNichol nodded in agreement. "Obviously, someone knew she'd be on the river, probably on one of the Mersey Ferries, and wanted her out of the way. The question is, why?"

"Not giving away any secrets, Dan, but we were already aware that Ryan wasn't working alone in carrying out the series of murders she was wanted for, so it's pretty obvious she arranged to meet with her partner in crime and he'd decided she'd become a liability and the result is lying there in front of us."

"Phew! The bastard wasn't taking any chances, eh? Do you guys have any idea who he or she might be?"

"Nothing definite, but we have a short list of likely suspects. Our people back at headquarters are working on narrowing it down as we speak."

"Well, I wish you good luck, Izzie. I just wish there was more I can do to help you." McNichol said with genuine feeling in his voice.

"You've done what you could by identifying the body and immediately getting word to us, Dan. That's all we could have asked of you, under the circumstances."

* * *

Ross, meanwhile, had moved to talk with Dr Winstanley, the Polar Star's senior medical officer who'd carried out an initial examination of Ryan's body as soon as it had been retrieved from the river, and brought on board. Noel Winstanley was, in appearance, a total contrast to the rotund and rather obese Medical Examiner. Standing at around six feet two or three, Winstanley was slim, had a full head of white hair, and even in his white coat, and with his dark blue dickie bow, he gave off an air of elegance in his movements and in his appearance. Ross could imagine him in private practice on Harley Street rather than being employed by the Manx Ferry Company. Ross guessed the doctor was probably in his late 50s or early 60s, though the white hair might be giving a false impression of age. His origins were easily betrayed by the presence of a not too strong Northern Irish accent.

"Is there anything you can tell me that you think might be relevant to the investigation into Miss Ryan's death?" Ross began.

"Not really Inspector Ross. Obviously, when our crewmen brought the body on board, my initial steps were first to ascertain if the woman was still alive, and once it became clear she was dead, I conducted an examination to see if I could find out the cause of death. Of course, once I saw the stab wound, I concluded that the woman had been the victim of foul play. At that point, I called a halt to my examination, ordered the woman's bag and belongings to be held in a secure location together with the body, and requested that Captain Woodley inform the police and request that they meet us as soon as we docked."

"Well, you certainly took all the right steps," Ross congratulated Winstanley on his professionalism.

"Thank you, Inspector. I'm afraid I got sadly used to dealing with the dead during the height of the troubles back home in Belfast some years ago."

"I imagine you did Doctor," Ross said, sympathising with what the doctor must have witnessed. By comparison, one dead body pulled from the river, though no less important, could be said to pale into insignificance.

"I'm sure your Doctor Nugent will also notice one other significant fact," Winstanley added.

"What would that be, Doctor?"

"Either simultaneously with the stab wound or perhaps

immediately following the inflicting of the wound, the woman appears to have been struck on the back of the head, what you would term a blunt force trauma, I believe."

"Any chance that she might have just hit her head on the side of the ship as she fell over the railing?"

"Unlikely, in my opinion, but Doctor Nugent will doubtless look into it in more detail during his post-mortem examination."

Winstanley could add nothing else of significance and Ross thanked him again and asked that he give a statement to one of the detectives in the sick bay waiting area.

* * *

Meanwhile, DC Gary (Ginger) Devenish had been speaking to Seaman Clark and PC Hewitt. Robert Clark, known to everyone on board as Bobby, sat beside PC Hewitt with a blanket draped around his shoulders. As he and a colleague had hauled the woman's body from the cold waters of the Mersey, the two men had received quite a dousing, and as yet, Clark hadn't had the opportunity to go below and change into dry clothes. After Devenish and Hewitt exchanged introductions, Devenish simply asked Clark to explain exactly how he came to see the body in the water, apologising if he'd already told Hewitt the same story, but explaining that he needed to hear it for himself.

"Yeah, sure," Clark began. "I was just doing a tour of the deck, prior to us docking at the terminal. The skipper likes everything to look neat and tidy when we come into port. He's a bit old-fashioned like that, probably 'cause he used to be the skipper on a cruise liner. Probably thinks he's still bringing the Pacific Princess into harbour," he laughed.

"Anyway, I was at the bow of the old girl, when I thought I saw something in the water about 100 yards off to port. At first, I thought it might be a dolphin or a seal, so I tried to focus on it. As we closed on the object, I realised whatever it was, wasn't moving, and then I saw it was a human being. Thinking he or she might be alive and in trouble I sounded the alarm, and the skipper brought us to a halt within about twenty yards. Me and Ronnie Evans lowered a boat, well, a dinghy really and we went and pulled the woman from the water. We could tell she was dead. We're not doctors, but at least we thought she was."

"Could you see any marks of violence on the body?" Devenish asked.

"Sorry, no, but then to be honest we weren't looking for such things. We just wanted to get the poor woman out of the water, if you know what I mean."

"Yes, I understand, that's okay. I just wondered if there was anything that stood out about her."

"No, nothing. I'm sorry I can't be more help," Clark said, apologetically.

Ross and Drake, accompanied by Sergeant McNichol walked out into the waiting area as Devenish completed his questioning of Seaman Clark. Ross looked questioningly at Devenish who shook his head, indicating he had learned nothing of use. Clark was dismissed and allowed to finally go to his quarters to change into dry clothes.

"I suppose you two would like five minutes to catch up on old times," Ross said, as he and Drake left Devenish and McNichol to chat while they conferred with the rest of their team. They soon found Officer Ford who led them to the ship's saloon bar where the rest of Ross's detectives had been talking to the officers and crew.

Dan McNichol and Ginger Devenish exchanged their respective news of their careers since Devenish had left the Port Police after being recruited by Ross for a place on his Murder Investigation Team. Devenish began by congratulating his old friend on his promotion.

"Cheers mate. Remember Sergeant Price?" Devenish

nodded. "Well, about two years ago he suddenly announced he was taking early retirement. Him and his wife had decided to move to Australia to be near their son, who you might remember married an Aussie girl. Next thing I was offered promotion and I took his place on the unit. But what about you? I bet life is a bit more exciting for you since making detective and working with the Specialist Murder Squad?"

"You could say that, Dan. No two cases are ever the same and it can get a bit hairy at times. We lost one of our lads a while ago, killed by a murderer we'd cornered in a field," Devenish replied, referring to the loss of Nick Dodds a few months previously."

"I heard about that, terrible thing to happen, poor bloke."

"Yeah, Nick was a good lad and a top detective too."

"Just goes to show, you never know what's going to happen when you get out of bed in a morning, eh?"

"That's true Dan, but we just have to carry on and do our jobs, you know?"

PC Hewitt, who'd been patiently sitting a few feet away, asked Devenish a question.

"How long had you been with the Port Police before you were head hunted by DI Ross?"

"Five years," Devenish replied, and the two men went on to have a discussion about the differences between working for the two forces.

* * *

Church, McLennan, Curtis and Sinclair felt that their time had been wasted in talking to the other crew members and the passengers who had been up and about so early in the morning.

Curtis spoke to one passenger who'd been on deck as the drama unfolded.

"I was taking a turn round the deck, having a cigarette, when the alarm was raised and I felt the ship kind of shudder, like, as I suppose the engines went into full reverse or whatever it is they do to stop a ship quickly," Eric Paisley, a schoolteacher, en route to Liverpool to visit his elderly parents. "I saw some crewmen running around and then they lowered a boat or a dinghy, hard to tell from where I was, and I saw them pull the body from the water and then return to the ship. Others were waiting to help them haul the body aboard, and from what I could see, the crew handled everything smoothly, no panic or anything."

"Did you see any other ships, or maybe a small boat near the ship in the few minutes before they saw the body?"

"Nothing at all, detective, but I wasn't really looking for other vessels, so there might have been."

Paisley turned out to be the only passenger to have seen the operation to haul Ryan's body aboard the ferry.

Sinclair spoke to a couple of other passengers who hadn't seen anything that had transpired, being below decks when the excitement began.

Church and McLennan felt their time had been pretty much wasted after speaking to the rest of the bridge crew who'd been on duty and the crewmen who'd assisted in recovering Angela Ryan's body. Fenella Church had, however, picked up on something in Derek McLennan's demeanour that morning, something that told her he was holding something back.

"Can I ask you something, Derek?" she asked when they were alone.

"Sure, anything."

"You're not yourself today. I can see it in you, as if you're hiding something."

McLennan knew she was a first-class judge of people and highly empathic too.

"Come on Derek. Spill it. You've got a poorly hidden

smirk behind that look on your face. You know something the rest of us don't, admit it."

"There is something," McLennan admitted, sheepishly.

"I knew it. Come on Derek, out with it."

"I was going to say something in the squad room, but when news of the murder was announced, I thought it best to hold on for a better moment. I only found out last night."

"Found out what, for God's sake?"

"Well, it's good news, great news, really, Fee. Debbie told me she's seen the doctor and she's pregnant. We're going to have a baby."

"Really? Wow, that's amazing news. Congratulations, Derek, to both of you. I bet you're walking on cloud nine this morning," Church said as she stepped forward to face her colleague and hugged him, as well as planting kisses on each of his cheeks.

"Thanks, Fee," he grinned, relieved to have told someone his news at last. "I was on cloud nine till the murder kind of took the edge of it."

"Sod that, mate," Church said, firmly. "Good news like that comes first for you. It's not every day you learn you're going to be a dad, Derek."

"I suppose you're right," he agreed. "Can't wait to tell the others."

"So tell 'em, soon as you can. They'll all be made up for you, especially the boss and Izzie."

"Yeah, you know, I was thinking on the way to work about how when I first started working for the boss, I was still a pretty wet-behind the ears DC. DI Ross had obviously seen something in me and gave me a big break when he selected me for the team. Now look at me, married and a baby on the way, just amazing really."

"And don't forget promotion to substantive rank, full Detective Sergeant when the expanded team comes into being."

"That too," Derek smiled. "When they made me an acting DS, I honestly thought it would be temporary and that I'd go back to being a DC one day."

"Well, there you are then. Good news all round, eh?"

"You're right, Fee. Definitely, great news."

"Now then, what are you looking all conspiratorial about?" The voice of Andy Ross broke into their conversation. Neither of them had seen him enter the room as he'd come to see how their inquiries had been progressing.

"Oh, hi Boss," McLennan blushed. "I was just telling Fee…"

"He was telling me that he and Debbie are going to have a baby," Church interrupted, fearing McLennan would try and skirt the issue.

"Really? That's fantastic Derek. When did you learn about it?"

"Just last night," McLennan replied, giving Church the 'dead-eye' as he spoke.

"Why didn't you tell us before we left headquarters, you daft sod?"

"Well, with the news about the murder and everything, I thought it was news that could wait, sir."

"Don't be daft, Derek. You should have told us as soon as you walked into the squad room, soft lad."

"Sorry sir, but…"

"No buts, Derek. We'll have to arrange a get-together for the team to celebrate the news. Meanwhile, unless you guys have learned anything useful, we need to get back to the office. There's not much more we can do here. Doc Nugent has arranged for the ambulance to take the body to the morgue, and he'll carry out the autopsy as soon as he can, but it looks pretty straight forward. Ryan's killer must have arranged to meet her somewhere, I'm guessing on a ferry, then knifed her from behind, bashed her over the head, and threw her in the river. They probably didn't expect her to be found so soon."

With little more to be learned on board the Manx Ferry, Ross and his team soon left the *Polar Star* and made their way back to police headquarters. The priority would now be to identify the 'brains' behind the killings as it had now become clear that Angela Ryan had been nothing more than a willing dupe, the weapon that carried out her master's wishes, while he or she orchestrated the whole affair from a place of safety.

Meanwhile, Derek McLennan became the happy focus of attention as the rest of the team joined in congratulating him and his wife, Debbie, who most of them knew, having been present at the couple's wedding.

Behind the jollity, however, Ross knew that with their chief suspect now deceased and an unknown enabler lurking in the background, they would need to push harder on their investigations into the previously peripheral suspects. The next team briefing would probably prove crucial to solving the case.

CHAPTER 23
AUTOPSY

The latest gathering of Ross's team began with the squad still buzzing with Derek McLennan's baby news. As a long-time member of the squad, the detective sergeant was not only well-respected, but was immensely popular, and his colleagues were all delighted for him and his wife Debbie. Ross allowed a few minutes for them to talk about his news, asking when the baby was due, how Debbie was and so on and then, brought the meeting to order.

"Okay, people, let's get down to business. We're all excited for Derek and Debbie and we'll definitely have to arrange a get together after work one day soon, but for now, we're nowhere nearer identifying the brains behind these killings. You all know we originally had Angela Ryan in the frame for the murders, and I still have no reason to doubt that she did carry out the killings, but, and it's a big but, as we'd begun to suspect, there had to be someone behind the scenes, someone with inside information relating to the trial of Howard Blake. Izzie's going to review what we know so far."

With that, he handed the briefing over to his second-in-command and Izzie Drake stood, as he sat down.

"From what we know so far, regarding the death of Angela

Ryan, somebody managed to get behind her and stabbed her in the back, then pushed her into the Mersey. From the position in the river where she was found, we have to assume she was travelling on a vessel at the time of her murder, possibly a Mersey Ferry, so I think it's safe to assume she agreed to meet with a confederate who she expected help from, and who got rid of her instead. Anything to add?"

Fenella Church was the first to speak up.

"Yes, one thing we don't know, if she was indeed on a ferry, is whether she was heading from Liverpool to Birkenhead or vice-versa, and if so, where she'd been holed up since her escape. I think someone was hiding her and if we can find out who that person was, we might get a clue as to who she agreed to meet."

"Right, Sarge," said Tony Curtis, "and if we can identify who that was, we should have our 'Mr Big'."

"Or Miss or Mrs Big," Sam Gable added.

"So, we need to go back and look at everyone involved in the case from the beginning and try to establish a link between one of them and Angela Ryan," Ross declared. "So, I suppose you all know what to do?"

A collective groan went up around the room. This was potentially turning into a long and boring slog.

The next twenty-four hours saw the team of detectives hard at work, engaged in going back through every report, every statement, and every piece of paper, no matter how insignificant it may initially have seemed.

The general consensus was that their number one suspect had now become Clive Evandon, the former chief clerk at solicitors, Metcalfe and Dunn. From all the information they possessed so far, Evandon had appeared to be the number one adherent to the beliefs of Adrian Metcalfe, Blake's solicitor. He certainly fitted the bill, Ross agreed, having had access to all the court papers relating to Blake's trial, down to having had access to the names of the jury members.

Going back to the day before the murder of Angela Ryan, it was decided that they needed to try and locate Evandon, possibly by speaking with the solicitor, Graeme McCain, at one time a junior member of the firm of Metcalfe and Dunn. Church and Curtis would take up where they'd left off, Church having spoken with Gerald Dunn, the retired former partner in the firm, who had been able to help them in their search for McCain, by suggesting the name of the charity for whom he thought the solicitor had at one time worked for. McCain now rose to the top of Church's list for an urgent visit.

Curtis meanwhile, had failed to find any record of Evandon being involved in any criminal or traffic offences in the ensuing years since the trial and had enlisted the help of Paul Ferris. If anyone could unearth any information relating to Evandon's whereabouts, Ferris was the go-to man.

Derek McLennan suggested they go back over the statements of the Blake offspring and if necessary, pay the son and two daughters a repeat visit. Ross readily agreed with his idea and placed McLennan in charge of reinvestigating the Blake family, aided by Sam Gable, Mitch Sinclair and Ishaan Singh, with Davy Grant providing them with logistical back up through the computers.

Following a lunch of sandwiches and coffee, Ross and Drake decided to pay the morgue a visit, Ross having received a call from Doctor Nugent to say he should have the results of the autopsy on Angela Ryan's remains in the afternoon. As it was a warm day, with a good deal of sunshine, Ross decided that it would do him and Drake good to get out of the office for an hour or two.

"Oh, yeah, that's just great," Drake smiled ruefully at him. "I love your idea of a bit of a day out. A visit to the morgue, just the thing to cheer a girl up."

"Yes, well, at least you'll get a chance to say hello to that husband of yours while we're there."

Izzie Drake's husband, Peter Foster, was the Administration Manager of the city's mortuary. Izzie had worked together with Andy Ross for so long and was known within the force by her maiden name, so when she and Peter married, they agreed that she'd continue to use her maiden name for work purposes, but out of hours, she'd be Mrs Peter Foster.

"True, but it still wouldn't be my first choice for a couple of hours out of the office. I'll never get used to the smell of the mortuary, even after all these years."

"I know, Izzie, but it's not so bad in Fat Willy's office, away from the autopsy suites," Ross referred to the Pathologist by his nickname among the detectives, derived from the doctor's chronic obesity. As much as he'd tried dieting over the years, Nugent's love of a good meal always ending up torpedoing any real efforts to lose weight.

An hour later, Ross and Drake, having been buzzed in through the security doors, were greeted by Peter Foster, who was delighted to be able to spend a couple of minutes of his working day with his wife. Their infant daughter, Alice was in the care of Peter's mother, a qualified nurse, during his working day. Unlike Izzie, he at least worked regular hours and returned home at the same time each day, so his mother didn't mind helping the couple, in fact, she loved every minute she spent with her granddaughter.

Peter walked them to the door of William Nugent's office, with which they'd become extremely familiar with over the years. After showing them in, he said his goodbyes and left them in the company of the pathologist and his assistant, Francis Lees.

"Inspector, Sergeant, good morning to you both. Please sit down. Francis, would you mind getting us some coffees, oh, and a plate of biscuits if you can find some, somewhere."

"Of course, Doctor. I presume coffee is ok for you both?" he asked the detectives, in response to Nugent's assumption.

They might have asked for tea, but they both indicated coffee would be fine.

"I take it the autopsy is finished, Doc?" Ross asked in response to the Doctor's 'good morning.'

"Aye it is," Nugent answered, gruffly. "Ye seem a little tense this morning, Inspector."

Whenever he felt stressed or angry, William Nugent had the unconscious habit of reverting to his native Glaswegian accent, which was hardly noticeable in his normal day to day dealings.

"I am, sorry Doc, I didn't mean to sound as if I'm pee'd off with you. Just this damned case. We seem to be taking one step forward and two steps back at present. I hope you've got something that might help us."

"Aye, well, ah'm nae so sure on that one. There's nothing that really stands out about the lassie's death. Her killer obviously struck from the rear, using what I estimate to be a slim, stiletto type of blade approximately seven inches in length. Whether by design or pure luck from the killer's point of view, the blade entered the back and penetrated through the rib cage, missing the ribs themselves and pierced her heart, which led to massive internal bleeding and was the actual cause of death."

"What about the blow to the back of her head?" Drake added.

"Aye, gimme time, Sergeant, ah was just comin' to that."

"Sorry, Doc, please carry on," she apologised for interrupting his report.

"Aye, well, here's the thing ye see. Yon bump to the head was in all likelihood caused by her head banging against the side of the ship as she went overboard. I'm nae saying her killer didnae push her, in fact it's highly likely he did push her immediately after stabbing her, but I found colour traces in her hair and in the wound which appear to correspond with the black paintwork of the ship's hull as if her head hit and probably scraped against the hull, in a bouncing effect as she went over."

"What makes you feel certain that the killer pushed her over immediately after stabbing her? Ross asked. "Was there not a chance she could maybe have turned and tried to grapple with her killer before he pushed her?"

"Aye, ye have a point, Inspector, but Francis and maself examined all the deck surfaces, not knowing exactly where the killer struck and we couldnae find even the smallest trace of blood on any of the ship's decks or on the, whatever they call the sides of a ship. It's always possible she may have struggled but in my opinion that's extremely unlikely, given the size and depth of the wound. A quick and strong stab, and then pulling the blade out immediately would have at least led to a drop or two of blood falling on the deck, if not from the wound itself, then from the blade, do ye see what ah mean?"

"Aye, I mean yes, I see," Ross replied, almost falling into Nugent's use of the Glaswegian vernacular.

"So, as I said," Nugent had calmed down considerably, "it's nae certain, but it is highly probable that the killing happened as I surmised. Francis photographed every ich of the decks incidentally and we took a fair few scrapings from the decks and there's nae a trace of blood to be found as far as we can see."

"So, there's really nothing you can tell us about the killer?" Ross said, disappointment clearly evident in his voice.

At that point, Lees knocked and re-entered the office carrying a tray, with the coffees and a large plate of chocolate digestive biscuits, which he placed on the almost empty left side of Nugent's desk.

With Lees back in the room, Nugent decided now was the time to deliver a hypothesis he'd been considering.

"Francis, your help please, dear boy, as we discussed earlier."

"Ready when you are, Doctor," Lees replied, walking to

one side of the office, where he was able to lean forward, resting his elbows on a mid-size filing cabinet. As he did so, Nugent rose from behind his desk, picking up a ruler as he did so, and approached Lees from behind.

"This is just a theory, you understand," he said, closing in on Lees. "Imagine I'm the killer, walking up behind Francis, and this ruler is a knife. Under normal circumstances, if I approach from directly behind him, leaning over the ship's railing, if I'm a right-handed person I'd grab hold of him with my left arm, like so, and stab him like so," he demonstrated, his arm placed around Lees's throat from behind. "Do you get my point?"

"Not yet, Doc," Ross said, as he and Drake waited to see what came next.

"Now, imagine I'm a left-handed person," he said, having swapped the ruler into his left hand, and performing the same act, but this time 'stabbing' Lees from behind using his left hand.

"I've got it," both Ross and Drake said in unison. Ross voiced their thoughts. "Angela Ryan was stabbed from behind and the weapon penetrated on the left side of her body. Under normal circumstances if the killer walked up directly behind the victim, to ensure the knife went in on that side, they would have had to grab her with their right hand, meaning that in all probability…"

"The killer stabbed her with the left hand," Drake finished his sentence.

"Which means, unless the killer is naturally ambidextrous, the bastard is left-handed," right Doc?" Ross said, feeling the pathologist just might have something.

"Aye, that's what I'm thinking," William Nugent smiled as he spoke, a rare enough occurrence for Ross and Drake to look at one another in surprise.

"I'd say you're turning into something of a forensic

pathologist, Doc," Drake said, and Ross added, "You been talking to our old friend, Christine?"

He was referring to their old friend, Doctor Christine Bland, the Home Office Forensic Pathologist who'd been called in to assist the squad in a couple of their previous cases.

"Och, I dinna think I'm quite up to her standards when it comes to such things, but I'm nae exactly a numbskull on the subject, as ye well know," Nugent said, as he thanked Lees for his cooperation with his demonstration and returned his ruler to its place on his desk.

"You've definitely given us food for thought, Doc," Ross said, sipping his coffee, that by now had cooled considerably. Drake had already finished hers, and her cup lay empty beside a side plate containing the crumbs of two of the biscuits, her sweet tooth satisfied for the moment.

"Anything else you can tell us, Doc?"

"Aye, though I don't know if it's of any importance to you. Examination of the stomach contents shows that the woman ate her last meal approximately two to three hours before her death, a meal of spaghetti Bolognese, and a glass or maybe two of red wine."

"As you say, Doc, I don't know if it's important but thanks for letting us know."

With that, the detectives took their leave of the mortuary, saying a quick goodbye to Peter Foster on their way out, pleased to leave behind the antiseptic smell of the morgue, the pair of them taking a few large gulps of fresh air as they made their way back to their car.

"I'm always glad to leave that place," Ross said as he seated himself in the passenger seat, leaving Drake to drive the short distance back to headquarters.

"I know, I'm the same," she agreed.

"Doesn't it bother Peter, working in such close proximity to all those dead bodies?" Ross had often wondered. "I mean, the Doc, Lees, and the other medical folk who work there don't have a choice and probably don't even notice the smell, but Peter?"

"It doesn't bother him," she replied. "Never has. Working in admin, he's not really in contact with the bodies, so doesn't really spend much time around the smell. Anyway, what now?"

"Now we throw everything we've got into a detailed examination of those we've identified as potential suspects for the Mr Big role."

"Especially if any of them happen to be left-handed?"

"Right, *especially* if any of them are lefties."

CHAPTER 24
PROGRESS?

Oscar Agostini sat behind his desk as he addressed Andy Ross and his senior team personnel, comprising Izzie Drake, Fenella Church, Paul Ferris and Derek McLennan, who took up virtually all the available space in his office.

"Okay everyone, the reason I've asked for this meeting is that in two weeks' time, we begin interviewing for personnel to join the expanded team. I'm not putting you under any pressure, but it would be to everyone's advantage if we could put this case to bed before we begin those interviews, which we'll need you to participate in, Andy," he addressed Ross.

"Oh, right, no pressure, just catch this bastard before you steal me away to sit behind a desk interviewing would-be recruits to the team," Ross was grinning as he spoke.

"Hey, we're used to a bit of pressure anyway, aren't we, Boss?" Church chimed in.

"We work best when we have something to aim for," Ferris added.

"It shouldn't take us too long, sir," McLennan spoke next. "With our main suspect herself murdered, we only need to find whoever was behind her and we'll have it all wrapped up."

"You make it sound so deliciously simple, Derek," Agostini responded.

"Well, sir, if Derek says we can do it, who are we to contradict him?" Drake said, and added, "Can we quote you on that one Derek?"

"Well, I…I…"

"I'm kidding, you daft bugger," Drake laughed.

"We're probably closer than we think to solving this one," Ross announced. "There are only a finite number of people who could be behind these murders, and we're going to delve into the recent past of each and every one of the possibilities. We'll get him, Oscar, I know we will," Ross said with a determined set of his jaw.

"Or her," Church corrected him.

"Or her," Ross acknowledged her point.

Knowing the case was in the best possible hands, Agostini brought the short meeting to a close.

"Okay everyone, I know you're doing your best. Don't let me keep you, go get the bastard, whoever it is."

Over the following twenty-four hours the team gradually began to gather additional background information on every person they'd already contacted in relation to the case. It was Ross's contention that they were literally a hairsbreadth away from identifying whoever was the 'brains' behind the spree of vicious murders.

"We know Angela Ryan was responsible for the three murders and attempted a fourth, but what we have to be on guard against is the possibility that our Mr or Mrs Big may have someone else lined up to take over where Ryan left off, and we need to collar this bastard before they have the chance to let another killer loose on our patch."

"Clive Evandon and that solicitor, Graeme McCain are top of my suspect list," Izzie Drake confidently stated.

"I must say, I tend to agree with Izzie, Boss," Fenella

Church agreed, which very soon became the general consensus of opinion.

Ross agreed with the rest of his team and every effort was now put into tracking down the two men, one of whom just might be an extremely dangerous and clever criminal.

Fenella Church's earlier call to Gerald Dunn, the retired former partner in the firm of Machin and Dunn had failed to bear fruit. Dunn had no knowledge of the current whereabouts of either McCain or Evandon, as he'd previously intimated, and any hopes Church harboured that he might be able to put them in touch with any potential contacts who might point them in the right direction in tracking them down were soon shot down in flames.

"I've tried to be as helpful as I can, Sergeant Church," he'd informed her, "but I'm afraid there's nothing else I can tell you that might assist in your inquiries. Believe me, if I knew anything, I'd tell you, but I'm afraid the cupboard is bare when it comes to any information relating to the former employees of the firm. Since you and your colleague visited my home, I've tried to recollect anything that might help you, but there's nothing. I'm sorry."

Dunn's apology sounded a hundred percent sincere, and she could do no more than thank him again for his time, after which she passed on the bad news to DC Curtis, who'd carried out the previous interview with the retired solicitor.

"At least it wasn't a complete waste of time, Sarge," he responded positively. "At least we have the two names, and it shouldn't be impossible for us to track them down."

"That's true Tony. Let's go and have a word with our computer geniuses and see what they're doing to locate these guys."

With that Church and Curtis moved across the squad room and entered the domain of Paul Ferris and his newly expanded computer team, comprising Kat Bellamy and newcomer, DC Davy Grant.

Sergeant Paul Ferris quickly assured them that he was already doing everything he could do, in order to locate the former junior solicitor and chief clerk but Davy Grant did have a small success to report.

"I've been looking for these former schoolmates of Angela Ryan and I think I've found current addresses for the two names we were given as her best friends in her schooldays. I've just informed the boss and Sergeant Drake."

"Well done, Davy," Church complimented him. "Where do they live?"

"One's in Norris Green and one's over the water in Birkenhead. Sam and Mitch had already started looking for them but got side-tracked after Ryan's murder I just took it up from where they left off and found this Imogen Garside in Norris Green and Eloise Parker in Birkenhead. I think the boss has already sent Sam and Mitch out to question them."

"Still, it's good work, Davy." Church reiterated, purposely wanting to help the new man feel he was an integral member of the team.

* * *

DC's Gable and Sinclair had indeed been dispatched by Ross to talk to the two close school friends of Angela Ryan. He reasoned that if either or both of them had seen her in the time between her escape from the squad car and her death, it might help him and the team to piece together her last hours and possibly lead them to the person, man or woman, behind the murders.

Their first stop had been the home of Imogen Garside, in Norris Green, who was just about to leave for her shift as a bus driver for Mersey Transport, and who confirmed that she hadn't seen Angela Ryan for some time, years in fact. With no reason to disbelieve her, they next set off to visit the next name on their list, Eloise Parker.

Within seconds of being admitted to Parker's neat home in Birkenhead, with Sam Gable mentioning the name of Angela Ryan, both detectives felt certain 'vibes' being given off by Eloise Parker. It was obvious to them both that Eloise knew something, but what exactly?

"When did you last see Miss Ryan?" Gable asked.

"Er, well…"

"Miss Parker, you need to tell us the truth," Sinclair told her, very firmly. "If you've seen her or had any contact with her recently, its vitally important that you tell us about it."

"You've seen her, haven't you?" Gable pushed her a little more.

"Why? What has Angie done?" Eloise asked, nervously.

"We need to trace her movements for the last forty-eight hours Miss Parker," Gable informed her.

"Oh God, I knew it, she's in serious trouble, isn't she? It's about those murders, isn't it?"

"Come on, Miss Parker," Sinclair smiled as he spoke to her, trying to get her to open up to him. "Whatever you know could be very important?"

Eloise Parker wasn't used to speaking with the police, much less being interrogated by two detectives. She suddenly grasped her head in her hands, and she blurted out exactly what they already suspected.

"Yes, she was here," she said at last. "She turned up the other day, saying she needed a place to stay just for a day or two. She told me the police were after her, but that they, you, had got it all wrong, that she was innocent, and so, I helped her, just by giving her somewhere to stay for a couple of days."

"Did she speak to anyone, or meet anyone while she was here with you?" Gable asked.

"No, nobody, but there was one thing. She made a phone call not long before she left. She said it was to someone who could help her get out of the country for a while."

"And do you know who that person was?"

"No, honestly, I've no idea, she didn't tell me, and I didn't ask."

"Were you the one who helped her change her appearance?"

"Yes, just a bit of hair dye, but hang on, how do you know she changed her appearance? Have you found her, arrested her or something?"

Gable knew they couldn't keep the bad news from her any longer.

"I'm sorry to tell you, Miss Parker, but Angela Ryan's body was pulled from the Mersey. She'd been murdered, I'm afraid."

Eloise almost fainted on the spot at the news of her friend's death.

"Oh God, no. Poor Angie. Who could have done such a thing? How was she killed?"

Sam Gable responded, as Eloise stood with tears streaming down her face.

"Your friend was bludgeoned around the head and tossed into the Mersey to drown, Miss Parker. You have to understand that Angela was responsible for at least three gruesome murders, but we believe she was being aided by someone else, who probably met her and disposed of her, probably as she crossed the river on the ferry."

By now, Eloise was visibly shaking, and Gable was adept enough to know that the young woman was likely going into shock. She knew they weren't likely to get much more from her before she broke down completely.

"Listen, Eloise," she said with as much compassion as she could muster, "It's really important that we find out who she spoke to on the phone. Whoever it was is likely to be her killer, and we have to find that person and get them into custody as soon as possible. Do you remember anything about that phone call?"

Sinclair added, "Was it a man or a woman she spoke to, for example. Could you hear anything she said?"

"No, I'm sorry. I left her to talk in private. I'm not one for listening into other people's phone conversations."

"That's okay," Gable replied, "but did she give you any hints as to who it might be?"

"No," Eloise sniffed, through her tears, "but I got the impression she was talking to a man, don't ask me why, I just felt it was a male. She seemed to really trust whoever it was because she seemed relieved and kind of hopeful when she got off the phone."

"Have you made or received any calls since Angela made her call?" Gable asked.

"Yes, I spoke to me Mum last night and a couple of friends earlier in the day."

"Does your phone show the last few numbers dialled?"

"No, it's just a basic phone. It has last number redial and that's about all. I use my mobile most of the time. I only have a landline because I need one for the internet."

There was nothing else of use to be gained from the woman and Gable and Sinclair left her to her grief, and perhaps to her conscience.

"At least we're sure there's someone else involved in all this," Sinclair said as the pair made their way back to headquarters.

"Yes, and as soon as we get back to the office, we need to get onto BT to see if they can give us a list of the numbers called from Eloise's phone on the day Ryan left for her meeting with her killer."

"That's why you asked her if she'd made any calls," Sinclair caught on to Gable's thinking. If she hadn't called anyone since Ryan left a simple press on the Last Number Redial button would have taken us straight to the killer."

"Possibly. If not to her actual killer, at least to someone who was in communication with the killer. We need that number, Mitch. It could be the key to finding the bastard behind all these murders."

"Good on yer, Samantha," Sinclair exclaimed. "You're bloody right. Let's hope British Telecom play ball about revealing Eloise's call records to us."

"If they do, I think we'll just be one step from catching this bastard," Gable stated with confidence.

On their return to headquarters, they found other aspects of the case had been moving along in what Ross considered to be a positive vein.

CHAPTER 25
JEAN

Andy Ross and Izzie Drake were ensconced in Ross's office, reviewing the files pertaining to the case, looking for something, anything, they might have missed in the various interviews with family, friends and acquaintances of the murder victims and those connected with the original murder trial of Howard Blake.

A hurried knock on the door was followed by the entry of Tony Curtis. Ross looked up from the file on his desk.

"Forgotten how to knock have we, Tony?"

"Sorry Boss," Curtis blurted out, almost breathless, "I think we can forget about that solicitor, Graeme McCain, as a serious suspect."

"Oh yes? How so?" Ross looked quizzically at his DC.

"Did some serious digging around to follow McCain's career after he left the firm of Metcalfe and Dunn. As Mr Dunn thought, he did end up working for a charity, but it seems Mr McCain couldn't keep his grubby fingers to himself, and it wasn't difficult to find his current address."

"Go on, Tony, out with it, man."

"Our friend, Graeme McCain's current address is at 68 Hornby Road, Boss".

"He's in bloody Walton?" Ross exclaimed, referring to Liverpool Prison, formerly known as Walton Jail, and still referred to as such by many of the city's police officers.

"Yep, he's doing a five year stretch for fraud. Somehow a few thousand pounds of charity funds found their way into McCain's bank account."

"So, he's nothing but a thieving scally," Drake almost laughed at the irony of the former solicitor being behind bars, along with possibly many of his former clients. "So, I assume we forget McCain as one of our chief suspects?"

"I think so, Izzie. Let's concentrate our efforts in locating the whereabouts of Clive Evandon. I really want to talk to that man."

Soon after, Gable and Sinclair returned with the news about Angela Ryan's mysterious phone call. Ross's intuition immediately told him that this could be the breakthrough they were seeking. The task of trying to trace that call fell to Sergeant Paul Ferris and his computer team. In response to Ross's fears that British Telecom might not be too cooperative in handing over information relating to Eloise Parker's telephone account, Ferris quickly reassured him.

"Don't worry, Boss. Once they know this is a murder inquiry, I think they'll be only too happy to help."

"I hope so, Paul. This could be the case breaker we've been looking for."

Even as they spoke, DC Davy Grant was already on the phone to one of his contacts at the Telecoms company, his dulcet tones clearly audible as he conversed with an obviously friendly person at the other end of the line. By the time Ross and Ferris ended their conversation, Grant's contact had already set the wheels in motion. She promised Grant that she'd have the number he was looking for in double-quick time. Grant delivered this information to Ross who was instantly impressed with the efficiency of the latest addition to the team.

"Jean's been helpful in the past, sir," Grant told him. "She's holds quite a senior post and cooperated with the murder squad a couple of years ago in tracing a series of threatening calls made to the victim and his family in the weeks leading up to his murder."

"Sounds like a useful contact to have Davy."

"Aye, she is, sir. I don't think she'll keep me waiting too long for a response."

For some reason, Ross felt that there was a little more than a purely professional relationship between Grant and his contact but didn't pry at this time. He didn't really care who 'Jean' was, as long as she could provide the information they were seeking.

Meanwhile, the rest of the team pressed ahead with their own individual lines of inquiry. Going back over everything related to the murders, every statement, from witnesses, although they were in short supply, to the members of Howard Blake's family, prison officers, the lot. Somewhere, Ross felt, they'd missed something, something that might lead them to the man or woman who'd been pulling the strings that manipulated Angela Ryan and turned her into a vicious, sadistic killer.

Izzie Drake walked into the office with two mugs of coffee and a couple of Danish pastries, placed them on the desk and sat opposite the DI.

"Seems like Davy Grant might be quite an asset to the team, eh?"

"Definitely," Ross agreed. "The whole point of this team, as you know is that we bring in new recruits with special skills or attributes, and that includes the contacts many of them bring with them from their previous posts. Look at Mitch, for example, apart from being a damn good detective he has a particular rapport with the ladies. He's got something in his manner, his personality, which makes them trust and open up to him, where many might be wary of reluctant to talk freely with a police detective. That's a skill you can't teach or train anyone in, it's just part of his nature."

"I agree completely," Drake concurred. "Mitch is something of a ladies' man for sure."

"It's more than that, Izzy. It's not like he tries to chat-up every woman he meets, for God's sake, even old ladies in wheelchairs seem to automatically come under his spell."

Ross laughed and Drake joined in. They both knew that DC Sinclair had a unique talent, which would possibly bear fruit many times in the future. Likewise, DC Grant had something of a network of contacts, which Ross had been informed about before he'd even interviewed the young Scottish-born detective.

"Well, it'll be interesting to see if and how long it takes for the mysterious 'Jean' to get back in touch with Davy Grant," said Drake.

As if on cue, the sound of knocking on Ross's office door was followed by the entry of Davy Grant.

"Got something already, Davy?"

"Yes, I have sir. Jean just got back to me to say the number Angela Ryan called the other day was to a mobile phone, a pay-as-you-go phone with no account attached to it, so no immediate way to identify the owner, I'm afraid."

"Damn and blast," Ross cursed, but Grant wasn't finished.

"Hang on, sir. Jean has another trick up her sleeve. She says she can trace any other calls made to that number, and also any calls made by that number."

"Bloody hell, Davy, that means…"

"That Jean can hopefully give us a real lead to whoever is using the phone, and that's not all, Boss."

"Come on then, Davy, spit it out man," Ross urged him on.

"Jean says that by doing whatever it is they do, some sort of triangulation or whatever, they can use the cell towers, you know, the mobile phone masts, to get us an approximate area where the phone's being used."

"My God, the woman is nothing short of a genius," Ross exclaimed. "I think you'll possibly end up owing this Jean of yours a meal at a fancy restaurant or something similar."

Davy Grant laughed at Ross's comment, much to Ross's surprise. The DI responded by asking, "Have I just said something amusing, DC Grant?"

"I'm sorry, sir. I know I shouldn't have laughed, but I don't think I'll be taking Jean out on a date anytime soon."

"Why not? Has she got a wooden leg or something to put you off?"

"Oh no, nothing like that, sir, but it's just that Jean is old enough to be my Mum and has three grown-up kids and four grandchildren. I doubt her husband would be very well disposed to me whisking his wife away to a posh restaurant or a nightclub for the evening."

Ross and Drake immediately saw the funny side of Ross's erroneous assumption and spontaneously burst out laughing. The mental picture of the young detective constable escorting the helpful grandmother on a 'date' was amusing enough to give them both a moment of light relief in the midst of a serious investigation.

"Sorry, Davy, I honestly thought there might be something more to your relationship with the mysterious lady than just a professional one."

"So did I," Drake added.

"I thought you might be thinking along those lines, but no, she's just a really nice lady who goes out of her way to help the police," Grant replied. "The one problem she pointed out though is that if the person we're looking for is tech savvy they might have thrown the phone away after using it to connect with Ryan or just changed the sim card, giving it a new number."

"So, no guarantees," was Ross's conclusion.

"No, sir. But we have to hope whoever we're after isn't too clever," Grant concluded.

"Okay, Davy, keep me informed if Jean gets back to you."

"You'll know straight after me if she calls," Grant promised, and was soon back at his desk working with Ferris and Bellamy looking into the nooks and crannies of the case.

An hour later, he was back, knocking and entering Ross's office.

"Jean's located the phone, sir," he announced excitedly. "It was used less than an hour ago from an address in Huyton. As far as she can tell, it hasn't moved since."

Within minutes, Ross and Drake, accompanied by Church and Curtis, followed by a police patrol car with two uniformed officers on board, were speeding through the streets on the way to Huyton, where they soon found themselves outside a nondescript home on a housing estate, that definitely didn't look like the home of someone like Clive Evandon who would certainly be expected to live somewhere a little more up market. Ross himself knocked on the front door, as the others stood ready to charge in and apprehend a desperate criminal.

They were taken by surprise when the door was soon opened by a young man, perhaps fourteen or fifteen years old, wearing scruffy jeans with 'designer' holes in the legs, a Liverpool football shirt, and a pair of shabby once-white trainers. In his hand was a cheap, throw away mobile phone. His short, dark, greasy-looking hair looked in need of an appointment with a bottle of shampoo and hot water.

Ross quickly identified himself and Drake, and the boy immediately appeared to adopt a defensive pose.

"I ain't done nothin' wrong," were the first words out of his mouth.

"Nobody says you have, yet, young man," Ross tried to adopt a non-threatening attitude. If the boy knew anything it wouldn't help to alienate him. "What's your name?"

"Barry, Barry Knox," the lad replied.

"Okay, Barry, we just want to ask you a couple of questions, that's all."

"What about?"

"Is that your phone for example?"

A guilty look appeared on the boy's face, with Ross and Drake immediately knowing this was the phone they were looking for.

"Yeah," the boy replied, sheepishly.

"Are you sure, Barry?" Drake asked in a quiet, non-threatening voice. "We really need you to tell us the truth about that phone. It's very important."

At that moment a door to the rear of the house opened and a woman, they presumed to be the boy's mother appeared, presumably dressed for work, in the uniform of a well-known fast-food outlet.

"Who's this, Barry? You in trouble or something?"

"Mrs Knox?" Ross asked.

"That's right, and you are?"

"Detective Inspector Ross and Sergeant Drake, Merseyside Police. We need to know where your son obtained the mobile phone he's holding in his hand."

Susan Knox took three steps towards her son and without warning slapped the boy across the back of his head, as she verbally berated him.

"You miserable little scally. Didn't I tell you to hand that phone in to a teacher at school? And why aren't you at school anyway?"

Ross and Drake looked at each other, their faces silently communicating their astonishment at this 'unusual' style of modern parenting.

"I got a belly ache Mum, I was going to hand it in, honest I was." Barry said to his mother, who clearly didn't believe a word of his excuse.

"I can't help it if I have to work stupid hours, can I? At least you could help by getting yourself off to school in a morning, and not making pathetic excuses. I'm sorry, Inspector," she said, as if suddenly remembering that Ross and Drake were listening to her conversation with her son. "I've just got home, after working the night shift, came in the back door and heard the kerfuffle out here. What's the little toe-rag been up to now?"

Gradually, Ross and Drake managed to calm the situation down, it having been some years since Ross had been involved in defusing a 'domestic' as the police referred to such a situation. Susan Knox explained that she was a single working mother, since a divorce from Barry's abusive father three years previously. She'd worked in her current job for nine months, and though the hours weren't perfect, Barry was nearly sixteen and quite capable of being left alone for the few hours she was absent when on the night shift. She apologised for losing her temper and explained that her son had arrived home with the phone two nights ago, and she'd immediately told him to hand it in, as someone would probably be looking for it. Barry chimed in again,

"But Mum, it's just a cheapo pay as go thing. Someone probably chucked it out. That's how I found it in a rubbish skip, didn't I?"

"The phone obviously has some credit left on it, I'm presuming, eh Barry?" Drake asked him, thinking that the boy had tried it and found it was live and connected to a network. "Were you going to hand it in when you'd used the credit up?" she asked, giving the boy a way out of his awkward situation.

"Yeah, that's right. That's what I would have done," he replied. "I'm sorry if I used someone's credit. I only made a couple of calls."

Ross and Drake didn't take long to relieve Barry Knox of the phone, after first ascertaining exactly where he found it, in a skip on a building site not far from home. Young Barry had already received a considerable telling off from his mother before they left, and the two detectives agreed that they could foresee young Master Knox being kept on a very short leash by his mother in the next few days. Ross contacted Scenes of Crime Supervisor, Miles Booker and he in turn arranged to have his team carry out a forensic examination of the skip, although neither he nor Ross held out much hope of finding anything useful. As Barry Knox had succinctly pointed out, someone had 'chucked it away' and the phone had outlived its usefulness.

The important thing, however, was that the police were now able to compare the numbers called from the phone, as saved in the call memory, with those provided by Jean at the telecoms company. They could easily eliminate the calls made by young Barry to his mates and could then get Jean to identify the recipients of the other calls made from the phone.

CHAPTER 26
CLOSING IN

"The net's tightening," Ross said as he addressed the team at the following day's morning briefing, then qualified his words with, "I can feel it, but the trouble is, I'm not sure who it's tightening around."

There were a couple of suppressed giggles from Sinclair and Curtis, but they quickly fell silent as the DI continued.

"Everything is now pointing to whoever Angela Ryan called on the thrown away phone, which the telecoms people are investigating as we speak. If we find out who the recipient of her call was on the day she died, we can be virtually sure we have our evil mastermind in our sights."

"But what if she called someone who then called someone else, sir?" DC Singh decided to play devil's advocate.

"That's a good point, Ishaan," Ross replied. "That's a possibility of course, but if that's the case, then whoever she called was clearly acting as a go-between and identifying them will still take us a step nearer to the man or woman we're seeking."

Singh nodded, pleased that Ross had seen some logic in his suggestion.

The next positive news was provided an hour later by Fenella Church and Tony Curtis, who together had been looking deeply into the eventual disposition of the former employees of Metcalfe and Dunn, the now defunct firm of solicitors. Together, the sergeant and the detective constable had diligently traced the entire list of ex-employees, aided by the fact that it was quite a small law firm, employing a small number of people.

It was Church who finally made the breakthrough in the search for Clive Evandon when she called a former legal secretary of the firm, Mrs Hillary Miller, formerly Hillary Taylor. As soon as Church brought up the subject of the search for Evandon, Mrs Miller virtually exploded over the phone.

"Clive Evandon? You want to find that little pipsqueak?" she snapped down the phone to the Detective Sergeant. "I can tell you where to find that bastard, sure enough."

"You appear to harbour some negative feelings towards Mr Evandon," Church prompted her to tell more.

"I'll say I do," Mrs Miller continued. "First of all, he doesn't call himself Clive Evandon nowadays. He goes by the name of Clive Evans now. He was a total pillock when he worked for Metcalfe and Dunn, but I didn't realise it until later. I was young and impressionable and fell for his smooth-talking patter."

"Go on, please," Church encouraged her.

"Yes of course, first I can tell you he's known as Clive Evans nowadays, not a big change but big enough. I was a junior when I began working for Metcalfe and Dunn, and Clive was something of a big-shot in the office, always sucking-up to the partners. He was a handsome guy, always well-dressed and I was very naïve back then. Of course, when he began paying me compliments and asking me to meet him for drinks after work, I was fool enough not to realise all he really wanted was to get in my knickers. After about half a dozen dates, I agreed to go for dinner at a nice hotel one night and he talked me into staying overnight with him. We ended up in bed of course and this happened about six times in the next few months, until one day I found out I was pregnant. That bastard told me it couldn't be his and that I must have slept with someone else. I couldn't believe it. I thought he really cared for me. Anyway, that was the end of my relationship with him, but when my son was born, I made damn sure Evandon was named as the father on the birth certificate and by then, he'd accepted his responsibilities on condition I didn't tell anyone at the firm he was the father. I'd left the firm when I was six months pregnant but went to work for them again when Ryan, my son, was older, after I'd met Roger, my husband, who's brought Ryan up as his own. Clive the swine has at least paid a small amount of maintenance for Ryan over the years, and he notified me when he changed his name by deed poll, because, he said, he didn't want to be associated with the failed firm of solicitors in his new job."

"And where does he work now, Mrs Miller?" Church asked.

"He manages a newsagent's shop in Whiston. He lives above the shop with a woman, but all I know about her is her first name is Kelly. Bit of a come down from his time at the firm, isn't it?" the woman laughed a bitter laugh as she appeared to take delight in Evandon's new position in life.

"Does your son have any contact with him, Mrs Miller?" Church inquired, at which the woman shook her head as she replied, "Not a chance. He didn't want anything to do with me when I was pregnant with Ryan and he never wanted anything to do with him when he was younger, and now Ryan definitely doesn't want to have anything to do with his rat of a father."

She paused, and Church heard the sound of a drawer

opening and closing. Hillary Miller came back to the phone, then read out the full address and telephone number of the man they were seeking.

Having thanked her for the information, she turned to look at Curtis, then pumped her fist into the air, and almost shouted, "Got the bugger, Tony." Ross was delighted with the information and immediately despatched Church and Curtis, together with McLennan and Sinclair to hopefully take the man into custody.

The village of Whiston lies just 8 miles from the city of Liverpool, close to the town of St Helens, just 3 miles away. The two unmarked patrol cars took little time arriving outside the First News combined newsagents and convenience store. Church and Curtis led the way into the shop, with McLennan and Sinclair holding back in case they were needed, if Evans put up any resistance.

On entering the shop, they were greeted by a harassed looking woman of around thirty-five years, who they presumed to be Kelly, his live-in partner. About five-feet-two or three, Kelly had obviously dyed blonde hair, shoulder length, and wore a tight-fitting white open neck blouse teamed with a bright red knee-length skirt and a pair of black high-heels, which weren't exactly what Church would have selected for working behind a counter all day.

"Can I help you?" she said, from behind the counter, which ran the length of one side of the shop floor, ending not far from the entrance, where the till stood ready.

"We're looking for Clive Evans," Church replied.

"You and me both, my love," the woman replied, a wry smile on her face as she spoke.

"Surprised at the reply, Church asked, "Are you Kelly?"

"That's right, and who might you be, coming here looking for my fella?"

"Detective Sergeant Church, Merseyside Police," Church identified herself, holding up her warrant card to confirm her identity, "and this is Detective Constable Curtis. Tony Curtis flashed her one of his 'knock 'em dead' smiles in an effort to put the woman at ease. "Are you saying you don't know where Mr Evans is, Kelly…I'm sorry, we don't know your surname?"

"Weeks, it's Kelly Weeks, and no, I haven't seen the lazy git for two days. He's left me here to do all the work while he's off doin' God knows what. Probably got into a heavy card game with some of his no mark-mates or even gone with another woman. If I find out he's shacked up with some tart with big tits, long legs and a skirt up around her arse, I'll chop his bleedin' nuts off with a carving knife when he eventually shows up. I mean it."

Church and Curtis exchanged a look that had them in agreement. Kelly Weeks was not a woman to cross.

"When did you last see him?" Curtis quickly asked, his brain trying to ignore thoughts of Kelly Weeks attacking a man's private parts with a very sharp carving knife.

"Two days ago, on Tuesday," she replied, "around six in the evening. He said he had to go and meet someone. He didn't say when he'd be back, just buggered off without another word."

"Could he have been going to see his son?" Church inquired.

"What? Ryan? He couldn't care less if he ever sees that lad of his and his mother doesn't want him seeing his dad anyway, not as I blame her. Clive isn't exactly father material, if you catch my drift."

"What about friends," was Church's next question. "Anyone he might have stayed with after a heavy night's drinking, perhaps?"

"His best mates are Jock Wilson and Tommy Murphy. They meet in the Feathers two or three nights a week, but I've rung them and neither of them have seen him since last week."

"Has he got a mobile phone?" This was Curtis.

"Yeah, and don't think I haven't tried ringing him. It just goes straight to voicemail, as though he's turned it off. You watch, he'll turn up eventually with a bloody great hangover after a drinking binge with some idiots he's met up with, or a shagging session with some tart," Kelly whined, although she didn't sound convinced by her own theory.

Sensing the woman was worried, Church probed further.

"Has he ever gone out like this before, Kelly, and not come home for a few days?"

"No," Kelly said, emphatically. "The daft sod has sometimes stayed out till the early hours after getting boozed up and losing his cash playing poker, but he's never done anything like this before."

"Tell me," Church pressed her further, "has he recently been spending a lot of time away from the shop, or talking on the phone to someone you might not know?"

"Now you mention it, he has been very secretive in the last few weeks, taking and making phone calls on his mobile. Every time I asked him who he'd been talking to he told me to mind my own business."

"Did you ever overhear any of those conversations?" Tony Curtis now asked her.

"No, if he was in the room with me and he got a call from this person, he'd get up and leave the room so I couldn't hear what they were talking about. That's why I thought that he might be seeing another woman, but if I brought the subject up, he just told me to shut up or to not be stupid. There was just one time a couple of weeks ago when I overheard a tiny bit of a conversation before he realised I was there, and he quickly waved me away."

"What did he say, Kelly?" Curtis asked.

"I don't know who he was talking to, but I heard him say, *that's it, you've had everything I've,* and that's all I heard before he noticed me and shooed my away."

"Listen Kelly, it really is very important that we speak to

Mr Evans. If you hear anything from him, I want you to please call me on this number," Church said as she handed Kelly one of her cards containing her name and number. "Will you do that for me, but you must promise not to tell him you're calling me?"

"Why, what is it you think he's done?"

"I can't go into details but it's possible Clive could be involved in some very serious crimes."

"Oh God. Do you think he might be in danger?"

"It's possible," Church replied, having just thought of something.

"OK, I promise," Kelly replied, before the two detectives took their leave of the shop, leaving a worried woman standing behind the counter, looking rather forlorn.

Back in the car, Curtis immediately questioned the sergeant.

"What is it, Sarge? Something came to you in there, I can tell."

"Yes, Tony, it did. That little snippet of conversation Kelly overheard, could mean that Evans was himself providing information to someone else, who may be the real culprit behind the murders."

"So, he might be another puppet, with someone else pulling the strings?"

"It's possible, Tony. I'm going to have a word with the boss as soon as we get back. He said he thought we were missing something. I think he was right, and we need to go back to the beginning to find just what it is we've missed."

"And what about Evans?" Curtis asked.

"Yes, he's gone missing which according to Kelly is totally out of character. I've got a bad feeling about that,"

"As in, something bad could have happened to him?"

"Exactly." Church confirmed, as they parked the cat in the headquarters car park and made their way to Ross's office."

***

"I'm in total agreement with you, Fee," said Ross as soon as Church and Curtis reported to him. We've got the team going back through all the witness statements. And finding Clive Evans has just become a priority too, if for no other reason than to establish his safety and whereabouts."

Izzie Drake instantly volunteered to take over the search for the missing man and selected Ginger Devenish to assist her with the search. Church and Curtis meanwhile, would continue the search for Clive Evans, formerly known as Evandon.

Drake and Devenish set to work straight away, with Admin Assistant Kat Bellamy being drafted in to help them in trawling through the original witness statements.

"Kat, please can you pull up the statements from the Blake family members, and then those from the prison staff? We'll begin with those. I have a feeling they're the most likely to contain what we may be looking for."

"No problem," Kat replied as she began typing information into her computer keyboard. Devenish had got a hold of the original trial transcript and had already begun picking through it, in the hope there might be something there that could illuminate the fog of apparent disinformation that surrounded the Howard Blake trial. Blake had always protested his innocence despite all the evidence pointing to his guilt. Had someone, somewhere missed something in the original investigation?

Izzie shared Ross's belief that they were very close to solving this case. They just needed a break, and she was determined to find it. After Kat had printed off the statements Drake had requested, she started reading, taking care to take in every word, every nuance in the language used by those who'd been interviewed. She was sure that one or more of their team had at some time during the investigation, spoken to whoever lay behind the murders. If by some chance they'd been wrong, and Clive Evandon, aka Evans was innocent, then who was orchestrating the whole thing?

As the day drew to a close, nobody was aware that a major development was about to take them all by surprise.

CHAPTER 27
AUTOPSY

Fenella Church was tired. The current case was definitely mentally taxing as well as physically exhausting with all the team putting in long hours in the search for the as yet unknown 'brains' behind the murders of the Howard Blake jurors. For the first time in what seemed like ages, but was in fact just a few days, she was attempting to relax at home, after Ross had ordered her and the rest of the team to go home and recharge their batteries, ready for another hectic day tomorrow.

For three nights, she'd been so tired that after eating either a take-away or microwave dinner, she'd fallen asleep on her sofa, eventually waking up on the sofa, with a crick in her neck, the TV softly playing in the corner. At least she'd turned the volume down before dropping off to sleep. She locked her door and decided to take a long, luxurious bath, in an effort to soak some of the stresses of the case away. She added her favourite bath foam to the hot water and was soon lying back, surrounded by the soft, fragrant suds. After soaking her weary limbs for half an hour, she reluctantly climbed out of the bath, the water beginning to go cold by now, wrapped an extra-large bath sheet around her body and made her way to her bedroom, which almost felt like alien territory.

Feeling better after the hot soak, Fenella was about to flop onto her bed when she noticed the mirror above her dressing table. There, just where she'd left it, was her message to herself to 'call Alan Deal'. She'd promised to think about his dinner invitation but felt a little guilty for not having given it any thought whatsoever. She suddenly made a decision. Surely, she was entitled to have some fun in her life, and Deal had seemed a perfect gentleman on each of their contacts so far. She had his home number on her phone's call log and before she could think about changing her mind, she dialled the handsome doctor's number.

Alan Deal was about to sit down, put his feet up and watch a DVD when his phone began ringing. Wondering who could be calling at this time, he looked at the phone screen and his heart skipped a beat when he saw Fenella's number. He'd saved it to his phone's memory quite some time ago and had hardly dared to believe she'd actually call him back after his call the other day.

"Fenella, I'd given up on you calling me back. I thought maybe you just weren't interested. I hope it's good news."

"Well, Doctor Deal. If you call me asking you if you still want to treat a poor starving copper to a meal sometime good news, then yes, I suppose it is," she laughed, a little nervously. It had been some time since she'd dated anyone, and Fenella found herself feeling as nervous as a teenager.

"Name the time and place, and I'll be there," he said, almost unable to contain the excitement in his voice.

"You're sure you want to drive all the way to Liverpool for an evening with me?"

"I honestly can't think of a better way of spending an evening, Fenella. If you know of a good quality hotel that has a reputable restaurant, I can stay over afterwards; no ulterior motives by the way," he quickly reassured her.

"The Richmond Hotel in Hatton Garden is nice, Alan. I had a lovely meal there with my parents a couple of months ago. I'm sure you'll be comfortable there."

"If you have the time to spare, maybe we could go to the theatre, see a show?"

"That'd be great. If only we could get this case wrapped up."

"I know, I'm not trying to pressure you or anything. I know how busy your life is."

"Well, if all goes well, Saturday night should be free for me, though I'm not sure about the day, just in case."

Deal quickly agreed to meet with Fenella on the coming Saturday night, work matters permitting, and the pair chatted amiably for another five minutes, forgetting their earlier awkwardness as they relaxed over the phone and by the time the call ended, Fenella Church found she was no longer nervous about meeting the handsome Manchester psychiatrist. She was now positively looking forward to her first real date in ages and after climbing into bed, she was asleep in no time.

* * *

The following morning's briefing was fairly routine, if such a word could be used to describe anything to do with the Specialist Murder Investigation Team's cases. With no progress having been made since the previous day, Ross reiterated the need for all of his detectives to continue pressing their current lines of inquiry. He confessed to a feeling of frustration, with the investigation apparently entering a phase of stagnation, while he remained firm in his belief they were on the cusp of a solution.

Despondency was not an emotion Ross had ever allowed his team to adopt, but he did admit to Izzie Drake, over a cup of coffee in his office shortly after the briefing, that he felt some of the team were also heading in that direction.

"I think it's because everyone feels as you do," Drake offered in response. "Everyone knows that with the information we possess, we probably have everything we need to solve the case, but we seem to be missing that one 'missing link' that will tie it all together for us."

"That's it, exactly," Ross said, unable to hide the annoyance in his voice.

"Maybe the team's reassessment of all the previous witness statements will reveal something, maybe an inconsistency we missed first time around, that we can exploit to get at the truth," Drake replied.

Their conversation was interrupted by a firm knock on Ross's door. In response to his "Come" Fenella Church walked in. The look on her face told Ross and Drake that DS Church certainly wasn't the bearer of good news.

"What is it, Fee?" he asked.

"Just received some disquieting news, sir," she said, without preamble. "I just took a call from a Detective Inspector Tuohy."

"Irish accent, sounds like he's had a Guinness too many?"

"That's right, sir. I take it you know him?" Church replied smiling at Ross's description.

"Oh yes, I've known Pat Tuohy since we were both DCs, years ago. He's a top-notch copper, born here, but parents from County Donegal in the Republic. What's he got to say for himself, Fee?"

"Well, sir, it seems that DI Tuohy has been looking into the alleged disappearance of Clive Evans, reported by his girlfriend, Kelly Weeks as a missing person. He and his oppo, DS Crundell, questioned all the man's friends and as many acquaintances as they could identify, and Inspector Tuohy say he had a gut feeling that something was 'off' about Evans suddenly disappearing like that. He's apparently a bit of a prat, but for the most part, pretty regular in his habits."

"Why do I have a feeling you're about to drop a bomb on our investigation?" Ross interrupted.

"Because I suppose I am, sir, or rather, DI Tuohy has."

"Go on," said Ross, looking resigned to receiving more bad news.

"Inspector Tuohy thought it odd that none of his mates had seen him after he'd left home that last evening. It wasn't like him not to have contacted any of them. He'd usually text one or more of them at least once a day. It was Sergeant Crundell who finally found someone who'd seen him that evening, virtually as soon as he'd left home. A man who lived not far from Evan's newsagents' shop, who didn't really know him, but knew who he was, saw him getting into a blue Ford Focus at the end of the street. The witness, a Mr Berry, told Crundell that he was sure the car was waiting for Evans, who gave a small wave as he approached the car. He got straight into the car, and it drove off straight away. That, as far as they could work out was the last time anyone had seen Clive Evans, the former Clive Evandon."

Ross was becoming frustrated, and he urged Church to come to the conclusion of her news.

"Fee, come on, out with it," he pleaded. "Don't keep us waiting."

"Sorry, sir. Seems last night, uniform and the fire brigade were called out to attend a car blaze on waste ground near Bootle Golf Course. The assumption was that it was a stolen vehicle, probably torched by joyriders. Our people had to wait till the brigade extinguished the blaze and that's when the fire chief informed the attending officers that there was a body in the car."

"Not Clive Evans!" Izzie Drake exclaimed loudly.

"They didn't know who it was at first. You know the effects of fire on the human body," Church grimaced as she spoke. She, more than anyone on Ross's team, knew the agony of being caught in a flaming conflagration. As soon as it was safe to do so, the body was removed and taken to the mortuary, where it's currently being examined by Doctor Nugent. However, one of the fire fighters managed to save a couple of items from the car, including a wallet and a mobile phone, both from the badly burned body. He got them out knowing our people might be able to use them to identify the victim. The phone wasn't in a very good state, but the wallet had survived the worst of the fire. Inside were a bank debit card and a Mastercard, both in the name of Clive Evans."

"Shite, shite and triple shite," Ross shouted, filled with disbelief.

"Obviously, there's a chance the body isn't his," Church said, "but it looks as if our main suspect has just literally gone up in flames."

"This is bad," Drake could hardly believe what she'd just heard. "If Evans is dead, it means we've been barking up the wrong tree all the time."

"You're right, Izzie," Ross responded, trying to calm down and think logically. "We need to know for sure if the body is that of Evans. Fee, will you get down to the morgue and see what Doc Nugent has found, if there's any way of identifying the remains?"

"Of course," she responded. "I'll take Tony with me if that's okay with you."

"Take him, he could do with the experience."

Church turned on her heel, left the office and wasted no time in whisking DC Curtis away from his desk and heading for the city mortuary.

Ross and Drake quickly left his office and informed the rest of the team of the new development. There was a collective feeling of disbelief from his detectives, and he now pushed them to dig deeper and faster into the available evidence and witness statements. He knew the answer was in there, somewhere.

* * *

A short time later, as they entered the autopsy suite where William Nugent was still at work on the remains of the body found in the burned-out Focus, Tony Curtis suddenly placed a hand on Church's arm, bringing her to a sudden stop.

"What's up, Tony," she asked. "You not feeling well or something?" She thought perhaps the all-pervading smell, present in the room might be affecting him. His next words took her by surprise.

"I'm just wondering if you're okay, Sarge, you know, with you having been so badly burned yourself in the past. I thought maybe this might be bringing back some bad memories, you know?"

"Well, bless my soul. Tony Curtis, you're nothing but a big softie at heart, aren't you? Thank you so much for your consideration and your caring thoughts, but I'm fine, really I am. What happened to me was a terrible experience and I'd never want to go through something like that again, but I'm over it now, and if I was to let my bad memories of being caught in the fire affect me every time I'm faced with a victim of death by similar circumstances, I wouldn't be much use a copper, would I? Seriously, I appreciate your thinking about me, but I'm okay, honestly. Thanks for being so thoughtful, I appreciate it. Now, let's get on with the job, shall we?"

"Yeah, sure, whatever you say, Sarge," he smiled at the attractive sergeant. Everyone on the squad knew he was carrying a torch for Fenella Church, but they also knew he'd never take it any further due to his respect for her superior rank.

They began walking again, to where William Nugent stood beside the usually gleaming stainless steel autopsy table, now stained by the grisly remains of the as yet unconfirmed Clive Evandon. Despite the fact they were both wearing protective face masks both detectives could detect the smell of scorched flesh and though Church didn't seem bothered by it, or any memories it might be triggering, Curtis found himself gagging behind his mask.

"You alright, Tony?" Church asked, noticing his facial pallor.

"Yeah, Sarge. I'm okay, thanks. It's just that smell."

"Aye, it's been a long time since I've seen you here, DC Curtis," the pathologist said, seeing the DC hanging back slightly. "This'll be you're your first death by fire, I'm thinking."

"It is Doc," Curtis replied. "But I'm okay, really I am."

"Aye, well, don't forget, there's nae shame in leaving the room if it gets too much for ye."

Curtis just nodded, and Nugent carried on with what he was doing as they'd entered the room.

Sensing he was busy, Church refrained from saying anything, initially, until Nugent stood up straight and took a step back from the table.

"Anything you can tell us that we don't already know, Doc?" she asked.

"Possibly. We've instigated a check of dental records which might clarify the identity and this person had suffered some injury in the past that necessitated the left elbow being pinned. The pins and metal plate managed to survive the conflagration. Your suspect's family should be able to tell you if he had such an injury in the past. The body's been badly damaged by the fire, but Ah have an idea yon chappie was probably unconscious at the time of his actual demise."

"What makes you say that?"

"Take a look here, Sergeant," Nugent beckoned her to approach the table, which she did, with Curtis a step behind her. Nugent indicated a depression in the victim's skull. "Ah think it's safe to say we have evidence of blunt force trauma here. Probably the result of being struck with a hammer, maybe an ordinary, everyday claw hammer, with a one-inch diameter. Church and Curtis could now clearly see the area indicated by the pathologist. Whoever had struck the victim had hit him hard enough to actually leave a dent in the skull that would correspond with a wound as described by Nugent.

"Unless the assailant was sitting behind him, I'd say that blow was struck by someone who knew how to wield a hammer," Curtis added a thought.

"Well done, young Curtis, ma thoughts exactly," Nugent agreed.

The two detectives exchanged a look. They both knew they had someone in mind who might just fit that description.

CHAPTER 28
A COUNCIL OF WAR

Soon after Church and Curtis returned to headquarters and after they'd reported to Ross, the inspector called an emergency briefing, having told everyone to stop whatever they were doing. This was going to be important.

As soon as the team was settled in the squad room, with much quiet muttering and speculation buzzing around the room, they were joined by Detective Chief Inspector Oscar Agostini, who Ross had asked to join them. Saying nothing, the DCI took a seat next to DC Gable, smiled at her, and sat back to listen to Ross's words.

"Okay everyone, listen carefully," Ross began. "I've asked DCI Agostini to be present for this briefing because, bearing in mind the recent developments in the case, I think we need to look at everything in a slightly different direction. Take a look at the whiteboard everyone."

Behind and to the side of him, Izzie Drake was standing in front of the whiteboard, which she'd hastily drawn up on Ross's instructions.

"As you can see," Drake spoke as Ross nodded to her, "every witness, and everyone we've questioned is on the board. We've kind of played 'join the dots' as evidenced by the lines you see here," she indicated with a ruler. "We've taken the information each one provided and tried to indicate where it led us in terms of how it connects with the others involved. As you can see, most of them appear to lead nowhere, with little or no sign of them having intimate knowledge of the other people involved in the investigation. In short, DI Ross, DS Church, DS McLennan and I believe most of these witness statements lead exactly nowhere."

Ross once again took up the narrative.

"In the end people, the only ones who link up using this method and who we haven't yet applied any real pressure too, are these three," he said, pointing to the three offspring of Howard Blake."

"But I thought we'd effectively eliminated them from the inquiry, Boss," DC Sinclair interrupted.

"Nobody was ever eliminated from our inquiries Mitch," Ross responded grimly, "and now it appears we were led down one blind alley after another by a very clever manipulator who, through a series of red herrings, led us to chase our tails while they orchestrated this whole thing. Angie Ryan was effectively handed to us on a plate, like sacrificial lamb, and when we were getting too close to her, she was disposed of. After that our whole case seemed to rest on the shoulders of Clive Evandon or Evans, whichever name he went by. Now it looks like he's out of the way, which means we need to look at the only people who realistically could have sufficient motive to set this whole thing up."

"I take it you have a new prime suspect, Andy?" Oscar Agostini broke in at that point.

"We do sir, in fact we have three. The Blake siblings."

"The son and two daughters, correct?"

"That's right sir," Ross was warming to his subject now. "We've recently concluded a meeting in my office, and these are the conclusions. Forget prison officers, girlfriends, ex-partners and the like. None of them would have had such a close connection to Howard Blake to inspire such vicious and personal retribution. It therefore stands to reason the people most likely to be behind this would be his closest relatives. Either singly or together in some kind of unholy conspiracy we now believe that that's where we'll find the person truly responsible for the murders."

"Bloody hell, we never thought of a conspiracy," Sinclair blurted out.

"The conspiracy theory is the wild card here," Ross said. "It's far more likely to be just one of the siblings pulling all the strings. Here's what we have so far. Derek, will you summarise what we have on the eldest daughter, please?"

Detective Sergeant McLennan rose to his feet, cleared his throat and began his summary.

"Okay, the eldest daughter is Mrs Jacqueline Elson, known as Jackie, lives in Formby, originally interviewed by Tony and Mitch. She's the least likely suspect, being confined to a wheelchair since an RTA some years ago. She still believes in her father's innocence, but her disability limits her mobility and it's unlikely she could be the instigator, unless she's simply the brains behind the killings and working in cahoots with one or more of the others. Apart from that, there's not a lot we can discern about her?"

"Why are you so sure she couldn't be the brains behind the whole thing, Derek?" Church asked.

"I'm not sure," McLennan replied. "I'm merely going by what Tony and Mitch said in their report."

"And were you guys certain she couldn't be involved?" Church directed her question towards Curtis and Sinclair, who looked at one another, Sinclair nodding to Curtis, giving him the okay to respond to the sergeant's question.

"We were never certain," he responded, but there was nothing in what she said that might have led us to believe she was in any way involved, right Mitch?"

"I agree with you, matey, though we did agree that there

was no reason why she couldn't be assisting her brother behind the scenes if he was involved." Sinclair concurred with Curtis.

"In other words," Ross showed signs of irritation, bordering on anger, "you had minor thoughts, which possibly irritated you at the time, but neither of you did anything to scratch the itch that irritation might have been causing you. You're both experienced detectives, for God's sake. One or both of you should have dug deeper into the life of Jacqueline Elson. Don't tell me: you felt sympathy towards her because of her disabilities, right?"

Both Curtis and Sinclair were silent for a few seconds, their faces registering some hint of guilt at possibly missing something important that could have helped the investigation.

"Sir, I'm sorry. We…" Curtis began, only to be instantly put down by Ross.

"Save it, Tony. What's done's, done and can't be altered. For God's sake, the pair of you, in future try to look past what's presented to you without questioning it. This Jacqueline Elson wouldn't be the first and definitely not the last wheelchair-bound convict in one of Her Majesty's Prisons, got it?"

Both men nodded, each feeling suitably chastised and hoping they hadn't allowed their sympathy for Blake's eldest daughter cloud their professional judgement. Moving on, Ross called on Fenella Church to present her thoughts on the second daughter, Gillian Spalding.

"Mrs Gillian Spalding is, on the face of it, completely in the clear. She and her husband are both Captains in the Salvation Army, and being located in Great Malvern, down in the Midlands, would be an unlikely candidate for the role of criminal mastermind. She turned to religion soon after her father's conviction and has had minimal contact with her brother and sister over the years, although she and her husband did travel up for her father's funeral. She's very small, not that that would preclude her from being an organiser rather than an actual killer. She had alibis for the nights of the murders, and she was the first person to intimate that her brother has a violent side to his nature. Going by what Sam and Ginger found from their interview with her, I'd personally put her in the clear."

"It wouldn't be first time a supposedly religious person was responsible for brutal killings," Ishaan Singh ventured an opinion.

"That's true, Ishaan, but somehow I don't think that's the case here," Church replied, and Singh nodded in acknowledgment.

"Okay, let's forget the Sally Army connection for now," Ross said, and indicated for Drake to profile the last of the siblings.

"Izzie, what do we have on the brother?"

"Darren Blake, lives in Huyton, he definitely did make various threats at the time of his father's conviction. He later said it was all a heat of the moment thing and that he'd never hurt a soul in fact. That's something of a fallacy as evidenced by the fact that his girlfriend, Sally James actually showed Tony and Mitch a bruise on her arm that she said Blake caused in a fit of temper against her. If he'll do that in a domestic situation it's possible he could do worse, if provoked or the motive was strong enough."

"Excuse me," DCI Agostini interrupted. "Izzie, if we had possible evidence of a violent nature against Darren Blake why was he never brought in for questioning under caution?"

"Because at the time he was spoken to, sir, our main focus was on looking for a female killer, not a male. This is why we now think he could be a clever bastard, by setting up Angie Ryan as the killer, and having us seeking a female killer, we wouldn't have thought he could have been responsible for the murders."

"Point taken. I stand corrected," Agostini responded.

Ross took over again.

"It's only since the death of Angela Ryan that we realised there was someone else pulling the strings in this damn case. Putting it mildly, we've been playing catch-up ever since. The way things are going, it looks like the real brains behind the murders was staring us in the face all the time. We were just too stupid to see it and recognise it. We allowed this bastard to lead us down the garden path and like idiots, we blindly followed his false trail."

"From what I've heard here, it looks like Darren Blake is definitely our man," Agostini commented. "I suggest we bring him in for questioning immediately, without wasting time."

"Yes sir, I agree," Ross concurred. "Izzie, Tony and Mitch, we'll head over to his workplace, where he's likely to be. Fee, Derek, you two take Sam and Ginger to his house in case he's not gone into work. Ishaan, go see Evans' girlfriend and see if she can give us anything that will help a positive ID of the body."

"Yes sir," Singh replied. "I take it she's already been notified of his death?"

"All taken care of by uniform division, so just go and be sympathetic about it."

Singh nodded his acknowledgment.

"Okay, Andy, I'll let you get on with it," Agostini said, "Good luck everyone. Let's bring this evil bastard in and put an end to this killing spree."

With that, The DCI left the room and Ross first of all arranged for uniform back-up at both their target locations, before giving final instructions to his team.

"Listen up everyone. If Blake really is the man behind these murders, we have to assume he's dangerous and might even be expecting us to pay him another visit. He might feel we don't have enough evidence to arrest him, and it's true that we don't actually have anything that connects him with Ryan or with the murder of Evans. We're going to have to get him in an interview room and sweat him, in the hope he'll crack. On the other hand, he might try to make a run for it and give us something to make a definite case against him. But, and this is important, I don't want anyone taking unnecessary risks with this man. We've lost one good man in the last twelve months, and I have no intention of losing another one, got it?"

Murmurs of assent and acknowledgement could be heard around the room. They knew Ross was referring to the loss of DC Nick Dodds during their last major case. No one wanted to emulate the tragic ending to that one, and all agreed with Ross's sentiments. Great care would need to be exercised in the arrest of Darren Blake.

CHAPTER 29
ARREST

As the others prepared for the apprehension of Darren Blake, DC Ishaan Singh arrived at the newsagents' shop run by Clive Evans' girlfriend, Kelly Weeks. Entering the shop, and being greeted by the grieving woman, Singh felt a little apprehensive, not having been faced with a similar scenario in the past.

After expressing his sympathy at her loss, he explained that he was looking for anything to confirm the identity of the body found in the car.

"So, are you saying there's a chance it wasn't Clive, that it might be someone else?" she asked with what he knew to be hopeless optimism.

"I'm sorry Miss Weeks, it's virtually 100% certain the body is that of Clive. It's just that, because the body was so damaged by the fire, the Medical Examiner wants to make sure that there's no doubt, quite normal in such cases, I assure you," he lied, trying to put the blame for his unwanted intrusion on somebody else.

"Oh, I see. What can I tell you? Oh yes, when he was a teenager at school he suffered a very bad injury, and he shattered his elbow joint, the left one I'm sure it was. It had to be all pinned together. He used to joke he set off the security alarms at the airport if he was ever going on holiday, not that the tight bugger ever took me abroad. Best I got was a week in a caravan at Skegness last year."

As she told Singh about that last holiday, she was brought back to the tragic reality of her situation and tears began to run down her cheeks. Singh couldn't help feeling intense sorrow for the woman's plight. Losing her partner in such a particularly terrible way was probably the most difficult thing she'd had to contend with in her life, and he knew that nothing he could say or do could help to alleviate her grief. At least, from a professional point of view, her information about Evans' elbow was all they needed to confirm that the remains found in the car were those of Clive Evans.

Singh did his best to calm the woman and asked if the uniformed officers had arranged for her to be visited by a family liaison officer.

"Yes," she replied after loudly blowing her nose, using a tissue from an open box on top of the counter. "They told me someone will be coming later today."

"That's good. I'm sure the officer will be helpful, Kelly. But please don't hesitate to contact me if you think of anything that might help us find whoever did this to Clive," as he handed her a card with his name and number at headquarters on it. With little more he could discover from Kelly Weeks, Singh did his best to make sure she would be okay until the FLO arrived, not leaving her until she'd ceased crying after which she assured him she'd be fine, and that she had the shop to run on her own in the absence of her partner.

* * *

As Ishaan Singh was making his way back towards headquarters, Church, McLennan, Gable and Devenish, backed up by two burly uniformed constables, were arriving at the home of Darren Blake. Not wanting to take any risks in the case of their suspect being there and violently resisting arrest, Church decided to split her forces. As she and Devenish, accompanied by uniformed PC Carter approached the front door, McLennan, Gable and PC Harris simultaneously arrived at the back door. Devenish knocked loudly at the front door but received no reply. A second attempt brought a similar lack of response. Church whispered into her radio to inform McLennan, who was instantly alert for any attempt by the suspect to flee through the rear of the house but again all remained quiet.

Alerted by the loud knocking and by the presence of the police vehicles on the street, a stoutish lady, in her fifties stepped from the front door of the house next door and instantly announced, "There's no one home, love. He's out at work."

"Oh, thank you, Mrs…?"

"Fisher, Maggie Fisher," the woman responded to Church's inquiry.

"What about his girlfriend?" Church asked.

"Gone, over a week ago," Mrs Fisher informed the DS. "I saw her go meself, suitcase in her hand. She was limping and she had a black eye. That bastard probably beat her up once too often, poor girl. I don't know why she stayed with him so long, but they do, don't they?"

"They?" Devenish asked.

"Yeah, abused women. I've read about it. They stay with men like him until they get badly hurt before they make a move to get away. You should know about it, being police and all."

"Yes, that's very true in some cases. Mrs Fisher. Thankfully, not always though.

"Well, that's why that young lass, Sally took off, for sure," the eager-to-be helpful neighbour announced with surety.

With Sally James no longer living in the house, and Darren Blake ostensibly at work there was little to be achieved by waiting around outside his house. Church quickly radioed

Ross with the negative outcome of her team's visit to Blake's home.

"Okay, Fee, leave one of our lads and the uniform constables to keep a watching brief on the house, just in case Blake's not at work and suddenly shows up there. That'd be typical of our luck with this case, devoting all our resources to this place, only for him to evade us by turning up at home."

"Will do, and what about the rest of us?"

"Get over here as fast as you can. If he is here and tries to do a runner, the more bodies we have to stop him, the better."

Church decided to leave DC Ginger Devenish with the two PCs at the house, while she and the others made their way to join Ross at Fuller's Woodyard.

Ross's team had already arrived at Blake's workplace, and Ross lost no time in assigning his people, not only to detain Darren Blake, but also to cover any potential escape routes, should he decide to make a run for it. They quickly ascertained that were only two viable exits from the small site which contained a number of small business units; Fuller's Woodyard being situated close to the main entrance to the site, double wrought-iron gates painted bright red, and propped open, being the main entrance. At the rear of the site, DC Curtis found the other means of entry and exit from the site, a single large gate, similarly painted to the main gates, which he presumed acted as the entry for deliveries to the businesses on-site, which included a paper wholesaler, a small foundry, a private courier company and other sundry units, a total of twelve altogether.

Ross gathered his people together outside the main gates, out of sight of the woodyard and he decided to go ahead with a direct approach. He, Drake and Curtis, who would recognise Drake from their previous meeting, would simply enter the woodyard and inform Blake that he was wanted in connection with the murders, and they required him to accompany them to police headquarters for questioning.

Sinclair was tasked with guarding the rear exit/entry just in case Blake made a run for it once he was aware that the police were on to him.

Before they made their entry to the site, Church, McLennan and Gable pulled up a few yards from their position and were quickly added to the take-down team, with McLennan assigned to the rear gate in company with Sinclair.

In fact, the arrest of Darren Blake was far easier than Ross had anticipated. He was quickly spotted by Curtis, feeding long, large planks of wood into a circular saw which was cutting them into smaller, measured planks, presumably for a sales order. Ross and Drake positioned themselves behind the man while Curtis walked around the machine and waved his arms to catch Blake's attention, his ears being covered by a large pair of ear defenders.

Seeing Curtis frantically waving, Blake turned the power off and the saw blade gradually slowed to a stop. Removing his protective eye goggles and pulled his ear protectors off, allowing them to drape round his neck.

"You again?" he said, as he recognised Curtis from his earlier visit. "Something else I can help you with?"

"Yes, there is," Ross announced from behind him, startling Blake, who wheeled around to see the DI and Izzie Drake no more than three yards away, with Church and McLennan positioned not far behind them, spread out in a line twenty feet from end to end. "We'd like you to accompany us to Police Headquarters, Mr Blake, for questioning in connection with the murders of Clive Evans and Angela Ryan." Ross deliberately left out the murders of the Blake jury members for the time being. They could be introduced once they had Blake under interrogation and under caution.

"What?" Blake exclaimed loudly. "Are you out of your minds? We dealt with all this when that one," he pointed at Curtis, "and the other bloke talked to me before."

"Ah yes," Curtis provided him with a reply, "but that was

before certain facts came to light, and certainly prior to the deaths of Ms Ryan and Mr Evans."

"Facts? What bloody facts? You lot are out of your minds."

"We'll see about that, Mr Blake. Now, are you going to come quietly or not," Ross said, firmly.

"Do your worst, copper."

"Oh, don't you worry, we will. DC Curtis, would you do the honours please?"

With that Curtis moved in and placed Blake in handcuffs while cautioning him as required by law. With Blake officially under arrest Curtis and McLennan escorted him, one to each arm, to one of the unmarked cars, where he was placed in the back seat, ready for the journey to Headquarters.

As the car containing Church, McLennan and Darren Blake pulled away from the woodyard, and the rest of the takedown team quickly followed, Ross and Drake stood and pondered on the way the operation had worked out, having first radioed DC Devenish and instructed him and the constables at Blake's house to stand down.

"That went well, wouldn't you say?" Drake said to which Ross responded.

"Yes, it did, Izzie," Ross replied, with a slightly quizzical look on his face.

"Something's bothering you, I can tell," she instantly saw the look and knew he had something on his mind.

"Yes, don't you think it was almost too easy?" he asked her. "He was so passive, almost as if he was expecting us. I know he made a bit of a fuss but that was such a weak response. I expected at least a minor struggle and maybe an attempt to leg it, but he just allowed Tony to cuff him, caution him and lead him to the car, like a lamb to the slaughter."

Drake allowed Ross's words to sink in for a few moments before she responded.

"Come on, out with it. You've got you devious head on, and your mind's somewhere else, I know it is."

"Why would he just meekly surrender like that? It just doesn't feel right."

"He's obviously guilty," Drake emphasised the point. "Maybe he realised the game's up and just decided to give up and take what's coming to him."

"Yeah, maybe," Ross stood rubbing his chin, his mind trying to come to terms with the strange feeling he was harbouring. As he and Drake followed the rest of the team back to Headquarters, they drove in silence, as his mind continued to pose questions he couldn't quite answer for himself. Drake, having worked so closely with him for years, knew when to remain tight-lipped, and patiently gave him time to work things out before they began the questioning of Darren Blake at Headquarters.

For Ross, it was akin to having an itch he couldn't scratch, and that itch wouldn't go away until he and Drake were well into their interrogation of Darren Blake a couple of hours later, in interview room one.

CHAPTER 30
END GAME

Ross and Drake had spent over an hour in a fairly fruitless interrogation of Darren Blake. Both of them knew they had very little substantial evidence with which to charge the man who sat, almost impassively opposite them. Blake simply sat there, stubbornly denying any connection with the murders of either the jurors from his father's trial, or those of Angela Ryan and Clive Evans. He denied ever having met or known Ryan and though he admitted knowing Evans, who he referred to as Evandon, he categorically denied having obtained information from him, much less killing him.

Until, that is, two things happened which turned the case against Darren Blake from a purely circumstantial one, into a firm one. The first break came when Devenish knocked on the door, popped his head inside and asked if he could have a word with Ross, who promptly suspended the interview, stopping the tape recording, rose from his seat and joined Devenish in the corridor.

"What is it Ginger?" he asked as soon as they were alone in the corridor.

"I've been looking through all the evidence we have which might pertain to our friend in there, sir, and I came across something interesting in the items we removed from Angela Ryan's home after her murder."

"And?"

"And as you know we found enough physical evidence to link her to the jurors' murders, but on looking through everything again, I just found these," Devenish said as he handed a pair of photographs to Ross. There's also a video tape, sir, which is obviously a home movie which is definitely Triple X rated. There's absolutely no doubting the 'stars' if you can stomach watching it."

Ross took one look at the photos, smiled and gave Devenish a clap on the shoulder.

"Well done, Ginger. How come nobody noticed these before?"

"To be fair sir, we were looking for connections between Ryan and Howard Blake, not his son, and you have to look really closely to recognise the pair of them in these pictures. I only found them because I expanded the search parameters."

"Thank God you did. Now we'll see what Mr Stoic, Darren Blake has to say for himself." Ross replied as he turned to re-enter the interview room.

As soon as he did, he took his seat, quietly whispered something to Drake after showing her the photos, and then immediately threw them down on the table between themselves and Blake.

"Still denying you ever knew Angela Ryan, Darren?"

On seeing the slightly faded Polaroid photographs of himself and a near naked Angel Ryan in what could only be described as compromising positions, Blake's face visibly blanched. For the first time, he appeared to be lost for words.

"Nothing to say, Darren?" Drake asked. "Looks like the two of you were once more than just good friends. Didn't you know she still had these? I'm guessing they were taken a fair few years ago. In fact, I'd be surprised if Angela was over the age of consent when you took these. Who actually took them, by the way? You couldn't have done it yourself, not with a Polaroid camera, and not with the two of you in that position."

Beads of sweat appeared on Darren Blake's brow, a sure sign to the two detectives that they had him on the back foot. He was clearly rattled and was now on the defensive.

"Come on, Darren," Ross added. "You seem to have been pretty close, considering your earlier assertion that you never even knew the woman."

Unused to being in the position he now found himself, never having been under close scrutiny by the police, the cracks began to show.

"Yeah, well, so I knew her years ago. That doesn't mean I was still involved with the woman."

"What I find hard to believe, Darren, is that suddenly, almost out of nowhere, Angela Ryan appeared on the scene as your father's girlfriend when he was in prison. You know what I think?"

Blake sat motionless, apart from a slight shake of his head. Ross continued.

"I think you put her up to it. Encouraged her to visit your father, become close to him, making it easy for you to eventually pressure her into going along with your plans. You knew your father was something of a ladies' man, and it wouldn't take long for her to fall for him and his stories of his innocence. Having hooked her, he probably filled her head with his thoughts of getting revenge on those who he felt responsible for putting him behind bars. Angela wasn't bright enough, nor did she have access to the trial records, so she could only have learned the names and addresses of the jurors from someone who did have those details and was willing to provide her with them. Between you, your father and you gradually groomed her and then when you felt she was ready you unleashed her like a loaded weapon. How am I doing so far?"

Blake was by now sweating profusely and Ross and Drake

couldn't help noticing his hands had begun to shake. They knew they were getting close to cracking their man, who continued to sit silently shaking his head in denial. Their years of working in partnership in situations such as this now began to pay dividends as the two detectives fed off one another. It was Drake's turn.

"What intrigues me, Darren, is how you managed to plan it all and put everything into operation. No disrespect, but you don't appear to me to be clever enough to have done all this without help. Then again, I suppose you had help and input from your co-conspirator, Clive Evandon, as he was before he changed his name."

"I, er, that is…" Blake sputtered as he searched for something to say in response to the increasing barrage of questions and highly accurate suppositions from Ross and Drake. He was suddenly granted a temporary reprieve by another knock on the door, with DC Ishaan Singh's head appearing through the crack in the open door.

"What is it Ishaan?" Ross asked, frustrated at being interrupted when he felt they were close to getting Blake to finally break down and confess to his crimes.

"Need a quick word in private, sir. It's important," Singh replied in a quiet yet firm voice that Ross knew meant he had something that needed to be said. Once again suspending the interview, the recorder turned off, he rose from his seat, leaving Blake once more to the tender mercies of Izzie Drake.

Alone in the corridor with Singh, Ross listened carefully to what the DC had to tell him.

"When I previously visited Clive Evans's partner, Kelly Weeks, I left her one of my cards and asked her to call me if she remembered anything that might be helpful. I stressed that we urgently needed to know if she could remember any of his friends or contacts."

"And I'm guessing she's remembered something, Ishaan?"

"She has sir, and I think you might like to hear what she

had to say. She called me less than ten minutes ago and gave me what I think is vitally important information."

"Okay, don't prevaricate. Spit it out, man."

Singh did just that and it was a much happier Andy Ross who returned to the interview a couple of minutes later, having instructed Singh to take Sinclair with him to arrest the person involved. Before confronting Blake with his new intelligence, he sat and leaned in close to Drake and whispered something to her, giving her the gist of Singh's call from Kelly Weeks.

"Well, Darren, looks like we were wrong about you."

Before Blake could relax, thinking he might be off the hook, Ross went for the jugular.

"We've just received information that on at least four occasions, Clive Evans or Evandon, whatever you want to call him, left his partner at home to run their shop while he went out to take part in a series of so-called business meetings. He always came home late at night and would never tell his partner what the meeting were about. She asked him if the meetings were just an excuse to meet up with his drinking buddies at the pub, but he told her they were with somebody important that he had to visit at her home because the lady was disabled and couldn't come out to meet him. When she asked what was so important that he was visiting a woman at home, he told her it was none of her business and was about something that happened a long time ago when he was working in the legal profession. Kelly Weeks, his partner, had virtually forgotten those meetings until one of my detectives planted a seed in her mind and luckily, she recalled them and had the good sense to call my detective a few minutes ago."

"So? What's that got to do with me?" Blake asked, unaware exactly what Ross had learned.

"It's got everything to do with you, Darren. I was hesitant to believe you had the intelligence to plan and put such a complex plot into operation. I felt there had to someone else involved, someone pulling your strings as you then did with Clive Evans and Angela Ryan. I'm still not sure how you lured Evans into your plans, whether he did it purely for money or because you somehow had information you used to blackmail him into revealing all he knew about your father's trial, including the names of the members of the jury that convicted him. I daresay we'll find out soon enough. I have two detectives on their way right now to bring your sister, Jaqueline in for questioning. I doubt she'll withstand the pressure of being arrested, interviewed, and charged with conspiracy to commit multiple murders for very long."

Blake's face collapsed into a mask of hatred.

"You fucking bastards," he shouted. "You leave my sister alone. She had nothing to do with it." With those words, Blake as much as confessed to the murders and Ross and Drake knew they had their man, and that Jacqueline Elson was the brains behind the whole murderous plot.

"Oh, but I think she did, Darren. She's an intelligent woman who's had plenty of time to nurse her hatred of those she and you held responsible for your father's conviction. You believed his claims to be innocent despite overwhelming evidence to prove his guilt, but you just couldn't accept it, and when his appeals failed, and then he died behind bars, your sister hatched the plot for you to exact revenge. I'm sure she'll soon crack under interrogation and reveal just how you brought Evans into your scheme. Don't try and tell me you were the brains behind it all. You're just not clever enough."

"Come on, Darren, save your sister some grief," Drake pressed the man. "Tell us the truth. It'll go easier for you in court if we can tell the judge you've cooperated with us."

At that point, much to the surprise of both Ross and Drake, Darren Blake collapsed into floods of tears, and as the tears ran down his face, he sobbed,

"Okay, I admit it. It was just like you say. Jackie was the one who planned it all. She had plenty of time on her hands after her accident. Can you imagine what it's like being trapped in a wheelchair with your career, your life basically finished? The whole idea was hers, and I went along with whatever she said. Around the time of Dad's trial, when she was younger and a good-looking young woman, she had an affair with Evandon as he was called back then. Somehow, she found out he'd been embezzling funds from one of the firm's clients, a large amount apparently, and she always held that knowledge in reserve in case it came in handy one day, which of course it did. What she knew could have put that sanctimonious sod away for a long time, so when she hatched her revenge plot, she simply used that knowledge to blackmail him into revealing what we needed to know. That bugger had kept records of every case he'd been involved in over the years, and it wasn't too difficult to bring him on board. Of course, once your lot identified Angie Ryan, she had to be got rid of. We couldn't take a chance on you catching her and breaking her down. She'd have soon broken down and revealed Evans as her contact. After she'd had the lucky escape from the police car, she stayed at a friend's house for a couple of days, and when she called him to supposedly help her get out of the country, we told him what to do, and he simply arranged to meet her on the ferry and then gave her a good whack over the head and pushed her overboard."

"So, why did you kill Evans?" Drake asked.

"That was pure self-preservation," Blake confessed. "Jackie said he was the only person who could tie us to the murders, so I arranged to meet him, with the promise of giving him a wad of cash to ensure his silence. You know what happened next."

"Yes, we do Darren," Ross replied, quietly. "I think we'll leave it there for now. We'll talk again later."

With that, Ross terminated the interview and Drake stepped out and called for two constables to escort Blake to the charge office where he was formally charged with murder and conspiracy, before being locked in a cell.

Jacqueline Elson was brought in soon afterwards, and when faced with the information her brother had confessed to, she readily admitted her part in the whole vicious and inhuman plot. She showed no remorse, simply asserting that they all "got what they deserved."

* * *

At their trial, some months later, the evil brother and sister were found guilty on all charges and received life sentences. The trial judge described Jacqueline Elson as "One of the coldest-hearted killers it has been my misfortune to face across the court. You had no respect for human life and you have admitted that you ordered Angela Ryan to be as brutal as possible in the way she administered your twisted revenge against those innocent people, whose only misfortune had been to do their civic duty in serving on the jury which, in my opinion, brought in the correct and only possible verdict of guilty against you late father."

She will probably die in prison, as the judge gave no indication of how long she should serve before being eligible for possible parole. As for Darren Blake, the fact that he'd eventually cooperated with the police did in fact go in his favour as the judge recommended he serve a minimum term of fifteen years. With good behaviour, he could be released in ten.

In between their arrest and trial, Ross found himself heavily involved in the process of expanding the numbers and the scope of the Specialist Murder Investigation Team. With interviews to carry out and a couple of lesser cases to keep the team busy, names were soon being added to the team and the newcomers were gradually integrated into the squad. Ross found himself slowly getting used to his new rank as a Detective Chief Inspector, and Izzie Drake to her new position as a

Detective Inspector. The whole team knew there were likely to be exciting times ahead with more seemingly impossible cases to solve, but after all, that was their job, and they would, as always, give their all in bringing the perpetrators to justice.

Andy Ross and the team will be returning soon in the next Mersey Mystery, *Under a Mersey Moon.*

Dear reader,

We hope you enjoyed reading *The Mersey Ferry Murders*. Please take a moment to leave a review, even if it's a short one. Your opinion is important to us.

Discover more books by Brian L Porter at https://www.nextchapter.pub/authors/brian-porter-mystery-author-liverpool-united-kingdom

Want to know when one of our books is free or discounted? Join the newsletter at http://eepurl.com/bqqB3H

Best regards,
Brian L Porter and the Next Chapter Team

ACKNOWLEDGMENTS

The Mersey Ferry Murders actually owes its existence to my publisher, Miika Hanilla, at Next Chapter Publishing (Formerly known as Creativia), who, after publishing *A Mersey Killing,* said to me, "I like this. Do you think there's a series in it?" Miika, with the completion of the 9th book in the series, the answer is a resounding "YES". So, thanks for the suggestion. As all the books in the series have topped the bestseller rankings at Amazon, I thank you sincerely for the original suggestion.

As always, I must say a big thank you to my chief researcher, editor and proof-reader, Debbie Poole, who is often to be found in strange locations in and around Liverpool, even sometimes in, wait for it…pubs…all in the cause of researching subjects and locations for various parts of my books. Ah, hard work, but someone has to do it.

To my dear wife, Juliet, my undying thanks for the patience and extreme fortitude she has displayed during the long hours I've spent writing the book. How many times has she asked me to do something, only to be met with the reply, "Not now darling, I'm busy writing?"

Finally, as always, my thanks go to my growing legion of fans/readers who enjoy these books and have helped make the series the success it is today. I couldn't have done it without you.

ABOUT THE AUTHOR

Brian L Porter is an award-winning author, and dog rescuer whose books have also regularly topped the Amazon Best Selling charts, twenty-two of which have to date been Amazon bestsellers. The third book in his Mersey Mystery series, *A Mersey Maiden* was voted The Best Book We've Read All Year, 2018, by the organisers and readers of Readfree.ly.

Last Train to Lime Street was voted Top Crime novel in the Top 50 Best Indie Books, 2018. *A Mersey Mariner* was voted the Top Crime Novel in the Top 50 Best Indie Books, 2017 awards, and The Mersey Monastery Murders was also the Top Crime Novel in the Top 50 Best Indie Books, 2019 Awards Meanwhile *Sasha, Sheba: From Hell to Happiness, Cassie's Tale and Remembering Dexter* and *Dylan the Flying Bedlington* have all won Best Nonfiction awards. Writing as Brian, he has won a Best Author Award, a Poet of the Year Award, and his thrillers have picked up Best Thriller and Best Mystery Awards.

His short story collection *After Armageddon* is an international bestseller and his moving collection of remembrance poetry, *Lest We Forget*, is also an Amazon best seller.

RESCUE DOGS ARE BESTSELLERS!

In a recent departure from his usual thriller writing, Brian has written six bestselling books about the family of rescued dogs who share his home, with more to follow.

Sasha, A Very Special Dog Tale of a Very Special Epi-Dog is now an international #1 bestseller and winner of the Preditors & Editors Best Nonfiction Book, 2016, and was placed 7th in The Best Indie Books of 2016, and *Sheba: From Hell to Happiness* is also now an international #1 bestseller, and award winner as detailed above. Released in 2018, *Cassie's Tale* instantly became the best-selling new release in its category on Amazon in the USA, and subsequently a #1 bestseller in the UK. Most recently the fourth book in the series, *Penny the Railway Pup*, has topped the bestseller charts in the UK and USA. The fifth book in the series, *Remembering Dexter* won the Readfree.ly Best Book of the Year 2019. The most recent addition to the series is *Dylan the Flying Bedlington*

If you love dogs, you'll love these six illustrated offerings which will soon be followed by book 7 in the series, *Muffin, Digby, and Petal, Together Forever*

Writing as Harry Porter his children's books have achieved three bestselling rankings on Amazon in the USA and UK.

In addition, his third incarnation as romantic poet Juan Pablo Jalisco has brought international recognition with his collected works, *Of Aztecs and Conquistadors* topping the bestselling charts in the USA, UK, and Canada.

Many of his books are now available in audio book editions and various translations are available.

Brian lives with his wife, Juliet and his wonderful pack of nine rescued dogs.

FROM INTERNATIONAL BESTSELLING AUTHOR BRIAN L PORTER

The Mersey Mysteries
    A Mersey Killing
    All Saints, Murder on the Mersey
    A Mersey Maiden
    A Mersey Mariner
    A Very Mersey Murder
    Last Train to Lime Street
    The Mersey Monastery Murders
    A Liverpool Lullaby

Thrillers by Brian L Porter
    A Study in Red - The Secret Journal of Jack the Ripper
    Legacy of the Ripper
    Requiem for the Ripper
    Pestilence, Breathe if you Dare
    Purple Death
    Behind Closed Doors
    Avenue of the Dead
    The Nemesis Cell
    Kiss of Life

Dog Rescue (Family of Rescue Dogs)
Sasha
Sheba: From Hell to Happiness
Cassie's Tale
Penny the Railway Pup
Remembering Dexter
Dylan the Flying Bedlington
Muffin, Digby and Petal, Together Forever (Coming soon)

Short Story Collection
After Armageddon

Remembrance Poetry
Lest We Forget

Children's books as Harry Porter
Wolf
Alistair the Alligator, (Illustrated by Sharon Lewis)
Charlie the Caterpillar (Illustrated by Bonnie Pelton)

As Juan Pablo Jalisco
Of Aztecs and Conquistadors

Many of Brian's books have also been released in translated versions, in Spanish, French, Italian and Portuguese editions.

Printed in Great Britain
by Amazon